About the A

Life is full of experiences; some are beautiful, others perhaps less so, yet all of them become memories to draw from. For Hudson Dean, imagination has always been a saviour, a tool to overcome obstacles, a means to cope and sometimes even a way to forget and block out the darkness. Writing has always been a passion, a talent recognised in school, and now he is fortunate enough to share this gift with readers.

33 Houses

Hudson Dean

33 Houses

Vanguard Press

VANGUARD PAPERBACK

© Copyright 2025
Hudson Dean

A CIP catalogue record for this title is available from the British Library.

ISBN 978-1-83794-432-3

*Vanguard Press is an imprint of
Pegasus Elliot Mackenzie Publishers Ltd.*
www.pegasuspublishers.com

First Published in 2025

**Vanguard Press
Sheraton House Castle Park
Cambridge England**

Printed & Bound in Great Britain

Dedication

Be fun, be loud, be strong, be true; you know who you are. Let it be known deep love for you.

1

Quite simply, Pip could barely believe the scene being played before him in his kitchen. In fact, for a second or two, the surprise took away the ability to think, let alone speak or indeed have enough remaining mental ability available to instruct his body to perform those all-important tasks of inhaling and exhaling. All he could do was look, somewhat blankly, jaw dropped, as his brain slowly began attempting to absorb the scene before him and comprehend what on Earth might be going on. He consciously considered if it should, perhaps, be the duty of the cognitive part to jump in right now to make his body perform its primary duties of messages from the brain to instruct the pumping of his heart valves, as he feared the shock would remove the ability to allow his body to operate autonomously. He wondered if he had taken the stairs too quickly, and his oxygen-restricted brain was offering delusion because he was convinced that this could be nothing more than a fantastical image or a bizarre surprise play being acted out exclusively for him in his home, right here, his own front room.

2

Not that it mattered, but it was Friday, and for no less than the third time this week and probably the thirty-third time this year, that Pip had forgotten to pick up the car keys and had to walk back, retracing his steps to the penthouse to retrieve them.

"One of these days, I'll remember everything the first time," he muttered and smiled to himself.

As he had so many times before, he pondered about the logic of leaving the car key in his office, which being on the ground floor below him, was closer to the parking spaces or swapping the car completely to one with a keyless system that you could perhaps operate from an app on your phone or at least the type of key you could still put on the same ring as the house keys, which was normally possible. Still, he'd broken the part that created the loop from which it was meant to hang. The office idea made sense, but Pip contemplated the amount of traffic through there, so perhaps, it was not such a good idea; it was not that the staff weren't trusted but more as if some kind soul picked it up and put it somewhere safe thinking, he had left it around again. One thing was for sure; he was definitely going to replace the spare one that he'd dropped a 30 kg dumbbell on, shattering the casing and the internal circuitry. He thought, perhaps, he would try and invent something that electronically wouldn't allow you through your own front door unless you had everything you needed; car keys, house keys, office keys, wallet, the phone; maybe each item could be tagged by Bluetooth, and you could set an alert for each item; maybe it could run through your smartwatch? He pondered and glanced at his naked wrist; he chuckled and thought to himself how that would only work if you remembered to put the bloody thing on.

"Note to self, call Mini…"

In fact… he reached for his phone.

"Hey, Siri, set a reminder to call Mini at one p.m.," he said aloud to no one, smiling to himself again about his need to own the latest gadgetry. None of it was of any use unless you were in its vicinity.

I'll have a chip installed under the skin like in the movies, he thought as he re-entered the large hallway of the old mill, waving to Jackie through the heavy glass, who was attentively standing at the reception desk of his gym, here on the ground floor. She waved in response, and then her face changed as she clearly remembered something. She swapped her gentle wave of hand to a single finger point and then to a beckoning gesture. Pip removed his right foot from the first marble step and his right hand from the highly polished banister supported by the simple yet stunning snake-bent wrought iron balustrades and turned towards the double-height glass wall that housed the gym doors.

The wall was quite impressive and had been a dream come true when Pip secured the planning permission to expand the gym to the second floor of his building to incorporate the spa-like features he had envisioned since day one some fifteen years ago, and even now as he glanced at his ten-year-old wall of clear glass through which one could see the mezzanine balcony, home of the bustling coffee lounge that overlooked the buildings Victorian marbled staircase, it would still make him smile with pride at how he, this troubled kid from nowhere had made something of himself, by himself.

"Hi, Jacks, everything OK? I haven't got long. I'm supposed to be at…"

"Mr AJ Jackson's office in twenty-five minutes. Dearest Philip, I have been making your appointments for the last God knows how many years, reminding you to go to them and sorting the filing that's resulted from them, all whilst juggling gym timetables, stroppy members, suppliers and the bloody staff timetable, you don't have to tell me where you should be!"

Jackie's little rant was said with affection as she repeated her usefulness to him at least once every day. It was her thing, almost a mantra said only ever in jest. The truth was Pip wasn't sure he would be where he was right now without Jackie; she really was the glue that held his little empire and, indeed, himself together since his breakdown not six months after meeting her.

"Hun, you know I cannot live without you; that's why I pay you the big bucks, and you will be rewarded throughout eternity by the universe itself."

"Flattery, Mr Scot, will get you absolutely… everywhere…" Jackie flicked back her hair, stoked her lip and gave a warm, inviting and suggesting look to Pip who smiled as she continued, "… If only you would give up this silly obsession with boys and start liking girls."

Staring into what had to be said were alluring and beautiful eyes set into a classic and quite stunning face, Pip frowned, shook his head, and in his best American gangster accent, said, "Ain't gonna happen, sweetheart! However, if it did, know that you would be really high on my straight priority list of things to do. I mean take out, date, oh, you know."

"There's a list? Wait, hang in there, mister. High? Not first? I may advise being very careful how you respond to this. By the way, just a little heads up, let's say."

"Yes, high. At least in the top twenty. Maybe. Top forty-five definitely, well, the top forty-five to sixty bracket-ish. Remember, I have to put the icons first; Kylie, Madonna, Cher, Dolly, Celine – although, she could do with a burger or two – and that lot. It's a Gay Law; in fact, it's chapter three in the manual, right after the instructions of how to wrap gifts, how to coordinate items in the home, and where to source high thread count linens." They both stood there and giggled. Jackie applying for that job was the best thing that could have happened in both of their lives. As a relatively young widow, Jacks had needed someone to take care of but could never ever replace her true love and soulmate, Jonny, in the partner department, didn't want to; that man had ticked every single box, his humour, his academic ability, the charm, the style and the 'oh so good times' in the bedroom. They had never borne children, however, so when she met Pip, something magical happened. They had instantly connected and became the very best of friends almost immediately.

"Anyway, did you call me in for more than your reminder of how utterly brilliant you are, or did you once more just want to bask in my aura in a bid to positively charge your fading one?"

The look on her face showed her defeat in this ritualistic banter; a few seconds more and a witty retort might have been found, but the timing was lost. Pip smiled and raised his right arm straight out in front of him, clenched a fist, then opened his hand to a flattened stance, mimicking a mic drop, roast complete; he was today's victor.

"Where's your phone?"

Pip patted down the pockets of his jacket and trousers. *"Erm,* here, I've just myself a reminder about my car key, which, yes, I have forgotten; I was just running back to the flat to fetch it."

"Really, and is the reminder set? For I can see from here that your phone, my dear, is flat. You are so lucky to have me." Pip gave another cheeky smile. "Jackson's office called; it looks like you don't have to go into their office after all…"

"Oh, no! No! No! Oh, fuck!"

"Wrong!" Jackie said this, mimicking the ringing sound of a beaten gong.

"Wha…?"

"They called to say it is approved. You got it, Pip. Every last penny AND a £500 k contingency secured on the land attached to this place. Whatever fine detail you've put into the contracts since the last time I looked, I don't know, but I will, of course, check before I let you sign anything; I wasn't the wife, legal executive and secretary of a big city Lawyer for knocking twenty years without learning to oversee the fine print, but honey you have done it. The thirty-three houses development can begin; your dream of turning that scraggy old derelict reservoir land up the valley into something beautiful is going to be real."

Pip stood, face positively beaming, barely able to believe the words he had just heard, *Wow,* he thought, *Wow!*

3

Pip stood in the grand entrance hall and looked around. Before him was the great white marble staircase that curved up on itself as it rose through the five floors of this beautiful Victorian Paper Mill located in a valley of hills just across the English border from Mid Wales, offering beautiful vistas of lush green hillsides filled with sprawling fields covering acre after acre like a patchwork quilt. He had been somewhat besotted with the building since he was a little boy and used to escape here when his grandfather decided to start to taunt young Philip about being so sensitive. His nanna was a different kettle of fish entirely and loved her Pippy as if she had borne him herself, but alas, that was something Mother Nature had never deemed a possibility for her and despite endless trying, she simply could not conceive. She did her best not to feel incomplete and accept that her purpose was to take a different path, so when Nanna Greta and Grampy Geoff, her loving husband, heard the plight of an abandoned little girl who had been found sat on the steps of the fire station in the next village, they had stepped forward, fostered and eventually, adopted Nina by the time she was just two years old. They loved her dearly, and her arrival took their property from being just a house and made it a home in the town where they had met and married in Scotland back in the 1960s. Geoffrey Scot was a craftsman, a cutter of fine gemstones who moved his new family down to the Welsh border to answer the need for work following some kind of serious incident that had occurred whilst he worked for an exclusive Jewellery workshop near Glasgow that made bespoke pieces for distinguished design houses and jewellers around the world as well as individual private and state commissions including for a certain family of the name Windsor, the Jeweller that employed him carried a Royal Warrant.

If she could see me now, thought Pip, and in his mind, he imagined being interviewed or perhaps shaking the hand of a local dignitary, and he recited his family tale that had become a practised party piece of small talk that covered up the less desirable truth quite well. Not that his biographical recant was actually a lie in any way; that was something Pip was never into or indeed very good at – he was honest as his nanna wanted him to be and equally as kind and caring as she was. Grampy was different. Nanna and Pip would giggle and call him Grumpy behind his back just as a way to soften the blow and deal with his gruffness; it's not that he was a bad man in any way and would certainly never harm anyone intentionally, but if he read or heard of a situation or news article that he didn't agree with, he would start to mumble and then become enraged about it, positively ranting to anyone that could or would listen to him, voice his opinion in words and a hard Scottish accent that, despite Pip growing up hearing, and indeed still to this day, himself speaking with a soft Glaswegian twang, he often couldn't understand a word said by his grandfather if in full rage.

Yes, the party chat was good, required, and less painful to admit and comment about Grampy with his tenuous Royal connections who was actually usually a miserable, overbearing, opinionated, impatient grouch. The portrayal of a loving, hardworking man of simple needs was deemed more acceptable chatter than the true tale of how his adopted daughter was a complete tearaway her entire life who got knocked up the night of her sixteenth birthday and abandoned her loving parents and her baby son on his second birthday to never be seen again. Or that Grampy died of a heart attack eight years later, leaving Nanna and Pip to soldier on together with no income or family to depend on. That kind of small talk didn't go down quite as well. Besides, Pip was determined to be a success story and promised his beloved Nanna on her deathbed eighteen years ago that he would do his best for her.

When Pip was around fourteen, his nanna had won a little money. With Pip being old enough to be left alone, she found a little independence and began to go to the bingo hall in the next town and made a few friends there. Pip loved the fact that she was finally going out and making friends; his teenage imagination had panicked him into thinking they would grow apart and she would face existence in solitude, the typical teenager making melodrama out of everything. He would never forget the look of sheer joy on her face as she came in at ten p.m. that Wednesday night, taking off her coat, sitting in her favourite chair by the fire and announcing that she'd won the rolled-over jackpot of £48,421.

This was still the late '80s and that amount of money was life-changing for a lone woman and her Grandson.

The clothing repairs that she performed to make ends meet via the ad in the local paper and card in the post office window would continue, but be performed on a new sewing machine in a dedicated room of the house that she would now buy in cash from the local council and still have a fair sum to put away for a rainy day in one of those accounts that paid a lot of interest if you didn't touch it for several years.

Pip inherited the lot when she passed. The house at that point was worth over £450,000. The rainy day savings and investment shares that Geoff had set up plus a little more squirrelled away in cash hidden around the house and also several thousand pounds gained from the sale of off-cut gemstone fragments that Pip had found in a tobacco tin when clearing out the grumpy old git's tool collection from the shed that Nanna forebode anyone to touch saying, "Leave that place to him. It's how we all get a little piece and quiet."

In total, for a man who started with nothing, made a tidy sum that could have set him to be comfortable for life, the chance to sit back and relax, and enough money to buy a house with a dividend-paying nest egg, but Pip wanted a little more than a comfortable life, he wanted to see just how far he could grow his existence, maximising his experiences and his feeling of self-worth.

4

Following the day, the conveyancing solicitor confirmed it was his, Pip had sat in his favourite spot once more on the steps of the 'formerly' abandoned Mill, the place he'd escaped to, time and time again, far away enough from home to feel rebellious and a free spirit, yet close enough to make it home for dinner if he had lost track of time and the sun had begun to fall. In his hand, sat a tattered leather-bound notebook that was used solely for his ideas about what he would do with this huge imposing building, which, to his mind, was considered the finest structure ever built; he sat and, after many years of daydreaming, decided exactly what he wanted to do with his acquisition. Taking out his pen, Pip turned the front cover of his thoughts bible of ideas and wrote on the blank fly page the mantra that had kept him realised that his value on this planet was equal to everyone else's and only he could provide his own limitations.

He wrote, '*Aim high. Achieve higher. All or more.*'

"As he made his notes, Pip recalled the days his life took a turn. The last time he had sat and let his mind wander was the day, he had carried out his nanna's final wishes and had held a small ceremony at the crematorium, and after being stood thanking the attendees, nodding to acknowledge their best wishes, the endless shaking of hands, the faint – somewhat condescending – wrinkle of smiles that uttered the gratifying comments of a job well done by the members of gathered mourners who had known her from the village, plus one or two that did not know her personally but came to pay their respects yet in truth with such little to do for entertainment by the village's seniors, had attended for a day out. He had once again strolled here to the Mill without thinking; it was, after all, his safe space, his go-to, and now, he felt it would somehow also be home.

5

The perimeter fences had been in need of replacement for many, many years before Pip had even come into existence, so even as a young boy, it had been more than easy for him to creep through them to access his escape place. This was a huge brick-built five-storey paper mill that had stood since the 1850s or thereabouts. It was a finely finished and handsome building, red brick with featured work in terracotta and cream sandstone, simple carved yet elegant mouldings around the rows of black iron windows, floor after floor. Most of the outbuildings that needed fewer substantial structures had become derelict over time, but this beautifully engineered structure had stood the test of one hundred and seventy years of time, passing very nicely, indeed. Pip often wondered how, without being used or looked after, the Mill had survived and assumed – not forgetting the possibility of it magically being protected by pixies, hobbits and wizards – that it was the location in the lower part of the valley created by three connected hills at one end that perhaps had saved it from the elements. He could never quite believe that the place had never been re-developed and did ask people why not, only to be told it seemed that the trends of town steel-structured business parks and shopping malls were of favour, they were cheap with good traffic links from the recently built ring road so why would anyone come here? Shame! But then, surely, there was an advantage to all of that; those very buildings with shopping park and business provided the local village with so much more valuable footfall, the same body of souls that had driven the value of his family home so high.

He recalled his decision that day, poignantly dressed in his smartest suit and overcoat.

"I'll buy it!"

Such a simple phrase, yet the idea exploded inside the head of young Mr Scot with such a surge of emotion, he thought he might self-combust as his blood seemed to heat exponentially as it pulsed around his body, giving shivers that offered a cold sweat and tingling sensation upon his skin. His imagination ran wild with the thoughts and possibilities; he could live here, he could work here, he could, he could, he could… be here. The place he had found sanctuary could be the place he would always belong to. He knew deep inside that it must be possible. The money was there, surely enough for a deposit or maybe a section of it or find a business partner, or… the ideas would never cease. Pip had to, at least, try and follow this dream.

It hadn't taken long to discover the owners of the site or to have an offer accepted for it. Having ended up in a property portfolio of a French investment firm that had never even been there, it was not a great task to convince them to offload it. The sum to purchase was cheap, considering the size of the building, which took the bulk of the inheritance. However, it did include the land that stretched right the way to and included the now tattered high, arched railway bridge that joined the two side hills at the top of the valley at the back of what had once been a reservoir, built to feed the steam engines of the Paper Mill, the rail bridge and track leading to what looked like a bricked up disused tunnel, presumably there to hold the coal for the engines and process the transport of the finished products out to the world. Pip was presented with the deeds and the original plans for the main Mill building. They were pretty irrelevant to his future plans, yet really nice to touch and feel. He decided he would have the drawings of the exterior mounted in the grand entrance hallway if he ever somehow managed to open the building accommodating his ideas. His dreams. Pip wondered if he would ever recover from the shock of being the sole owner of this place.

Money was tight for the first couple of years. Pip sold everything he could lay his hands on to obtain enough money to begin to convert this huge building. To give it life, he decided the double height ground floor should be a fitness centre, the kind of posh gym he had seen the wealthy use on the TV but this one would be for everyone with a social side too, having grown up less than a mile away he was all too aware of the need for some kind of meeting place other than the two old man's pubs in the village, the kind of places where unless you have lived there for thirty years you will create a noticeable draft from the whip round of heads when you walked through the door unannounced and most definitely uninvited, it would then be a further five years of attendance before the deathly silences would abate upon your entrance providing your regular time and days of attendance were upheld without fail, then yet a further ten years of acceptance before even suggesting you would like a chair to sit on and if you persevered hard enough to obtain this goal, one must take the seat allocated and remember to never ever attempt even the suggestion of using 'Ol Westie's' chair that sat closest to the fireplace despite the fact he had passed some forty years before.

Making the building secure and watertight was the first priority. Fortunately, the ironwork of most of the windows was in good repair, so only glazing was needed and amazingly not that much either; the boards that had blocked the windows for who knew how many years had done the job they were intended to do Pip knew from growing up around the corner that although there was little to do, the village was so small that there were barely any kids to vandalise the place and teenagers either escaped to college or began modern apprenticeships to, hopefully, get enough money together to move away leaving the untouched abandoned buildings as just that, untouched and left alone. Power supply and clearing the grounds and cobbled access roads, however, depleted the rest of the inherited funds. So here he was left with a shell of a building and possibly an empty dream; he knew there had to be a way to get this going; all he had left was his car and the starter home-style flat in the village; it had to go, he needed to release the small amount of equity as desperation was setting in and the fear of failure loomed. Once the flat was sold, Pip experienced a surge of positivity. Talk had been wild since he began this mammoth task of resurrecting the old Mill, enough so to spark interest within the local community, who gladly supported his plan to sell advance memberships to the new gym; he was one of 'theirs' after all. Within days of the offering, many took up the offer, amassing just enough money to buy second-hand gym equipment for his new members to use.

Used rusted iron weights were cleaned and resprayed with car paint for a new lease of life, old boxing bags were obtained from an abandoned boxing club and covered in new leather stitched by his nanna's sewing machine and his skills learnt by keeping her company as she worked, weights benches from eBay were reupholstered and all of it sat upon a wooden floor which he had painstakingly relocated plank by plank from the top floor, re-laid and sanded and varnished with his own hands. Slowly but surely, this dream was becoming a reality. He could do this. Him. Philip Scot, the proud owner of the Old Paper Mill and the all-new leisure facility SCT fitness.

Despite the company logo being ■ ● ▼, Pip was disappointed that people assumed SCT was simply a fancy way of showing he owned the place and was being a smart ass by removing the vowel. He had spent night after sleepless night trying to come up with a name, bounced around ideas related to the valley, ones relating to paper and even ideas like Phoenix as the building was being resurrected before settling on SCT, which actually stood for Square, Circle, Triangle, Fitness for 'whatever shape you're in' as a supporting tagline. Yet still he bowed to opinion and simply agreed to the misconception of Joe Public and even called the property side of his new empire SCT Holdings, using the same logo but in a different colour as the organising company for the sale of leases for ground floor businesses and apartment dwellings in the rest of what would again become a glorious building.

Time soon passed and within a year, Pip had cleared enough money to begin investing in the development of the remaining half of the ground floor. His little coffee lounge had been a huge hit as a meeting place within the gym, so he thought that one of the four units he was going to develop, he would keep as a watering hole extension to his own site, enabling a little more work out space to be freed. It was a full further year, though, when Pip decided that sleeping in the gym office and using its changing rooms as his bathroom was time enough served. Two years of a cheap single bed hidden behind three tall metal office cabinets, getting up at five in the morning just so he could take a shower in private in the changing rooms was enough. It had taken two full years to gain enough money to develop the apartments on half of the second floor, all of the third and two-thirds of the fourth, but with the leases complete on the residential side, plus the rents from the newly opened boutique, restaurant and furniture showroom next to his coffee house; it was time to finish the last of the residential properties, moreover, finish and move into HIS, the penthouse, the last and the finest of all the conversions and he couldn't wait.

6

It was here in this very apartment where he now stood, having entered through the heavy black double oak doors and through either shock or disbelief, he'd averted his line of sight from where it had initially been drawn and glanced around his home instantly taking in everything in view and remembering the detail from each and every installation. To his left, at the rear of the building, was a wall of folding glass doors that stretched the full length of the apartment, opening onto quite an extensive balcony that he'd created by removing part of the roof and reducing the height of the original back wall. Pip had always thought the simplicity of the design enhanced this old building, not particularly to preserve its character for any other reason that he had loved it for so long. Open plan was definitely the theme here. Nanna had always said that the kitchen was the heart of every home and the most important room of the house as it fed you, gave you water and was the place you could always find a cup of tea and a chat. It was a saying he had heard a thousand times by many people, but in his mind, it was Nanna's voice that repeated it, so that's where his design began, with the kitchen exactly positioned in the centre of the floor plan. With the balcony being part of the overall footprint, one might say the kitchen looked a little offset when the doors were closed, as it left an odd little corridor between the glass and the left-hand island of units that contained the dishwasher and sink. A second island stood to the right of it, this one with a six-ring hob and the only wall stood behind them to give a home to the enormous fridge freezer and ovens, built-in microwave and coffee machine – that had been used once, incorrectly, causing a steam burn down his left arm a lot of cursing, the breaking of his favourite Superman mug, a stained white shirt, wet denim-clad thigh and a £65 fine for then forgetting his dental appointment. Needless to say, once clean, it was a very pretty and expensive kitchen ornament – the few wall tiles, that could be seen, were from the walls of his home office, original Victorian metro tiles not quite white, not quite cream, some with crackled glazing some still in good condition but all of them leading to the edges of the wall which had a softened curved edge which he had created just to use the curved tiles that had edged one of the double height windows on the ground floor. The rest of the same wall furnishings remained in his gym alongside the exposed brickwork and rustic panels made from reclaimed pallets and sheets of old riveted steel sheets.

Behind the kitchen wall a simple, narrow utility room and behind that, his bathroom with a copper roll-top bath sat next to an internal glass wall so he could bathe and bask in the glorious vistas of further down the valley. The master bedroom ran behind this, with another bedroom in the right-hand corner that he used for storage, bringing his gaze back to his lounge area filled with oversized leather upholstery, creating a comfortable area for the company, three sofas surrounding the large Fortnum & Mason wicker hamper upon which sat a reinforced piece of glass he'd had cut so as to use it as a coffee table. It wasn't that he couldn't afford a real piece of furniture; he was hardly struggling financially, not like in the old days; it wasn't even that it was a quirky feature; it was the fact he had been presented with it by the local chamber of commerce for best new business several years ago when SCT celebrated its first anniversary. Pip would sit and put his feet up on the hamper and spend hours daydreaming as he had for most of his life at the view up the valley where the reservoir had once been, the very same seat where he had studied what must have been the footings of the curved dam that had stood there holding back ton after ton of water.

Pip took several steps to his left and grabbed the back of one of the eight dining chairs to steady himself as he braved to turn his head back to what he hoped had been a trick of the mind.

His eyes moved across the oak floor that he had replaced with the original boards downstairs; he saw the clear droplets of water splashed aside the wet footprints that trailed heavily from the hot tub on the balcony, becoming smaller and fading as the water dispersed in the path they created on the kitchen floor, he could see in each droplet a reflection of the sight he'd seen after opening his front door, the image of a naked man.

The athletic silhouette was something to behold. The few remaining droplets of water that clung to the perfectly taught tanned skin did nothing but enhance the vision and bore emphasis upon the shadows offered by muscle from neck to calf and the fair hairs that stood erect upon his ass and his thighs which were exactly where his focus lay as the young handsome guy turned to face Pip, orange juice carton in one hand and a partly filled glass in the other which left him no immediate physical option of attempting to cover, even if he felt the need, his very erect and very ample dick.

"Hi, Mr Scot, Marcus said to help myself; by the way, this is empty. Do you want me to write a note to get more?" he said and shook the empty carton as if proof was required.

It wasn't really arrogance that made Chris say it; he quite genuinely thought he had the right to help himself as he had done for the last year, in fact, ever since Marcus had moved in with Pip and they had begun their affair. Chris was a fine-looking and fit man, however, not the most academic but couldn't be faulted at work, never late, a team player, always available at short notice, always nice to the members and being eye candy never hurt, so he was very popular with the 'ladies that lunch' overall quite the boon for any business. Or so Pip thought, which was why he had hired him as a gym instructor eighteen months ago. Pip was honestly unaware of Chris's sexuality; why would it matter? Until, of course, you walk in on him and your new husband sans clothing, clearly in mid-flight of a passionate encounter.

Chris was part of the final stage of the SCT fitness development, one of four extra staff needed to cope with the expansion to the second floor of the gym. Pip was overjoyed that this project would finish the whole building and he could offer full spa treatments and take his fitness centre to another level. Finally, his vast glass wall would offer home once more to his coffee lounge, moving it back to where it belonged but this time bigger, better and sexier; not only that, moving it released the front-facing unit, which would be taken by one of the major chain supermarkets for use as one of their express stores who had shown interest in the development many times via one of the gym members who was quite a big cheese with them.

7

So, this was how, two years ago, Marcus appeared on the scene and into the life of Pip. The plans for the upper gym floor had been drawn up for a while by the same trusted company he had used since the project began, Jackson's. A few tweaks were, of course, required to follow the ever-changing trends, including having the glass wall side look as if the floor behind it was floating to those looking in from the marbled staircase or the ground floor. With a change of ideas comes a re-drawing of plans to be submitted once more to the planning department and then the obligatory council inspector who would usually come out, nod, grunt, drink coffee and say something along the lines of 'Yes, we like what you've done here' before suggesting/demanding a small yet obvious detail to be amended which Pip was convinced was so the officer could brag about his involvement in the success of the business. Pip expected nothing more nor less as he stood and welcomed his architect, who was joined by an impeccably well-dressed chap that he presumed must be a new associate at Jackson's. Pip observed this unknown man as he walked with balance and confidence into the main lobby; he thought there was certainly an 'air' about him, something about the way he held onto his fine leather satchel that looked to be the perfect match in shade to his shoes. Light yet perfectly even, well-groomed stubble adorned his chin upon a face that was really far too pretty to be on a man. Pip thought to himself that this guy must keep the stubble to prevent looking ridiculously young and then found himself wondering how well the rest of this stranger was groomed beneath the fine-tailored clothing.

"Bet his socks and pants match his pocket square, and a fiver says, his watch strap matches his shoes…" The all too familiar tone speaking from behind his shoulder was, of course, Jackie who had watched Pip watch the man; she pondered momentarily about the future and for the first time since being part of this friendship, whether one day her bestie would settle down, but before she could decide on the outfit and new hat that would be appropriate to be the best woman at a gay wedding, Mr Jackson and guest had opened the heavy glass entrance door, stepped inside and were now exchanging handshakes and introductions.

"Marcus Bright, the new head of planning at the Valley Council," Jackson said as he almost ushered the man towards Pip's waiting hand, leaving himself the position to look over the shoulder of Mr Bright and mouth the words, "Check your phone," to Pip.

"Pleased to make your acquaintance, Mr Scot, I have heard much about you. Actually, you seem to be quite the modern legend in these parts, so I have looked into your files in great detail. I must say I do like what I see; I am really looking forward to working with you."

"The pleasure is all mine. I'm sure, and please call me Pip or at least Philip."

"Marcus."

He moved his satchel from his right to his left hand, briefly exposing his wristwatch, so he could once more shake hands to confirm the accepted first name terms, a handshake that lasted a whole three seconds longer than it should be accompanied by a non-blinking gaze into each other's eyes. Jackson moved forwards and began to gesture at some of the details of the previous works while Pip leaned behind the reception desk to grab his phone and whisper in Jackie's ear, "It's a steel bracelet strap; you owe me a fiver; I'll let you know about the underwear later…"

Although, once he had read the text sent by Jackson, Pip wasn't so sure about his last remark.

"Pip, the new bloke in charge of the council. London trained, I've asked around, and I'm told, he can be a right pain in the arse, really picky. Tread carefully later. Cheers AJ"

And then another message;

"FFS, do you ever pick up your phone? Call me before I get there! AJ"

Ah, that explains the seven missed calls then, whoops, he thought as he straightened his jacket and headed off to his guests.

"So here is where the steam rooms will be, the sauna, new changing rooms, then on the opposite side will be the therapy rooms, then front to back will be the new coffee lounge with the kitchen over there at the back; I thought it would be better there for deliveries etc. and then the internal stairwell will sweep down from here with a waiting mezzanine above reception."

Marcus nodded in agreement. Pip thought this was going to go a lot better than feared, but then, despite everything he had achieved thus far, he was always so inexplicably anxious. An hour had passed before AJ made his excuses and offered to remove himself, providing everything was fine with the plans. It was his way of judging the situation as well as teasing out any problem Marcus may have seen whilst they were all here on site. He felt like punching the air when he heard that all was well and gladly took the compliment of his standards of both design and execution of work so far. Once Jackson had left, Marcus turned to Pip and looked him square in the eyes as he stepped forwards into what was considered personal space.

"I want to see it all."

"Pardon?" Pip replied, feeling himself blush with the anticipation, hope and a little nervous dread that this handsome young man was flirting with him.

"I'd like to see the whole building, if I may?"

"Well, *er,* yes, of course, I would love to show you. I have even kept the sketches I made in my days of daydreaming; they aren't very good, I'm afraid. In fact, I don't know how Jackson ever translated them into what we see today." Pip chuckled to himself as he thought about the state of some of the scraps of paper he had once presented.

"You know what, Mr Scot, I would love that, as it goes, I am free for the rest of the day, time off by the firm given to explore the area after relocating here, but to be honest, there's not that much to see. I discovered that fact from exploring after moving last weekend, so perhaps after the guided tour, you could indeed show me your etchings."

"Seriously, they aren't good."

"No matter, it makes it more fascinating in a way. Besides, besides if what you say is true about the translation of rough sketch to this glorious outcome, it means your oral skills must be extraordinary."

Pip felt his face burn as it flushed with the realisation that he was indeed being flirted with. It wasn't that it never happened. He was, after all, a handsome chap himself who found it easy to keep in shape even before he owned a gym; he knew that maybe he should tidy his beard a little more often and maybe one day start to use or, at least, learn how to apply the moisturiser from the endless number of gift sets he would receive at Christmas from grateful gym members that always made him mentally recite the phrase, 'So what do you get the man who has everything?'

"Hmm, let's see… not the bloody stuff that you get complimentary from the reps that provide the soap in the changing rooms!" His tiny rant was, of course, only ever heard in his own head and then only thought in jest; anger was something so well hidden it never reared its head; he was really quite a humble man and was genuinely thankful for all that took the time to offer gifts almost as grateful as the boys' home where he re-gifted most of it every January.

Pip leaned across this pretty man's shoulder to swing the fire exit door open and hold it as they passed through onto the first-floor corridor that led back to the marble stairs. He could feel a positive surge of electricity between them as their proximity became closer; Pip thought he felt an underlying urge to grab this stranger and kiss him, entangle each other's arms and legs in a clumsy over, lustful grapple right here in the emergency exit, it caused quite the stir to his crotch making his cheeks flare red once more.

Marcus had a cheeky side to him. He was indeed a man who knew what he wanted, and throughout, his life had very rarely been said no to. He was a little cocky; he knew that, but he managed to portray himself as a cute and misunderstood yet caring and meaningful type whose perfectly aligned teeth created the smile that could win over most. The observation regarding his style was correct. Marcus was quite obsessed with his wardrobe and his image. From his work in The City, he knew that image was everything if you wanted to be noticed, and oh boy, did he. Marcus taught himself how to be the ultimate in a well-groomed male, his shoes imported, his suits tailored, his underwear ironed as impeccably as his London branded shirts that fit closely to his tidy body. Fitness wasn't his thing, but he would attend a gym four times a week for aesthetic reasons. In his mind, he considered nothing to be unobtainable; if he wanted it, he believed it was his right to have it. His target, right now, was the ruggedly handsome and naturally charming man who was holding the door for him, although he did look a little flushed, which delighted him and caused his inner devil to move his body even closer to Pip, deliberately brushing his thigh against the man's hardening member.

"C-C-Coffee?" Pip suggested as the pair approached the main stairs, which they descended to the shop and took their order in take-out containers.

"Tell you what, why don't we walk a little way over there? I can show you where I used to get in as a kid; you can see what I saw."

"Love to," replied Marcus. "I find this place really interesting. I was trying to find out more about it, but there are only the plans that you've submitted over the years, and even the land registry isn't complete just that after the First World War, the land was given to a French dignitary and no clue as to why. It's as if it didn't exist before 1918."

"You don't have to tell me, I know. I've spent so many hours poring over history books and wading through old documents in the reference library and there is so little to find, no plans, no drawings, no photographs. It's as if the only copies in existence are the set I was given after the sale. I nearly gave up looking and drew a line under the history of it, presuming that records had been destroyed in the Great War, when one of the gym members overheard Jackie and me chatting about the possible background and politely butted in with valuable information, albeit handed down hearsay."

"I'm more than intrigued, do tell."

They wandered around the grounds for nearly two hours before re-entering the building and casually strolling up the vast stairs.

"Possibly my favourite part of this place. These stairs feel so grand and, dare I say, a little out of place in a Paper Mill. Are you sure, that is what it was? Or did you have them installed?"

Pip responded, "You know, I've never really thought about it. They're original, apart from some minor repairs to one of the handrails and being cleaned. Of course, they are basically in the same condition as the day I first saw them. In fact, apart from the missing glass in the windows, the whole place was in really good condition behind the boards someone put in to seal it off; I imagine that's when they removed the printing presses and engines and put the boundary fence up. With only two tiny villages close by, I thought there were simply not enough adventurous kids around to wreck it, or they were too scared about the ghosts left from the flood."

Marcus paused and placed his hand on Pip's forearm to halt the stroll.

"Flood? Ghosts? Are you for real?"

"Oh yes, very much so."

They reached the top floor, and Marcus commented on how impressed he was with the layout. To the left of the building were three large apartments, and to his right, a set of very heavy-looking black doors. Pip once more held a door for his guest, who responded again with a deliberate invasion of personal space. "Welcome to my humble abode! Not quite finished yet, but nearly."

"Oh wow, look at this view!"

"Yep, the terrace faces south down the valley, and if you sit here, you face north, and well, obviously, at where the reservoir used to be."

"Reservoir?" questioned Marcus. "That's not listed on any plans anywhere."

Pip took the takeaway coffee cup from Marcus's hand and replaced it with a mug of steaming hot coffee made with the bags he'd seen advertised during one of his very rare times of watching television. He sat next to him on the sofa that faced the front windows and began to explain, "See that curve over there, no, look down a little, yes by that line of trees, that is the foundation of what was the dam wall and over there on the left there's a road that travels from that bricked up tunnel right down to where some of the old sheds used to be, I think it must have been for coal or maybe to take out the finished paper, anyway, if you look up on the right just near the top of the road that brings you down here you can see where the bridge used to connect and run the train track next to the road."

"I'm loving this!" Marcus reiterated. "Please tell me the rest."

"Are you sure?" asked Pip. "I know I can go on and on when it comes to the Mill. You're being very polite to listen to me ramble on; most folk would have done a runner a good couple of hours ago."

Marcus felt he had this guy right where he wanted him, under his control, just to make sure he leaned across, so his face was no more than an inch away from his host. and said, "Hey, I know we only met this morning, and I know that was for official business, which, by the way, is all fine, and I will rubber stamp it all tomorrow, but I honestly am enjoying spending this time with you and hearing all about your passion for this place, it may seem sad, but I work in planning and building control for a reason; I love architecture. Especially buildings that have a tale to tell and especially when there's a handsome man telling the tale."

Marcus leant into the last space between them and kissed him. "Now, if it's all right with you and not too bold, may I suggest a bottle of wine or two and a takeaway, my treat for my first new friend made, although somewhat bizarrely, I feel like I've known you for years. Could I ask one favour, though? I have an overnight bag in the car. May I use the gym to change?"

"Always prepared, are we?" Pip teased. "There's no need to use the gym when there's a perfectly good bathroom over there. Also, yes, oddly, I do feel like I've known you for a while; it's as if we have a connection somehow."

"Thanks, I'll take you up on the offer of using the bathroom for reference, though I was at a conference yesterday and stayed till this morning before coming straight here, hence, the bag. Mind you, I'm beginning to think a little preparation is a good thing. I might keep a permanent bag in the boot, you know, just in case."

They kissed more and a lot more gently than expected, moved to the bedroom and shared each other's bodies, which, with the built-up tension that had grown throughout the afternoon, didn't take long for either to climax. Both showered and Pip offered Marcus a robe, as he was still to retrieve his bag from the car.

They resumed position on the sofa, opened wine and ordered food from the restaurant downstairs, which twenty minutes later was delivered to the door by Jess, who helped as a waitress as well as being one of SCT's reception staff. Pip pondered as to how well house-trained Marcus was, at least, before their swapping of bodily fluids, that is, and instantly placed the food onto the dining table, fetched more wine and cutlery, and beckoned him to join. Pip watched as Marcus took the napkin from its ring – not a fuss that Pip had provided; it came with the plate from downstairs – and laid it gently across his left thigh before checking his posture and beginning to eat.

"Yep, no fish and chips out of the paper on your lap for this guy!"

Pip smiled to himself at the confirmation and glanced across to his guest, who was also grinning. "To new friendships." Glasses raised and a toast was made.

8

"So, tell me more about the guy who interrupted in the gym, the one with more information."

The guys had finished their meal, their first bottle of wine, and after Pip loaded the dishwasher, he had moved to join Marcus back on the sofa with the view.

"Oh, yes, right, sorry I'd become distracted..."

"Well, seeing as I was the cause of the distraction, you are whole-heartedly forgiven; in fact, if you play your cards right, you might get distracted again later. Now, come on. Tell me."

"Adrian Mitchell, that's his name, membership type Circle since we first opened. Pleasant chap, divorced, with two kids, both at university; he restores vintage cars from the sixties, I think. Is that old enough to be called vintage? Or do they have to be from the dawn of motoring? Anyway, he said to Jackie and me that his great-grandfather was the village priest, going way back to the 1890s and was sure that in the church ledgers, he had seen a mass entry of over one hundred deaths when he was riffling through old cabinets in the vicarage. He offered to show us, so I invited him to dinner, and the three of us met up just a couple of days later. Turns out, the vicarage was sold off when the church combined the parishes of here and the next village and Adrian's grandfather took advantage and bought the house that he had been raised in. So, Adrian, a bored teenager sent to stay with Grandad one summer, was on the hunt for loose change so he could get the bus to the cinema; Grandad had said to him that if he sorted out the old office, he could keep any money he found and on top of that he would pay for his cinema ticket. Adrian was always keen on old things, which I imagine is why he has cars as a hobby. Am I wittering?"

"A little, let's call it, an endearing charm."

Marcus topped up the glasses as Pip continued.

"So, Adrian was having a good old rummage when he came across this old ledger. I don't have that, but I do have photocopies of the pages showing ninety-eight registered deaths on July 17, 1852. Every name was neatly entered, clearly by the same hand. There were, I think, four other deaths reported on the same day, but it was the ninety-eight that stuck out, not just because of the high number but the fact that they all bore the same description as the cause of death. Every single one had met their end by drowning. Now, the really odd thing is, as you pointed out earlier, there are no other records to show or explain what happened. Well, no official records. Adrian was quite the teenage investigator; it seemed and had set himself the task to ask every elderly person he could find if they had any information. It didn't take too long before he could piece together what had happened and his grandfather helped where he could."

Pip paused and sipped his drink before continuing. "So, now bear with me. It might not all be in the right order, but hopefully, you will get the gist of it. For a start,

I know it was built as a paper mill because Adrian found quite a by-mistake one of the paper press things at a scrap merchant whilst hunting for a set of wheels for his first car. He said this giant piece of black iron was just sat there and according to the man, who owned the yard, had been there for as long as he could remember, and thought, his uncle had lifted it from that old place in the valley. It took Adrian a few days to work out what it was and a lot more questions to find out that this place was thought to have been built as a paper mill, not just any old mill, either this was steam-powered and planned to be the biggest and most productive of its day – a factory that would be a jewel in Queen Victoria's crown. Indeed, rumour had it that her husband, the Prince Consort Albert, had been a big part of the idea as yet one more of his adventurous projects to prove his worth and power to those who accused him of lacking backbone and hiding behind his wife's petticoats. Anyway, I think that bit is pure fantasy added to spice up an old village tale that continues with sadness. That curve I pointed out was the footing for a dam wall that I've walked upon many times; it's so big it gives almost a flat bottom to where the water would have been and the whole thing is very circular in shape. I've never looked but from upon high, it must look like a giant paddling pool."

"Hang on, did you say circle?"

"Yes, and right in the middle, there's this kind of monolith, which I guess is some kind of memorial."

"No, not that; earlier, you said Adrian was a circle member. What the fuck is that? Are you running some kind of cult here?"

Pip laughed. "Don't be daft. Honestly, I put so much effort into marketing and nobody ever notices. The circle is from the company logo; I used the circle to denote an anytime all-access membership, you know, like a circle, round and not ending, then the Square, which, by the way, is what the S stands for, which is the weekday access before six p.m., then the triangle one is any time access including studio classes and yoga but limited to three hours a day three times a week, that one is definitely the most popular but the seniors tend to buy squares."

"I wish I'd never asked. Is there more wine?"

"Left-hand island, reds are in the cupboard next to the bottle fridge, back in a sec' Pippy gotta go peepee."

He returned to the sofa to find Marcus had dug out not only a further two bottles of Malbec but also the cheese box from the fridge and a box of charcoal and cranberry crackers. "Hope you don't mind."

"Not at all, so where were we? Oh yeah. The dam wall was erected at the same time as this place went up. It seemed excessive when I first heard about it, but then, to be honest, I haven't got a clue how much water is needed for steam power. Or coal. All I know is with the sheer size of this building, it was meant to be a showpiece; maybe that's why the staircase is so extravagant? Makes sense when it's all said out loud. I'm told that the reservoir was left to fill naturally from the three hills that surround it, making the other containing banks, and everything ran very smoothly and planned for a while after completion, in fact, right until that July day. During the very early morning hours, there had been some kind of tremor. Not many folks had ever experienced such a thing, so the topic was hot gossip as the men and women walked into the mill to start a hard day's work and from the steam whistle blowing at seven a.m., the shift began as usual. Only thing was not a soul had thought about checking if the earth tremor had caused any more damage than shaking a few plates from their displays and the loss of a pane of glass from the Post Office window."

"Thought you said there were no fine details."

"There isn't. I added it to set the scene and build up the drama, and also to see if you were paying attention. You passed the test. Well done to you! Now pour more and let me carry on. Turns out, a little shaking of ground had caused some damage—"

Clutching his chest to show his dismay, Marcus interrupted, "Oh, no! Those poor people! The dam gave way?"

"Yes, no, sort of and a bit like earlier, you've peaked a bit too soon. The tremor had caused the railway bridge to split right at its start where it joins the road, up there on the right; I guess, to be fair, even if someone had looked, they would have unlikely seen anything. It was probably only a hairline fracture; no one of that day would have expected that fracture to be sheer and run right through the first brick arch or know that the ground that held the foundation had been loosened. Perhaps, if someone had pieced it together in the seconds before the arrival of the mighty steam locomotive pulling truck after truck of coal, they would have been able to avert disaster. I wonder if any of those workers knew their fate if they heard the screeching sound of metal as the track twisted away from the bridge and beneath the oncoming engine whose weight forced the structure to collapse, bricks tumbling as the brakes of the train were pulled far too late to have any effect whatsoever. In fact, it's likely the emergency stop caused the accident to be of such great magnitude. Rather than gliding to a halt, the pulling of the emergency brakes caused every single pulled truck, each piled high with tons of coal, to shunt into each other; imagine the force felt as each one hit the one in front. The continuous, repeated shuddering impact took its toll on the fractured brick below the engine. It wasn't the tremor that made the dam give way; it was the train. Remember, I said the reservoir had been left to fill naturally. Well with, the constant use of the water in the mill meant that it only ever filled halfway. More than enough water. Only downside was because it wasn't full, there wasn't anything to break the momentum of a running steam train and its cargo now tumbling from the bridge and hurtling towards the dam. All the workers would have probably heard, if anything, I guess, would have been a soft thud as the engine hit the back of the dam wall, the sound muffled by the water, perhaps not even hearing that over the noise of the machinery they were working with and of course none were alerted by the hissing roar the water made as it broke through the cracks the training impact caused. No. I bet the first they knew about anything untoward would have been the tidal wave that ripped through the first two floors below us, glass exploding and cutting them as the water broke through the windows, bodies being beaten by waves, being hurled against machines, against walls, some crushed by the products they had taken such pride in creating. Ninety-eight souls lost in as many seconds."

"Christ."

"I know one accident of nature wipes out all those people, leaving this very space empty, an unused building empty for a hundred and fifty years until I bought it."

Marcus sat thoughtfully for a moment before commenting, "So if the res' had been full, the water would have broken the impact of the train and the dam would probably be here today?"

"Quite possibly, I guess, but also, if the train had still cracked the dam and the water was at maximum capacity, it would have knocked this place flat. Anyway, that's all I know; who cleaned up is still a mystery. I wonder if that monolith is made from the dam bricks? I've drunk too much; time for bed!" The wine consumption had given Pip a sense of bravado. "Joining me?"

9

"Harbridge!"

"Harbridge!"

"Your Highness."

"How long have you been my personal assistant?"

"Since one month before your first anniversary to Her Majesty, sir, it was I with whom you entrusted to locate the gifts."

"Yes, that's right. Now tell me, have you ever disclosed to anyone the finer details of those gifts? You know the more 'personal' items."

"Sir, I would never…"

"I know, I know, I'm teasing you, my friend."

"Friend, sir? I would never be so bold as to presume such a thing despite the honour it would give if it were so."

"That's why I like you, and I consider your dedication and loyal service to be as close as one can be a friend to the Prince Consort."

"Thank you, sir; I would and will never dishonour the crown or your family; my life is dedicated to my duty to serve."

Harbridge was, indeed, a genuine and loyal fellow who, like his father and grandfather before, had served the reigning British monarchs of their time, Queen Victoria and her beloved husband Albert being the current employers of this man who believed to his core that every fibre of his existence was created to serve the crown. James had never taken a bride, thinking that perhaps it would be something to consider if he retired from this royal service; however, in truth, he would prefer to perform in this capacity until the day he died. Now, these words suggest friendship with the man he admired and was so proud to be in the company of sealed his destiny. This was the only position he ever wanted until the end of his time.

His father was a trusted butler at Windsor Castle who had found happiness with one of the junior scullery girls; his position allowed them, once married, to take one of the cottages within the Bailey where James was born. James Harbridge was extremely proud of the fact he had been born not only in a castle but in the one considered the home of the empire's leading royal family. This inner pride was perhaps a tad misguided in that he felt his life was an integral part of the royal family and not just a servant, yet still he rose through the ranks quickly and accompanied Albert on most of his visits and assisted where possible. His job was totally his life, a fact which he equated to the role of the prince himself. His life is his duty and service.

Albert did trust Harbridge. Unbeknown to his loyal servant, he had tested him many times, the very first challenge to locate certain French garments of fancy which would be presented, privately, to his bride upon their first wedding anniversary, a mission performed with efficiency and discretion of this similarly aged man with whom he felt comfortable sharing company. Other juicy snippets of royal household gossip had also been offered several times as well as information invented by Albert, and then, fed to James to once again test to secure the knowledge of having this man's trust; never once had he been let down, and in the more recent times, the prince had allowed James freedom of speech in his presence as to ascertain castle and palace rumour which he was about to do once more.

"Harbridge, may I be permitted to call you James? Would you see that as being out of sorts?"

"Sir, I would happily respond to any beckoning you prefer."

"Then, James, it will be. You are my considered friend, after all, and to save you from struggling to find the courage to ask, you may call me Albert, as a true friend would. Although, I must insist that this is only when we are alone; in any company, including my wife or any staff or associates, the protocol must be adhered to. Is this to your acceptance?"

"Of course, sir, but may I ask why?" James thought this very question was impertinent and regretted saying anything despite this declaration of openness. However, his fears were soon allayed.

"James, please relax, come sit." Harbridge was still standing in his customary position to the right of the oversized double doors finished with golden decal to the private suite of the prince. He did as requested and relaxed his hands from behind his back and moved towards the pair of gilt chairs on either side of a small round table unusually inlaid with ebony, silver and glass offering the illusion of a moving spoked wheel as through the oversized window, sunlight reflected upon it from behind the moving clouds. He sat, trying not to show his uncomfortableness and escalating nerves. "Listen, I have admired your candidness in relaying news, both truth and gossip and expect nothing more as we progress."

"Of course, sir."

The prince looked at him and raised an eyebrow. James took a breath and, with a small smile, corrected himself.

"Yes, Albert, of course."

"Better! I will make a friend of you yet. Now, please understand our friendship is to remain secret for no other reason than my lack of trust in others, all others. Never feel the reasons are to do with rank or rights, royal or staff; I simply no longer can allow myself to give trust to anyone but my wife and you."

"I'm astonished to hear this and honoured at the same time. But why do you feel this way?"

"It has come to my attention that, yet again, there is a plot to assassinate the queen and most likely myself to boot. Now, the palace office is aware of this; however, they did try to keep it to themselves, yet, I uncovered the truth, although, quite by accident. These threats may or may not be serious, but I have a plan to protect my wife, my children and, of course, the crown at all costs. However, it will be a closely guarded secret, in which I will need your help. Firstly, you are, from this day, promoted to Official Senior Aide and trusted advisor to the Prince Consort and with the title comes free reign to access any office or archive that I myself would have; you are a well-deserved right hand. As a confidante, I will need you present at all meetings and gatherings as my eyes and ears to the things I would normally be shielded from. This very fact is why I wish for our friendship to remain private, should you be deemed staff. I feel you would still be trusted with such information if our companionship were known. I fear your isolation and not being privy to passing news. I will require you to travel with me also. Are you well with this?"

"Once more, I assure you my loyalty."

"Good man. Let us resume this conversation in the morning; we shall take a ride across the grounds. I'll have the appropriate costume sent to your cottage."

"Yes, sir… Albert, sir. Oh, this will take some getting used to. I bid you goodnight."

James left the suite and took the stone stairs that led to the rear of the castle and stopped for a second to gaze from the high vantage point across the deep floor of trees before walking around the chapel to the home in which he was born, where he lay on his bed wondering where this new level of responsibility may take him dubious about this somewhat sudden announcement of friendship. He lay for hours pondering. There was certainly no problem on his side about being a friend, over the clear advantage this alone could give him would bode prosperous, but he, of course, would never abuse the connection after all, he genuinely felt a love and admiration for him, and deep down, he knew it simply would be going against all instinct to take advantage.

As the cockerel crowed at dawn the following morning, James heard a knock at his door. He opened it to face no less than the prince's personal valet, Richardson. Behind him, a junior he recognised from the boot room, which was laden with not only riding gear but what seemed to be several other outfits.

"With compliments of the prince," Richardson said with almost a sneer. "I had to come and see for myself that this isn't an error. Why has his highness had us up all night preparing outfits for you and a new uniform?"

"Hello, William." James smiled at his colleague. "Am I not worthy of new clothing, old friend?"

"Come on, what's going on? Bellow stairs reckon you're a secret heir and that your Mam succumbed to Royal advances."

"Very funny! Tease as you will, Mister Richardson. You knew my mother well enough to know she would succumb to nothing and no one and only had eyes for Father. Truth is, I've been promoted to His Highness's senior personal aide, and it will be announced officially later today. I must say, though, I didn't expect a night shift for new clothing to be ordered just for me, sorry. Heck, I bet Polly and Miss Louise are fuming with me!"

"Not at all, not for you, James, you're far too well-loved around here. Cards Friday night? Or are you above that now?"

"Yet once more, you utter words of wit. I'll see you there, and I'll bring chocolate to say thank you."

With that, the junior placed the outfits on a hall chair, and the men left to continue their morning tasks. James bathed, dressed, and walked to the stables to be greeted by quite an excitable Albert.

"Harbridge! There you are, come on, you can mount Chester today; he looks in need of a good canter; I'll ride Duke."

Chester was a simply stunning creature. James patted him as he walked around to stroke his head; Chester responded by nuzzling into the kind man's neck, his long white mane gently ticking his face. Chester stood still as his rider took a seat in the highly polished fine leather saddle adorned with the embroidered royal crest strapped to his strong dapple-grey body. James realised he was sitting on one of Alberts's personal saddles and felt he should dismount and point out the error when he caught sight of a knowing nod from the prince, making it clear that a point and no error was being made by the selection of tack before raising and lowering his right arm indicating the start of the ride.

It was a clear but cool morning as they rode, making James think how grateful he was for the prince to provide suitable clothing. After around forty minutes, Albert headed towards a densely wooded area of the estate and guided his steed through the trees to a large clearing, in which in the centre sat a stunning fifty feet high iron framed domed orangery. The beautiful circular structure looked as wide as tall, and through the glass, James could see on the opposite side to the double entrance doors was a spiral staircase that led to a gallery landing around the structure. Although as impressive as the building was, it wasn't as immensely surprising as what happened next. Albert reached into his pocket and removed four keys.

"That's quite the novelty to see; I must say, sir, sorry, Alb… *ahem,* I don't think I have ever seen any of the monarchies carry keys before."

"There will be a few things that may surprise to become apparent, my friend. Please secure the horses while I set up."

James took the reins and led them to a water trough and tethered them while the prince unlocked the doors and carried them inside a hamper that had been left by the door, where he proceeded to unpack the contents of food and flasks onto the side tables that sat in front of the plants around the glass circumference.

"Help yourself! Get it whilst it's still hot."

"Thank you," said James, trying not to show shock that he was being served and not serving, and loaded a plate with warm fresh bread and preserves before joining Albert at the round centre table surrounded by four large leather winged chairs.

James felt a little tense and still unsure about the protocol of being a royal friend, but he thought, if he was in error at any time, his apology would be accepted, so he braved himself and opened the conversation.

"This is an impressive glass house; I didn't even know it was in the grounds."

"Thank you. I had it built three years ago. Castles and palaces are all very well, but this place is just mine, somewhere I can retreat and have my own thoughts without interruption. You may have noticed the food was left outside at the door. That is because I have the only keys, well, until today." Albert handed two of the four keys that James had seen over to him. "The square teeth key is for the top lock, the one with triangular teeth is for the bottom lock. At fifty-five feet high in the grounds of the Royal family home, this may not be a secret, but it is very private and is where you and I shall hold our most involved conversations. The beauty of here is not its soundproofing qualities, which are little, but more that we can see if anyone is trying to eavesdrop."

James was as flattered with being entrusted with access to this most private of places as he was bewildered by his new role, which he feared would be by far more complex than imagined.

"James. I said last night that I have a plan to protect my wife and my children; my friend, you are an integral part of this, and for my position dictates anonymity, I will be entrusting you with all the required dealings. Please use this place as often as you wish for personal use as well as an office for our combined dealings. The balcony above us has a hollowed chamber that runs around the inner handrail; it is in there we shall store our documents and where you will leave messages and packages for me that I may discover should we never have the opportunity to speak, the walls of Windsor do indeed have ears after all."

"May I see?"

The prince rose from his chair and led James to and up the spiral staircase and stood at the inner railing looking down upon the chairs and then across to the clearing the other side of the glass. "I do love glass. One of these days,

I'll have a huge glass building made that all can use. For now though, the matter in hand." He opened the first compartment and handed the contents to Harbridge. "There you will find your new papers, details of your new banking and investment accounts, a certificate of birth and assorted receipts from your tailor, with whom you have an appointment next Monday by the way, I am sure the ladies performed an excellent job in altering some of those spare suits that tailors almost throw at a Royal in the hope that he would be seen in them, but a man must have his own made for him, watch, rings and other pieces I will have sent over from my own collection, you must use them all as if they had no value."

"I'm confused. Why, sir? I respect your generous gifts; I presumed that the arrival of various outfits earlier this morning contained a befitting uniform and travelling clothes to suit my promotion. But for what purpose is this paper masquerade? Who is James Percival and why do I have his details?"

"Please get used to calling me Albert; it is going to be very important that you are comfortable relaxing when in the company of the gentry. As for the identification, my friend, outside of the castle walls, you will no longer be senior aide Harbridge but the wealthy son of an American gold mine owner, James Percival. I obviously cannot spend time in the city without my plan quickly being uncovered. Therefore, I have invented a new persona for you. There's plenty of money in those accounts to reward you after my project is complete, and don't worry, I have already set up most of the things we will require during the last six months, or rather Mr Percival has."

"So, um, I... you wish for me to pretend to be a wealthy man to set up a project on your behalf that may be needed to protect your family and here we use as an office?"

"Yes, and within that package are also the deeds to a house in the city, which is yours to keep as my small way of saying thank you for the performance that I sincerely hope you do not find an inconvenience, but it is more than just a gift, Percival will need a city address for deliveries or maybe the odd meeting, folk do become suspicious if public meeting places are often used and the gossiping gentlemen who frequent the private clubs are exactly who we are trying to avoid the prying eyes and ears of."

"But Albert, will the city set not recognise me as an imposter? Or, for that matter, know me as your servant? I have been in attendance for the majority of gatherings."

"James, do not be offended when I say you will never have been noticed as anything more than service staff. The vile, pompous, vain creatures that hang onto our coattails and pretend to be of standing are nothing more than jumped-up, rude and arrogant monsters that wrongly think themselves above and better than those who bring their drinks and serve their food. Believe me, it is only dressed in fine threads that they will see you, and I regret, will try and flock around the new boy in town. As for imposters, the city is filled with new money that cannot hold their own in a society where, whereas you, dear man, have been literally raised in the bosom of all this pomp and circumstance, I have thought it through, I promise. There is only Lord Cushing that gave me fear of our plan being unfurled, for as you know, he attends every single bash he can and has quite the attentive eye for our young male uniformed waiters, but then I thought with the amount of Spanish brandy he consumes it is most unlikely that he would recognise even myself the following day! Let us take tea and allow a little time for you to absorb things so far before we discuss what I need you to do and bring you to speed as to what 'you, James Percival Esq.,' have done so far."

10

James loved and hated central London at the same time. As the driver brought the horses to a halt, He looked from the cab window at his new 'home'. The three-floor Chelsea mews above a basement apartment almost shone in the morning sunlight. Alighting the cab and paying the driver who had courteously placed the trunk and two travelling cases at the door atop the eight white stone steps, James admired the gentle curve of this handsome street filled with identical houses with their wrought iron railings and simple white columns supporting a small flat roof creating porch shelter at each door. He took the time to acknowledge the hat tilt of a passer-by and wondered if the wearer would be a neighbour before reaching into the smart monogrammed document case the prince had presented him with as a welcoming gift to mark his new position. *Or to remind me who I am meant to be,* he thought as he caught a glimpse of the initials J.P as he removed the envelope containing the keys to the heavy black front door.

The simple elegance of the house was pleasing to the eye, James thought as he moved from room to room, admiring the rich, polished woods of the furnishings provided. The pieces were perfect for a gentleman's home, stylish for the periodic yet not overly fussy and limited in number, giving an air of extra space within the plain white walls which were ready for personal decoration; however, James thought he was quite partial to the stark finish and would delay his meeting with the decorating company from Mayfair, a touch the prince thought appropriate surely those Yanks would order the biggest and most expensive available. James began to think and worry a little about the monstrous task before him. The prince had trusted and expressed his faith in him, and he was sure that organising the project would not be difficult; the problems would be maintaining the secret and splitting his time between the city and the castle. Albert had assured him that now being his Senior Aide would allay suspicion as most would presume his Castle absence as nothing more than running official errands for Royal business or whim.

—

"One of four," Albert told him.

"Pardon?"

"The table is one from a set of four. I noticed you admiring one of its brothers in my quarters. They were a gift from the coachbuilder, four to represent the number of wheels on the carriage he was commissioned by the queen to build. I find them to be quite the novelty, the way the spokes are filled with glass to make a usable surface yet retain the illusion of a wheel. I find them inspiring. Should one ever be stuck for an idea, sit and look at an object that makes you think about its concept and build, it always gets one's brain ticking again. These tables are my muse!"

James recalled the conversation as he sat in one of the pairs of high-backed leather winged chairs not dissimilar to those used in the Windsor glass house and studied his very own gifted wheel table between the seats in front of the tall panelled sash window. The table was his new favourite possession, and James had decided, no matter what, that it would always be an inspiration, as he was sure was the intention of it being put here. As the morning progressed, the passing sun shone into the front room, creating three bright stripes upon the breast of the fireplace. James stroked the edge of the table and saw the stripes were a reflection of three vertical gold inlays, each around half an inch wide inserted into the table rim, it struck him that he had noticed a single golden stripe previously on another of the set in the prince's quarters as candlelight danced upon it. *Three of four?* he thought and took pride that just as his employer, he understood how an object could be a comfort and an inspiration, and once again, felt incredibly honoured to own such a personally valued piece.

James completed his exploration of the house and gave home to the contents of his bags and chest into the first-floor back bedroom, which one would presume was designed to be the master, yet he decided, it would be the best place for a study, so he could see from above any visitors that may impose upon his chosen solitude. An afternoon of moving furniture followed to create his workspace before taking the last package from the trunk and placing it on the heavy leather inlaid writing desk, which he had hauled each section to the room up the staircase from the middle reception room. Sitting down, he took the folding blade from a drawer and slit the coarse string that bound the brown paper covering the box. Unwrapping it to expose a lockable red case that James knew would have to be kept hidden from all eyes but his.

"My dearest Percival," the letter atop the box contents began, *"The contents of this box are to be used as a reminder of the plans, we discussed at our last meeting. You will also find a book containing the names of the architects I think we should use, some of which have already been contacted, and indeed, you will see from the enclosed diary that some appointments have been scheduled and will require your attendance. The sketches will further explain how I want this to look. Please study in detail; as far as anyone is concerned, the project is yours; therefore, you must appear confident in discussing the plans. Additional banking details are also enclosed for the project; a further two accounts for you to use as you see fit; perhaps dedicate one to each part of the project? I will leave the decision in your capable hands."*

A quick check of the diary revealed the first meeting was the very next day with French architect Jules Pascale, who, according to the notes, was a young protégé twenty years previously of the firm commissioned by Louis XIII for the renovation of the Louvre. Taking the sketches from the box, James prepared himself for a long night of study and preparation and recalled that first glasshouse meeting.

—

"Harbridge, the threats and assassination attempts are no longer tolerable; if I cannot wipe out those who make them, then my only choice is to protect. My plan is simple; I shall hide my family whenever I feel we are under attack. I shall build a fortress that no one can enter that will be hidden from view on the border with Wales."

The sketches were actually quite detailed drawings; it seemed the prince had rather an artistic gift when depicting his ideas. The structure to be created was to be subterranean at the foot of three hills; Albert had even suggested its construction would begin with excavation and then covering it rather than the more time-consuming tunnelling approach. He wished for a large factory unit to be erected a little further down the valley from the site that would initially be used to home the workers, builders and engineers whilst the project grew; all of those employed were to be brought in from France or Spain and not allowed to venture from the grounds until their short contracts were complete and they were replaced with other cross channel staff. Albert thought that this way, rumour would be kept to a minimum and knowledge of his bolt hole limited. The factory unit covering five floors would later be used as a paper mill, which is where James Percival enters as the frontman to the charade. The Mill would be fed by water from a reservoir contained by a strong circular dam, built between the side hills of the valley over the new royal safe house, access to which would be via elevator from a dead-end train tunnel to be purpose-built into the side of one hill and supplied by rail track that would sit atop a bridge high above the water's surface. Albert planned that the train would first be used for materials and manpower transport and then later to bring goods for the paper mill and export finished goods, the real intention, of course, being the secret passage of his family to safety.

James sat with Monsieur Pascale Abreo at their meeting place, a fine Mayfair hotel, the following day.

"Mister Percival, these ideas are ambitious yet achievable, but may I enquire as to their purpose?"

Grateful that this gentleman's English was near fluent as he could not himself speak a word of any other language; James responded with his well-rehearsed script.

"It is the wish of my Father. As you are no doubt aware, his success in America has given the family great fortune. Father wants this building as a vault, a fortress for his fortune and himself; he does not believe in banks, and I fear he suffers paranoia that everything will be lost, hence, wanting this remote location to house himself away from the prying world."

"I see you wish for this to be self-sustaining. We will have to work hard to create how this may be possible."

The men sat and discussed options for several hours, Pascale writing frantically notes after that would help him with the plans. He'd accepted that the project was to be a secret and that it was because of his connections to the French Establishment that discretion would be assured. With so many drawings and details provided by Albert, the redraw of the plans was expected to take only a few days for the deep underground construction; as for the factory building, a structure required as a masquerading business, Pascale suggested he duplicate a recently completed premises just three miles away on the bank of the Thames.

11

"Babe, can you pour me one?" The voice became louder and clearer as its owner moved closer to the kitchen. Marcus walked straight over to the handsome young Adonis-like naked man, dropped to his knees and went to take his lover's throbbingly erect penis in his mouth. Chris didn't move, didn't speak, didn't breathe.

Pip simply cleared his throat to indicate he was in the room.

Marcus hadn't even noticed that his husband had come home, and with his back to him whilst knelt on the floor, he uttered the words, "Oh, fuck."

"Erm, should I go?" questioned Chris to the silent room filled with tension so strong, it could almost manifest into a physical being.

"Might be an idea," Pip responded in a tone so calm it unnerved the other two men in the room. It was a voice that was controlled, one that should have been screaming instead of this simple, somewhat muted sound that gave a spine-chilling sense of power. Chris put down his juice and walked to the bedroom. Despite the situation, Pip had to admire the view of the strong thighs and firm round ass, taut torso and strong, broad back upon one of his gym instructors as he walked away, but right now, that wasn't the topic that required discussion.

A uniform tracksuit-clothed Chris strolled confidently past the married couple and to the heavy doors. "I'll call you later, M, see you at work, Mr Scot," he cheerfully said as he left the apartment. The door clicked shut before Pip spoke to his naked husband, still facing away from him, who sat back on his calves where he had shifted himself to a more comfortable position from being knelt on the floor.

"Would you like to tell me what the fuck is going on?" Pip said in the same overly calm tone.

Marcus stood upright and turned to face his partner. "You mean apart from how fucking amazing sex is with that beautiful young man?"

"What? What the fuck?" Pip was in total disbelief at this reaction, but then the last couple of minutes that seemed to have lasted achingly longer than had actually passed hadn't really given him a chance to fully process the rush of totally unexpected information, let alone the supercilious attitude with which it had been delivered. Marcus silently removed himself from the scene to the bedroom, returning momentarily, dressed in a simple mid-brown crew neck fine knit jumper, dark checked trousers and fine brown leather slippers; despite the hurried dressing, he still looked as if he had been dressed by a professional in a top end department store. The fitted trousers outlined his still near-hard member.

Pip, however, hadn't moved, and wasn't sure, that moving was actually an option; he felt glued to the spot. He stood focused on the tiny inverted reflections in the droplets of water on his highly lacquered floor. His mind could still see the images each reflective globule held, frozen there like a photograph, now permanently etched in his memory. As he eventually looked back up at his husband, he felt as if the world was about to sway out of existence. He felt himself begin to fall forwards and tightened his grip on the closest chair back. "I'm going to be sick," he announced and rushed past Marcus to empty his gut of the coffee and toast he'd wolfed down earlier.

"Don't make a mess in there! Peggy is off for two days, remember."

Pip sat on the floor next to the toilet, reached up and pulled the chain to flush away his breakfast. He couldn't help but wonder if all of this was real; perhaps, he would awaken to find all was well and he was having a stress-related episode, that he would arise from his warm bed, grab a robe and wander to the kitchen and grab a cookie that the cleaner, Peggy, who Marcus had insisted on them employing, would make her favourite boss, the 'other one' she found to be false, above his station, with a distressingly arrogant streak. He stood up and splashed his face with fresh water from the small hand basin. Then, he took a minute to gather himself. Often, he had found that distraction from a subject would help him absorb the original topic; he wondered if this was a skill or perhaps if he was deemed to be recognised on a spectrum other than the collection of colours used on the Pride flag, he smirked at his private little joke, breathed deeply in and out as his former therapist had shown him how to do in times where composure was required in stressful times at unfathomable, unavoidable events. He looked squarely at his reflection in the small oval copper framed mirror he had found in one of the rooms on the third floor that had inspired his entire bathroom design. Standing tall, re-tucking his shirt and checking the collar, he felt he was as prepared as he ever could be to confront his new husband and have one of the most awkward conversations of his life. Little did he know exactly how awkward the talk or the consequences of it were to become. He exited the bathroom and walked silently into the kitchen, poured himself a glass of tap water and leaned against one of the islands. Marcus stood casually next to the other island, sipping coffee made from the bean-to-cup machine he simply had to have, leaving the built-in machine once more without a chance of ever being useful; it simply sat there as a focal point that Pip would need through the next few minutes.

Looking like two opposing politicians stood at their rostrums, Pip broke the silence.

"Seriously, what the fuck is going on?"

"Did you make a mess in the bathroom?"

"What?"

"Did you make a mess in the bathroom? I don't want to use it if it's covered in bits of your breakfast, do I? Christ, do you never think about my standards?"

"What! Are you for real? No, I didn't make a fucking mess in the fucking bathroom!"

"Good, so what seems to be your problem?"

Pip was seriously trying not to cloud judgment or confuse his train of thought with rapidly building anger, yet this bizarre, sudden, arrogant attitude of Marcus was making that quite the challenge.

"Well, let's see, Darling Marcus, the problem looks to be about the fact I have just walked in to find you and a member of my staff in the middle of having sex. With me so far?"

Marcus was undaunted by the context of the sentences he was hearing.

"So?"

"So? So! Well, let's see now. You're married to me! Affairs are not allowed, or did you not read the handbook? For fuck's sake, we haven't even been married a year."

"Oh. That. Well, if it helps with timeframes, we've been having sex for a lot longer than you and I have been married; bloody good sex, too, way better than with you and as for under a year, really? Is that all? Are you sure? Feels like twenty!"

Pip was really not feeling anywhere near normal; the conversation was by far too surreal. He regained focus on the shiny, redundant coffee machine and discreetly pinched the inner side skin of his left wrist. He looked down to confirm his reality check and saw the indentation from his thumbnail redden as he felt the sting begin to subside. This was not a dream.

"Let me get this straight. Have you been sleeping with Chris since before we married?"

Marcus's frank response wasn't expected and not wanted, yet almost welcomed rather than hearing excuses and misplaced blame that one expected with the discovery of an affair.

"Oh, poor little Philip! Nanna's little Pippy! I've been with Chris since the day you took him on after the gym extension. He was mightily impressed to know I was behind the planning approval and even more so to know that the place would be mine and, Oh, that body! I tell you, that first time in the changing room shower is one I will always remember." Marcus smiled as he recalled the first moment, he had purposely brushed past the hot new gym instructor and, after some teasing words, leaned forwards and touched his still near erect cock through his trousers.

Pip raised his voice a little. "You fucked in my gym! A... and what do you mean yours? This place is mine; everyone knows that, lock, stock and barrel."

"Oh, darling, do let me explain; clearly, your tiny mind is having trouble with comprehension of the matter." The sarcasm and condescending tone that spoke Marcus's sneering nasty words were sickening. Pip had never heard anything like it from anyone, especially not the man he thought he liked enough to consider the feelings a kind of love, enough to offer marriage. He had surrendered to compromise after giving up hope of ever again finding the feelings of dizziness, lust, longing and completeness that he'd experienced in his youth; those chances are few and far between, he feared; it had been a long time since he thought that the love train only passes through your station once and once only.

"It's like this... actually, let's be civilised and sit; it seems a shame to waste the sunshine I was enjoying before you rudely interrupted."

Marcus took a large silver ice bucket from a cabinet and placed two bottles of crisp New Zealand Sauvignon into it, added ice, then grabbed two large glasses by the stems and led out to the roof terrace. He sat on the rattan garden suite and beckoned the man he had betrayed to join. Pip sat opposite and took a filled wine glass from the table between them.

"Now, where shall I begin?" Marcus purposely paused as if to contemplate his approach. "Chris is nothing more than a plaything, although I must say I am really attracted to him, and I have a hankering that he is besotted with me; we have such a giggle together; he's supportive, loyal and dependable. I know he may not be the sharpest tool in the box, but that is part of his appeal and my God, that cock of his! Drop that boy a Viagra, and he can reach parts I never knew could be pleasurable."

"He fucks you? Enters you? But you have never wanted me to do that, and since when do you need Viagra?"

"I don't need it; we take it for extra fun. Surely, you noticed the glorious effect when you came in."

"Couldn't really miss it, could I? Guess that explains the bulge you're still nursing, too."

"Aw shucks, thanks for the compliment. Chris loves to get his hands on it as many times a week as he can."

"Times per week? But you said you have a really low sex drive! I bet we haven't had sex ten times in the last twelve months!"

"Well, Pip, what do you expect? There's only so many times a week a man can perform, and what with the four- or five-times Chris and I are at it, there's little left. Besides, it's so difficult to be interested in sex when it's with an old fart like you. I like fresh, young, firm men, dear."

Pip was almost becoming immune to this barrage of nastiness. His brain had presented a filter to not take in the spiteful phrases. He wanted the episode over. Not knowing or understanding this unprovoked attack led his mind to conclude this was a sick kind of game, some weird test, perhaps. It wasn't as if he was old, being in his late forties, and knew from many advances and comments that he couldn't possibly be in too poor a body shape.

"I don't believe this is happening; why are you doing this to me?"

Marcus shifted in his seat, not through discomfort but moreover to perform assertiveness. His glass refreshed, and he flicked an imaginary piece of lint from his crossed leg before continuing.

"Well, Philip, please don't think that it's because you're special in any way because I can tell you right now that you ain't all that."

Pip was rendered speechless. He had never experienced such poison; the shock of the change in attitude, the discovery of the affair was sinking in as a reality quickly; the stranger he was married to continued, at least with his touch of narcissism. Pip knew that this monologue might be of length.

"Quite simply, my darling, you are nothing more than access to an early and comfortable retirement. I've always worked in planning and had really good positions, but it took me nearly a year to get this transfer; despite Daddy pulling the strings with his council friends, I needed to get things moving. One might say he would have done anything to get me further away from Mother to try and stop her giving me money." Marcus chuckled lightly to himself. "I don't know why they moan about money so much; they've got plenty, and it's their fault for showing me the finer things and sweetie to look this good cost plenty."

"Erm, yes, I know how you can spend; I haven't even paid for the wedding yet! Nothing left after your 'must have' new wedding and honeymoon wardrobe and not forgetting paying off your Chelsea Taxi loan with money that took me forever to save, you've had all of my personal money, spent it all, gone."

"Well, you will. Anyway, Daddy sort of cut me off a couple of years ago because I 'borrowed' £250,000. Well, it will all be mine one day. After all, I'm the eldest and the twins certainly don't have the style that needs supporting; Christ, they don't even have accounts with Harvey Nic's! Just a couple of barren spinsters, never got on with them, bloody embarrassment if you ask me? So Father says, I've been written out of his will because I 'stole' from him, but I think it's an idle threat, pretty sure Mother will sort him out. Anyway, it's never been difficult to access his computer so if necessary, I'll help myself again, what's he going to do? Be embarrassing for him to have bad press about his only son. Especially in those circles. Oh, speaking of the press…"

Marcus reached for his tablet, unlocked it, swiped to his files and selected one before handing it across the table. Pip took it, not knowing what to expect on this day of unwelcome surprises. The screen showed the front page of a Glaswegian newspaper from 1964 with a highlighted article on the right-hand side. He pinched and zoomed in to read.

Glasgow Bugle
14 March, 1964
Jewel Heist

At around ten p.m., last evening, Friday, 13 March, two masked raiders broke into Mackenzie's Fine Stone Crafts, Fife Way, Industrial Quarter, Glasgow and held late-night worker Mister Geoffrey Scott captive until his reluctant release of the contents of the company safe. Husband and Father of one Scot described the two men as tall, both possibly just over 6'3', wearing matching dark blue overalls, heavy steel toe-capped boots and black balaclavas. Both men held shotguns and threatened Mister Scot with being shot if he did not open and empty the safe contents into the red duffle bags with white piped edges and string. Additionally, he thought there may have been a third man waiting outside in a car as he heard one of the men shout loudly, "Keep it running!"

The safe contained several finished pieces of fine jewellery, including a sapphire and diamond necklace, several diamond rings, plus a large collection of uncut precious stones and metals belonging to the Royal Family of England, which the firm had been commissioned to craft into a necklace and other matching pieces as featured in the Monday evening edition of this paper entitled *Local Pride*.

Mr Scot's employers are devastated by the theft but are relieved and grateful that no harm or worse was caused and have offered full support and full pay while their master craftsman recovers at home from this harrowing ordeal. Scot, who was working late to get a head start on the royal project, said, "I feared not for my own life but for my wife and child if they had to survive without me. I tried to get the men to leave, but the sound of the hammer of the gun being cocked meant that they really meant business. I'm very sorry this has happened to the company. I feel that I have let them down."

Police are appealing to anyone who may have seen the men or the car they used and urge witnesses to come forwards.

—

Pip had never seen the article before. "Oh. Never knew that. I think that's about the time Grampy and Nanna moved around here. Certainly, makes sense now; he must have been so upset he couldn't face going back there. Hell, it might even explain why he was such a miserable git. Oh, I feel bad for him now. No wonder they didn't tell me; it must have been too painful."

Marcus smiled the widest of sneering grin, exposing his perfectly coloured and even veneered teeth. "Oh, you think that, do you?"

He reached behind the cushion he was sitting against and withdrew the 'thistle box'.

"What are you doing with Nanna's jewellery box?" Pip asked.

Marcus leaned forwards and placed the simple stained oak box with the relief carving of a wild thistle in the lid and slipped open the simple brass hook from its catch. Opened the box before Pip, who saw the very same contents it had always given a home; a pair of Pearl earrings, a small ruby engagement ring, a simple gold cross and chain, some plastic junk pieces from the eighties and a coin that she had kept from her very first date with the love of her life that they were going to buy chips with on the way home from the dance at the village hall but missed getting there before closing time.

"Tell me, do you think I chose you at random? Do you think our first meeting was a chance connection from official council business?" Marcus questioned. "Because it wasn't. I knew of you from the published article in Gay Business a few years ago. I'm sure you remember it, the one where the feature photo shows you sat on that fucking picnic basket that some two-bit self-elected business society gave you just for being a queen that can keep a business open for a whole year. Well, anyway, I liked the look of the building, and the plans in your outlined description looked quite promising to be profitable, so I kept an eye on the developments until I thought it was a good time to get into your life and take what I needed. I thought I'd get a few pennies out of you easily as it was clear you were a desperate, sad old fairy that would do anything for attention from a young, handsome man like me who would usually be considered way out of your league. Then, of course, with your easily opened mouth, you told me your dreams on the second date, looking from that very window facing the hills, telling me all about your wish to build outward-facing houses that would be taller in the front plots than the shallower buildings at the back to compensate for the rise in the hill where the reservoir had sat, so that the rooflines would appear on one level and could shimmer sunlight from the solar tiles resembling the reflection that may have been seen of light on the body of water in its original form. How the sun's energy could be stored in basement batteries and used cooperatively around the development, free power for all, et cetera et cetera, et cetera, fuck you did drone on and on. However, I must admit the idea was a good one; fine houses get fine money."

"Yeah, it would, but you won't see a fucking penny of it, you conniving little prick! I won't build the houses; you're getting nothing. In fact, get the fuck out of my house. You don't get to rip me off; you've had enough; go on, pack up and go."

"I'm not going anywhere."

"Marcus, I have literally just walked in on you having an affair. There's not a divorce judge in the land that will grant you a penny of my money, I'm sure. What are you doing with that old box?"

Marcus leaned forwards to the open box and twisted the brass loop kept at the front of the lid. Pip had no idea that it did that despite many times over the years taking a look inside the trinket box as he reminisced about his family, yet now watched as a hinged panel dropped from within the lid exposing a secret compartment lined with felt shrunken to perfectly cover tailored hollow shapes cut there to hold firm special items.

"Like I said, I won't be going anywhere, not least until I have what I want."

"Erm, am I missing something? Nanna's trinket box has a secret compartment; your point is, what exactly? Are we off to the antiques roadshow? Is there an inscription saying that a little bit of oak belonged to a highland prince? Give it here and fuck off."

"No, no, no and well, to be blunt, no. I won't be going anywhere for if you scroll down to the pictures on that iPad a little more…"

Pip followed the instruction to read a follow-up article, regarding the robbery, which stated that despite investigations, neither the thieves nor jewels had been found. Interviews with the victim, who had been held at gunpoint, expressed his fears for his life and the nightmares he'd had and now was suffering from nervous shaking leaving his specialist workmanship somewhat redundant so would be finding a fresh start somewhere safe for himself and family.

Below that, there was a photo of the trinket box, then another closer shot of the thistle, another showing the box open and then a final one showing the open box's false lid displaying in full HD glory each of the cut slots filled with fine jewellery containing the most exquisite large stones and others holding unmounted polished gems. The box lid was around the size of a sheet of A4 paper; Pip couldn't even imagine the value of this collection that filled every available square millimetre.

"Of course, I've taken them out," said Marcus. "They're very safely out of your reach."

"I don't understand."

"Look, Pip, it's easy. You told me about the house plan; so I stayed around to take the money; then you told me about the tobacco tin you found with the precious stone chips that you sold to help fund the gym and the purchase of the site, so I did a little, well quite a lot of digging of my own into your history. I'm amazed you never did; it's really easy if you know the right people. That grandfather of yours I must say I have a lot of respect for; he staged that robbery and made his excuses of having a fresh disability to relocate, hiding his booty right here. Think about it; a near-perfect crime, working alone late at night, the company's previous stupid boast of the work they'd taken on for the queen, no CCTV back then, just the statement from a loyal employee who had once again volunteered to work late alone to get up to speed on a project that he himself had purposely made behind schedule. Once you told me about the tin of gems, the clues slotted together, there simply had to be more, as no way would any company allow stones to be taken or bought if they could have used them to create other jewellery. Those stones must have been stolen over the years. Then I happened to watch an old film from the fifties and in it, a vial of the murderer's poison, which she had been dripping daily into her husband's food to slowly kill him, was hidden in a box with a catch just like this one, so I tried it, I bet your grandfather saw the same film. So, a little WD40 and a pair of pliers later, an anti-clockwise turn revealed the compartment. It was complete, all bar one piece, so I did a bit more digging and guess what? Your Nanna didn't win any money at the bingo; they didn't have prizes like that here or within fifty miles of here at that time; she must have discovered the compartment and sold one of the rocks, from the shape of the only empty holder I'd guess at it being a hefty number of carats."

"Wow, that's quite the story, but so what? I'm not being blackmailed by you; I'll hand over the gems and carry on. I never had them, so I'm not going to miss them, am I?"

"Irrelevant, my dear. Attempt to deny my requests, and I'll expose the fact you sold stolen jewels to fund this building. I'll swear to the fact that you blackmailed me into sorting and approving the plans for those houses, permission for the shop to open, alterations to this very balcony and of course the extension of the car park, so let's see, the money for the Range Rover will be seen as one payment, I'm sure I will be able to think of others, my Breitling maybe? I'll tell everyone how I felt pressured into marriage through constant abuse and then, of course, please don't forget that pulling out of the house deal will leave you broke. Don't try to say anything to contradict; you forgot your phone this morning. I answered the call from the architect and being who I am as a husband and planning executive, I was told in full about the funding approval that you pre-signed. Do anything now but build, and you will lose the very land we stand on to the investors. Also, please remember that if you make anything difficult for me in any way, I will halt building progress through my job so much and so often and for lengths of time that I see fit until I send you bust."

Pip sat, shocked. "You will never get away with this."

"I already did. I was going to wait until the houses were built before telling you, but you had to go and come home early and spoil the big plan, it matters not. There's no way you would risk losing everything. Now, to get me out, I want £20 million. I'm not greedy; I reckon it's about half of what the new development profit will be plus the value of this old shack. I'm sure by completion, a divorce lawyer would fight for and no doubt get the same. So, I will move into the front bedroom until the first house is ready, which will be a gift from you. By the way, the morning light in that balcony bedroom wakes me too abruptly, so you can keep it. Actually, I might just go and have a nap soon; all this chat is rather exhausting and boring, to be honest, could do with recovering from that awesome session you went and spoiled too."

"Why are you doing this to me?"

"Like I said, easy target, and I like money. No, there's no daytime TV story of mistreatment in childhood; mine was glorious. I had everything I wanted and more. I simply like money, and I'm going to take it from you. Oh, and don't think coming clean with the law will get you anything more than a prison sentence; those stones you sold are traceable and I'm positive they are the cuts from the pieces of the box collection, which, if you recall the detail from the article I've shown you belong to the crown, so guess from whom you have profited…"

12

The If Only

The rage built within Philip like something he had never before experienced. His heart pumped faster and stronger, pushing the blood through the veins of his body, causing heat to build in each muscle. He almost pictured himself sitting there seething, shaking, body hunched and ready to fight. He had never been a fighter, never found interest in people knocking several bells out of each other, never understood the hook of street fight movies. In fact, the only violent film he had enjoyed was 'Fight Club' and that was only because of the draw of Brad Pitt's tanned and toned and oiled torso.

But now the need to harm was here. Pip felt totally justified as he launched himself forwards, smashing the wine glass into the side of Marcus's face; he let go and grabbed the silver knob handle on the side of the ice bucket, curling it into his palm and making the vessel an extension of his arm and swung it towards his foe. The rim of the bucket struck Marcus in the upper chest and cut through fabric and skin, letting blood pour through. Marcus was on his feet in an attempt to escape the attack and stumbled across the balcony, yet only managed a couple of metres before feeling the mighty blow of his husband's fist strike the left side of his back, making him gasp for air and drop to his knees. Only a split second later, he received a blow to his head from Pip's boot; he crawled towards the outer wall on his hands and knees, leaving a trail of blood, sweat, tears and vomit. He grappled the brickwork and heaved himself up to stand. Using the wall to lean upon, he turned to face the man he had set out to destroy and said, "You'll pay for this one, fucker."

Pip saw red. The evil within this man seemed relentless and he ran towards him and struck him with both fists square in the chest, launching the weakened man over the wall where he tumbled and fell, smashing his head on the corner of the Range Rover that he'd made Pip pay for. The fall would have killed him with the injuries he had sustained upstairs. Smashing his head on his car made sure of it as his neck snapped and twisted his head to almost face backwards; blood spurted from his eye socket from where it had landed on the roof aerial.

Pip looked down on the sight devoid of emotion. He walked to the kitchen, took a fresh glass and another chilled bottle and returned to his seat. He topped up his glass and settled back.

—

Pip was shocked with himself that for the first time in his life, he had allowed himself such rage to fuel his imagination to such a level. He feared that he might even be capable of playing out such a fantasy as he took a sip from his glass, hiding the small smile that was forming on his lips, not in any way from joy about the imaginary fight and death of his betraying husband, but the fact, he knew damn well he would never and could never do such a thing. He recalled an attempt at the erecting of a bookcase in his office with Jackie some years before; she suggested he stopped fighting with it as it would be an embarrassment to lose to a piece of furniture saying, "Darling, please accept your limitations, you certainly don't have a black belt in the martial art of IKEA."

"Belt! Hun, they won't even accept my skills to upgrade from yellow to blue bag! I'm still on the hotdog novice level." The shared joke had continued and made him smile many times, as it was doing now; he could always rely on Jacks for that. Following furniture, shopping trips were always made together, giving the friends the opportunity to use their new grading system that now had categories from Allen key through to the fitted kitchen, passing judgment upon unsuspecting shoppers, making them giggle like children.

13

Pip stood under the two large copper rain showerheads and considered the last twelve weeks since the confrontation and the exposure of what his grandfather had thrust upon his family. He looked through the floor-to-ceiling sheet of glass that matched the one behind him at the old copper that clad the exterior of the white enamel slipper bath that sat in front of the balcony doors. He was proud of the bathroom after managing to create a unique design on the smallest of budgets. The bath was a stroke of luck. It was one of eight he had found in what must have been a washroom on the fourth floor with heavy sinks and toilets in an adjoining room. All of the fittings were reused as features in the apartments as they were developed, but this room was different to the others. The floor was made from the bricks of the original back wall of the balcony, the walls were polished black stained concrete, all of the taps and pipework were copper, and the simplicity was beautiful. The shower was in the centre of the floor, nothing more than two sheets of glass; he'd had all pipework hidden from view. To operate the flow and temperature of water, there was a digital control panel behind a small copper door next to the mirror above the sink. The toilet was behind a sheet of black glass with a door from the bathroom and inside the closet, another door that gave access to the main area of the part of his building that he used to consider his home. Random thoughts went through his mind as he stood there. Pip had desperately tried to keep positive over the last three months, took solace in the small things and kept his mind fuelled with endorphins by increasing his use of the gym after Jackie had found him drinking alone one afternoon a couple of days following The Reveal. He had returned from a dental check-up and passed the convenience store entrance, then doubled back to go in and buy a bottle of scotch, marched into his office and sat and drank a good half of its rich, warm blend whilst pondering the three metallic monkeys stuck to the shoulder of the glass bottle, 'hear no, speak no, see no', he'd said aloud to no one just before his best friend entered the room.

"You OK, Hun?"

"No, I…" He had panicked at that point, fearing that should he have told his best friend, she would have attempted to solve the unsolvable problem, causing Marcus to carry out his threats. "I… sorry. It's the building plans; what if I've bitten off more than I can chew?" He knew this must have sounded a little pathetic after all the conversation they'd shared about the topic, but Jackie humoured him.

"You daft sod, it will all be fine, you know it." She slapped the air in front of his face back and forth, mimicking a face slap and told him, "Now pull yourself together, go get an hour's sleep, a shower, then meet me in the bar later; I'll buy you dinner."

Since that day, he had been so busy there was little time left to worry about what Marcus would or could do. Pip had considered trying to raise enough extra money to pay him off, but everything he had was already collateral for the houses; there was little he could do but wait. At least, his husband left him alone; they barely saw each other and Chris was nowhere to be seen since the conversation they'd had in the gym changing room. Pip had begun his fitness regime and was reaching for his towel as he left the showers; with both hands, he raised it to his face and hair and was rubbing the water out when he heard.

"Hello, Mister Scot."

Lowering the towel, he saw the words spoken by the mouth belonging to a naked-toned young man with a pair of shorts in his hand, Chris.

Pip knew he had to tread very carefully. After all, Chris was one of his employees and he was sure that one wrong move would give Marcus more ammunition with some kind of lawsuit for illegal employer/employee actions that he could use to publicly attack him, but at the same time, he felt he would never rest unless he said his piece. Chris looked Pip up and down and smiled as he focused on his groin. "Looking good there, Mister Scot."

Pip hurriedly wrapped his towel around his waist, hiding his modesty.

"Oh, you've spoiled the view," Chris said with an even cheekier smile. "I thought I might finally get to play with you; I've been dying to fuck you since I started here."

As he spoke, he cupped his balls and stroked his cock which was becoming bigger and harder by the second.

"Put your shorts on and sit down. I think we need to talk."

Chris obeyed and put on the running shorts, taking his time to position his now fully erect member.

"Now, to start with, why the heck do you call me Mister Scot when everyone else calls me Pip?"

"Oh, *erm,* well." Chris began to flush as he started to explain, "Well, *erm,* Marcus said you got off on it, that you would be turned on by being respected as my master; I'd be more than happy to be your slave if that's what you wanted. Marcus said you liked to take your staff over the desk in your office whilst watching the films that he made of him and me fucking."

"Oh my God! He said what? Now look, to start with, I have never EVER slept with a member of staff and never would. I'm sorry, but you have been lied to. Marcus is using you in some way."

"But he said that to keep my job and get promoted when it came to us finally doing it, I should be sure to shout, sir, to make you cum."

"What?"

"You know, to help you get off because of that problem you have keeping hard enough to climax, he said you needed to feel fully in charge to keep going; that's also why it was OK for me and Marcus to keep fucking because you knew you couldn't satisfy his high sex drive with a limp dick, I kept hoping you would join in one day, I thought I might know a trick or two that might help you out, you're a really nice person. To be honest, you're my favourite out of the two of you; Marcus is pretty and good in bed and really generous with presents and money, but he does talk down to me quite a bit, sometimes makes me feel like I'm stupid, but you never have; around you, I feel relaxed and worthy in some way."

The phrase, 'I'll show you who can get hard, fuck hard and blast enough cum to drown a small animal' were words swallowed back and unheard as Pip bit the inner of his bottom lip. Instead, he somehow kept refraining and calmly spoke.

"Chris, none of it is true. Now look, you're a nice young man, and I'm sure your intentions were sincere. Believe me, I know how convincing the words my husband speaks can be. I've fallen for the lies, too, but that's all those words are; lies. To be clear, I don't have any problems in the sex department, none at all. It's true that we hardly ever had sex, but that was down to mister, 'I've got a headache', 'I've got an early start', 'I just don't feel like it', not me and I'm sorry, but I don't condone his affairs. Marriage, in my eyes, is loyally respected by the two people who swapped vows. But don't get me wrong, you're an extremely attractive man and in another time and circumstance, then I may be interested. Not presently possible, though."

Something clicked in Chris's mind, tears began to roll down his cheeks as the realisation of being used all of this time became apparent. "I'm so sorry, I got it wrong. Marcus said so many things; we would talk about you quite a lot of times. I would say if you were in a good mood at work, and he would tell me that it was because you both had sex whilst watching the sex videos of me and him. I asked him if I should talk about it with you, but he made me promise never to mention it because you were as shy talking about sex as you were a professional to not discuss such things during work. I can see now it must have been all lies; it makes sort of sense. I am oh so sorry, Mister Scot, *erm,* Pip. So sorry. I don't know what to say. It's wrong. I got it wrong."

Pip's inner fatherly nature felt the need to hug this young man, make him feel worthy and secure, to tell him everything would be all right. But he knew he couldn't. not that it would offer forgiveness for that was genuinely already given to this duped soul but for the fact that this exposure of emotion would lead to much more than an embrace if they touched and right now that would have been very very wrong and even more confusing to the situation. Instead, he stood and backed away just out of reach. "Chris, please forgive yourself. Yes, I was angry with you, blamed you and I was dreading the first time I saw you; I didn't know how I'd deal with it, but... that conversation is done and well... it's not your fault. I cannot blame someone who so clearly didn't know his response to Marcus's advances wasn't approved of by me."

Chris slowly stood, removed his shorts and redressed himself in the tight, fine, knit white jumper and blue jeans he had come to work wearing. After he pulled on his boots, he stuffed his gym gear and towel into the leather bag that had been given to him by the man who had made him part of an affair said, "I'm sorry." Once more and with head bent down walked out of the changing room, out of the gym and out of the lives of his boss and his lover forever. He didn't quit, didn't call, didn't even email an explanation, just simply walked away.

—

The water continued to fall over Pip's much-improved physique since his more regular stress-busting workouts. He had lost track of time as he stood there but thought perhaps breakfast might be a good idea. He knew the coast was clear, that he was alone after hearing Marcus leave earlier; he walked over to the sink, turned off the showers water supply and dried himself on one of his newly replaced towels, part of the cleansing shopping trip taken to remove the discovered affair from his touch, he couldn't bear the thought of wiping his face on something his husband's lover had wiped his ass upon such towels, robes, bed linens had all been swapped and the whole place deep cleaned, he was so grateful that the other bedroom had an en suite and there was no need for the scum with whom he was regrettably attached to use and contaminate his stuff.

Donning a pair of light grey sweatpants, Pip went to the kitchen and made coffee, which he carried to the front windows and sipped while he gazed at the housing development.

It had come on in leaps and bounds. From day one, luck had been shining on the project. A building firm had been readily available in the first week after the collapse of another business; the quote they gave was almost a third under the allocation in the initial budget due to already having a wealth of purchased materials from the other failed-to-build. Plans, of course, had been ready for a long time and despite being narcissistic, using, stealing, lying, well-dressed bastard piece of shit, Marcus had eased along any minor hold-ups at the council that would normally have caused delays with such a project.

The thirty-three concrete pad bases and foundations of the homes were all complete by the end of the third week and building the walls had begun. The most forward-viewed house was to be his own or, rather, his blackmailed gift to his worse half. Being at the front and in the deepest part of the slope, it was three storeys high and wider than all of the others, stealing five metres from the adjoining plots either side, which as the further two buildings each side of them would also be three storeys, seven properties. However, six being quite narrow to make the big centre house look even more imposing, Marcus's idea, of course. The set of stone steps had already been installed that led to the centre placed double front doors leading to a wide hallway that would eventually house an impressive stairway that snaked around the walls as it rose to the top, leaving an opening that would be filled with light from a glass section in the roof, despite the growing hatred for the man Pip had to admit to being fairly impressed with some of the design features he'd insisted on, although a tad flamboyant, Number one would be quite impressive. He looked on and tried to picture a more complete picture of when the walls would reach roof height. He wondered if his daydream of shimmering rooftops would give the watery effect he desired. He let everything slip away for a few moments and enjoyed the accomplishments so far achieved and wondered if his nanna would be proud of him, a ponder that bought all of the recent events crashing back into play. As he watched the buildings grow brick by brick, he knew that the time to find a solution to the Marcus problem would run out, and he would be handing over an enormous amount of money. He had a feeling that would not be the last of it either; he felt that as long as Marcus had that thistle trinket box and its ill-gotten contents, he would forever be able to demand whatever he desired. With a sigh, he turned and walked to the kitchen, put his mug in the dishwasher and dressed. He was ready to go downstairs for a meeting with Jackie to discuss the new personal trainer discount scheme.

Ten minutes later, the glass door of the gym entrance eased shut by the hydraulic closer arm behind him and he approached the reception desk and was greeted by David, who sat at the screen with Jackie stood behind him, giving him training on the updated CRM. She looked Pip square in the eye. "Someone looks tired."

"Yeah, I know, a lot on my plate."

"Do you want to skip today? I can compile a draft for you to look over tomorrow, maybe?"

"No, no, let's get it done, swallow the frog and all that. Besides, I promised the website guy it would be ready to launch by Friday."

"OK, sweets, tell you what then, pop over to the shop and get some of those ginger cookies; we deserve a treat;

a bit of sugar might put a smile on that handsome face of yours; it seems an age since I saw one there."

"Yeah, yeah, you're just trying to justify eating biscuits." And he blew his cheeks out to make like a hamster. Engaged in this simple conversation distracted him from noticing that behind him, the door had opened and someone had entered the gym.

"Hey, Squeak."

14

Hearing those two words spoken by that soft, deep voice with a hint of Mediterranean accent, it took being able to breathe momentarily away from Pip's list of natural functions. He felt his body produce a cold sweat and his muscles tighten; he had waited for fifteen years to hear that voice again, the sound that could stop him dead in his tracks, the noise he would obey the commands uttered by it. Panic. Joy. Fight or flight. Stay or turn. Cry. Laugh. Shake. Faint. Throw up. One of these surely must happen, but Pip's brain was feeling them all at the same time and couldn't decide which one to choose.

He turned around. "Bastard! Where the fuck have you been?" he said to the visitor as he leaned towards him and they exchanged a body-squeezing hug. Pip stood back, tears filled his eyes as his smile broadened and with nervous laughter in his voice, he said, "Fuck, I've missed you!"

"I'll draft the PT offer then, shall I?" questioned Jackie in a matter-of-fact way, hinting at sarcasm.

Pip hardly heard her call for him to regain position in reality. "Please, babe, you'd only correct my work anyway. Do what's needed and send it to the web guy."

"Of course, I can see you're going to be busy with your guest?"

"Shit. Sorry. Caught up in the moment. Jackie, this is Mack. Mack, Jackie, my best friend, confidante and my right hand, no, my right arm, well actually more like my right-hand side."

"Pleased to meet you, Mack," Jackie said to the handsome man, then whispered in Pip's ear. "Mack. As in Mack?"

He whispered his reply, "Yes. Now *shush,* I'll let you know everything later, thank you, love you, bye!"

Jackie smiled as Pip took a grip on Mack's upper arm and guided him into the lobby. "We need to talk."

"Hey, Brian, have you got a booth free? Need a bit of quiet for a meeting," Pip said to the bar owner as they entered it across the lobby.

"Far corner is free, nothing booked in, yours all day if you want it." Brian was a lovely, kind man. Before approaching Pip with a business plan and a prayer, he had operated a couple of pubs for other people. The bar was semi-industrial in its finish, which suited the feel of the building. It also cut costs to something he could actually afford; working for others didn't pay so well and he'd opened the business using every penny he'd saved, a small loan and several limit-maxed credit cards. Pip loved and admired his enthusiasm from their very first meeting and helped him as much as he could, giving him the use of stools and tables that had been found on the above floors and waiving the first six months' rent so Brian would have a chance of recovering his investment and make a realistic wage.

"Two Chilli Nachos, please. Can you stick it on the gym courtesy account? I've left my wallet upstairs."

Brian smiled; the landlord, who had become a friend over the last few years, was always forgetting something. "Order is in, sir. It shouldn't be long. Drink?"

"Just water for me, Mack? Sorry, how rude am I? Do you still eat chilli and nachos?"

"It's still my ultimate favourite, yes."

"And to drink?"

"Pip…"

Pip looked at Mack square into his deep brown eyes.

"I love you."

"What."

"I love you. I've come back to tell you I love you, always have, always will and as hard as I've tried, I cannot make the feeling change; I'm not going to build up some dramatic, winded story and sorry, but you know I'm more laughter over slush. I'm here to tell you I love you, hate me and send me away if you wish, but I promised myself, no messing; I'm telling you as soon as I find you."

Numbness struck Pip. He sat remaining in eye lock, trying to absorb the information received from the man who, a mere fifteen minutes before, had walked back into his life after being gone from it for fifteen years.

"Brian!" he shouted over to the bar. "Have you got a full bottle of monkey juice I can buy?"

"I've got a full bottle, yes, but you can't buy it; I'll give it to you and you can get me one back. I'll bring it over. Do you still want the water?"

"No thanks. I think it's going to be a day where I don't need my alcohol levels diluting."

Silence fell between them; neither man quite knew where to begin. The blended scotch and the food arrived; Pip took a breath, a sip and leaned forwards to quietly and simply said, "Talk."

"You can't walk into someone's life and say that after fifteen years of being missing. For fucks sake, that's the phrase I so desperately wanted you to say over twenty years ago! Why now? Shit, you don't even know me any more. Or I, you for that matter. I don't get it. Don't tell me you're after the goodies, too. Christ, I wish I'd never had the fucking idea. You know what? I'm going to pack the car, blow up the build and just fuck off somewhere."

Pip's mind had gone through so much these last few months; this random meaningless rant blurted out to a very confused person who had thought he'd been brave and true by coming back.

"Sorry, Squeak, I should go, look, forget I said anything, forget I was even here. I shouldn't have said that so soon. I should have explained first, written or emailed or something. I think I just wanted to sort of surprise you. I'll leave. Sorry."

"Don't you fucking dare move. Sit back down. Please. Sorry. So much is going on. Sorry. It's OK. Please, please, don't go."

"Thank you. Are you all right?"

"I'm fine, Mack. Sorry for the rage. Seeing you was the biggest shock. My head was spinning for a minute, joy, anger, confusion, attraction, need, and relief all mixed into one; for a second, I didn't know whether I wanted to punch you or kiss you or even believe it was you. Shit, am I having a stroke? Is any of this real? Fuck, is this what happens when you lose it or am, I dying and you're my stairway, my brain fantasy making nice of a terrible transition. Am I saying this out loud?"

"I deserve that."

"Oh really? Which one, the kiss or the punch?"

"Both."

—

The two men took several deep, reassuring, calming breaths whilst looking into each other's eyes, reaffirming the connection they'd had since university. Allowing Pip to fathom that this was indeed real.

15

They first met whilst moving into halls in their freshman year. The ever-forgetful Pip had locked himself out of his room by leaving his key on the bed. As the door clicked shut and locked behind him, he'd realised just that second too late what he had done. He stood there, back to the door, eyes closed and said, "Bollocks."

"Big fat hairy ones," a stranger's voice said as Pip opened his eyes to see who had commented on his swear. Holding a box stood possibly the most handsome young man he had ever seen, clearly of Mediterranean descent at least in part, with thick dark brown wavy hair, deep brown eyes, strong features adorning an otherwise simple classic face, the kind that would stay handsome throughout his life. At 5'9" with a naturally athletic body dressed in jeans, a sweatshirt and Converse, this soft-voiced hunk was right up Pip's street.

Pip smiled at the beautiful stranger. "Very funny! Isn't that part of an old joke? Or perhaps an observation?"

"You know the joke? The alphabet-swearing kid in the class?"

"Oddly enough, yes, I do. So, not an observation then?"

The stranger flushed with embarrassment at the comment, for indeed, he had checked out Pip as he'd approached en route to his own room just a few doors down near the bathrooms. Sexuality was something that this young man had been trying to avoid the conclusion of, being in total denial of the fact that when alone with cock in hand night after night, no matter what scenario his mind would attempt, the initial thoughts of sex with women dissipated and turned to sex with men after the first stroke of his hand upon the thick, veined eight-inch hard shaft and stayed that way until climax. Deep down, he knew it was men he wanted to talk to, men he wanted to hold, to kiss, to hug, to undress, to caress and to be held and loved by, but he was unable to be brave enough to come out and believe in himself.

He smiled, put down the box and offered his warm-skinned hand. "I'm Mack. Macaulay Phillip Gordon Sullivan at your service."

"No way!"

"Way! That's my name."

"Wow, I didn't think I'd meet another Macaulay, or do you mean you're a Sullivan?"

"Sorry, no, non, neither *erm,* I mean your middle name. I'm a Philip too, first name though, Phil Scot, but everyone calls me Pip."

"Ah, cool. How many 'L's?"

"One."

"Mines got two, close though."

They both giggled at the coincidence. "So, when did you move in? I only got here today, still unpacking the car," Mack said and indicated towards the box.

"This is day three for me and will also be the second time I have to track down the caretaker to let me in because I've locked my key in there. I can see the look on his face now; he wasn't impressed the first time; he's a bit of a mumbling old git."

"I can imagine, tell you what, I'll come with you. I could tell him it was my fault if you like, tell him you had gone to the bathroom and I decided I needed something and left the room without thinking about the keys."

"You're a star, Mister Sullivan, thank you. I'll help you unload the car to say thank you."

"Cheers, Mister Scot, The Scot, by the sound of your accent, that would be a great help."

"Welcome, sir."

The pair found much to chat about whilst moving Mack into his new room. Both felt instantly as if they had known each other forever and although neither would admit it, both found the other incredibly attractive. The following three days cemented the friendship; they discovered a mutual love of science fiction, Stephen King novels, but not the films, modern must-have gadgets and both favoured Coca-Cola over Pepsi. Monday rolled around and the first classes and timetables were announced.

"You're kidding, right?" Mack said to Pip as they collected the timetables. "Shit, I can't believe I didn't ask; you're really studying Sports Science? The same as me?"

"Well, yes," replied his new friend. "Can't believe I never asked either. Sorry, odd, isn't it? Starting Uni and not asking a new mate what they're taking, you'd have thought it would be one of the first things to say. We've spent too much time laughing, I guess."

"Well, I'm glad we are on the same course; it will make it a right laugh. I'm dead excited now," he said this aloud, but his mind was already considering that he now had the opportunity to see this man not only in shorts but also out of them in the locker rooms.

Mack took the timetable from Pip and compared the two with more scrutiny to discover that they shared all classes every day except for Thursday, where they were split for other chosen subjects, Mack for Introduction to Criminology and Pip for Modern Literature.

"Are we together much?" Pip enquired, looking at the two pieces of paper.

"Looks like we are stuck together all day, every day except Thursday; Christ, you're gonna be sick of the sight of me."

"Somehow, I doubt that very much; we get on too well."

"Agreed," confirmed Mack.

The first months flew by, it seemed. Both Mack and Pip excelled in their classes, most of which they were sat next to each other with their names being so close alphabetically. Neither complained; the partnership suited them; they bounced well off each other and helped each other study. Pip adored his new friend far more than he dared let on. His not-so-accident walk-ins on Mack in the communal showers and the gym showers following the live games practice gave his imagination fuel to assist masturbation most nights; he couldn't help it; he felt he might be falling in love. Little did he know, Mack was thinking along the same lines. Despite desperate attempts to imagine he was with a girl, it wasn't long into the new term, after spending most of the time with Pip, that he surrendered himself to his fantasies, starting with bumping into men, having a casual conversation before undressing them and taking their cock in his hands. Accepting his secret kept him going for a while, but those fantasies soon turned to involve just one handsome, intelligent, well-dressed, funny, artistic, fit and just about perfect in every way young Scotsman. Although he thought he could never publicly say it, he thought he loved his friend more than he was supposed to.

"Hey, Pipsqueak, you going home for Christmas?" Mack asked as December approached.

"Only for the day; I spoke to Nanna about it and said I had loads of study to catch up on, so I needed to be here for the library."

"What study? I thought we were ahead of everything?"

"We are! I just used it as an excuse. I want to see her, but really, a chat about the bingo, repairs to some old fat bastard trousers and talk of the extra dram of scotch she's putting in her tea to fight off the winter colds isn't exactly what I call fun, don't get me wrong, I love her to bits but one day is enough. What about you? Going to your dad's?"

"Am I bollocks? No chance. He was insufferable before, but with Mum gone, it will be an atmosphere that you'd need a chainsaw to cut through."

16

Mack's mother, Sophia, was an Italian beauty and certainly where her son had gained his stunning features. Her classic, somewhat timeless face, turned many heads over the years as she gracefully aged; it was such a shame that her husband gave up noticing so soon after their marriage began. From a young age, she had wanted to travel, to explore the world that her father told tales of from his time in the Italian naval service. She dreamed of strolling through the streets of Paris, London, and New York, taking in the sights and feel of the cities. As soon as she was able, the young woman left her home, her parents and her brother to indulge her dream; with the intention of starting her adventures in the Big Apple, Sophia flew to Ireland, where she intended to work for a short while to earn enough for her passage on one of the liners that travelled across the Atlantic Ocean.

Having a nurse as a Mother, Sophia took an unqualified orderly position within an Irish hospital; it wasn't long before her skills taught by her Mother were seen and she was encouraged to take training to become a qualified nurse herself. Flattered by the recognition, she decided that perhaps for the future, following her travels, it may be wise to have something to back on and graciously accepted the offer and enjoyed becoming a qualified nurse; she felt quite adult about making the decision to delay her dream for a couple of years.

Her charm and sense of humour, alongside her curvy figure dressed in a fit where that touched nursing outfit, made her very popular with patients. She offered several advances from some of the men to which she would smile and tease them by telling them they may be in with a chance maybe one day and simply walk away. That was, of course, until she met the man who would give her a child, Gordon Phillip Sullivan.

It was a wet Tuesday evening, the kind where the dark seems darker than usual, the raindrops large and heavy, the kind of night where no matter the use of Macintosh, Wellingtons or umbrella, one would still be soaked to the skin and cold to the bone. The newly qualified Sophia had taken an extra shift to cover her friend in the emergency room. Within an hour of the beginning of the shift, a man shouted for help as he entered through the automatic doors with another man beneath his supporting arm, coat over his head and his hand holding the other as high as he could. The men were wet through and left a trail of water and blood as they approached the desk. Sophia had heard the commotion and come to the desk to see who was making a fuss; she saw the bleeding hand before observing anything else and approached the injured man, taking him from the grip of the other who had brought him in and guiding his sodden body to a curtained booth. Here, she assessed the wound, a very clean cut on the left hand from wrist bone up the side of his index finger to near the tip. One of the doctors on duty joined them and between them, they compressed the bleeding to a stop and stitched the long wound.

"You may not think it, but you are one lucky man," said the doctor. "Any deeper and you would have lost the use of your finger and probably thumb, but apart from a scar, you will be back to what you were in no time at all."

"Thank you, Doctor."

"It's what we are here for now because of the prescription I gave you and the loss of blood; I'd like you to stay right where you are for six to eight hours, so I know you'll be OK, we don't want you passing out somewhere and causing yourself more damage, do we? Nurse will look after you and make you comfortable, perhaps offer you tea and a biscuit? OK with you, Nurse?"

"Of course," responded Sophia as she continued to clean and dress the freshly stitched wound.

"You are very kind. Thank you for your help," the young man said to his caregiver. "I'm ever so sorry to put you out."

Sophia flashed her dazzling smile. "It's my job; there's no need to apologise. Now, before you go any further, we need to get you out of those wet clothes; I can't have one of my patients catching pneumonia on my watch!"

The young man moved to get off the bed, but as he sat his upper body upright, he felt himself sway forwards. Sophia caught him before he fell from the bed. "I'll help you get undressed, I think." And before he lay back, she took hold of his jumper and T-shirt at the waistband and eased them over his head, revealing a toned torso wrapped in pale skin. "See, better already," she said to him.

"I can do the rest," the blushing young chap muttered and, without thinking, placed both of his hands on his jeans button. He screamed in pain as he tried to use his injured left hand.

"Allow me," said Sophia. "Don't worry, there's nothing I haven't seen before." She took firm hold of his waistband, undid the button and fly and began to lower the soaked denim and the white boxer shorts that had taken on some of the blue dye. The action caused more blushes as the young man's arousal became apparent; the nurse politely covered him with a sheet and then a blanket before helping him into one of the back-fastening hospital gowns.

Another nurse drew back the curtain a little and entered to offer Sophia the man's file.

"Gordon Sullivan."

"Yes, that's me."

"Nice to meet you, Gordon, I'm Sophia. You're one lucky man; not only did you miss anything debilitating when you cut your hand, but that friend who brought you in did so in record time; you will have to thank him for that."

"It's my dad. Sorry, he's my dad, Phillip. That's who brought me in, he was just getting out of his car when he heard me scream in the garage. It was such a stupid accident, I was using a plane on a cabinet I was making, not sure how but as I stood up after taking a look at the level of the wood, somehow the damned thing slipped from my grip, I tried to catch it and, well, you know the rest."

The nurse who brought the file returned with the senior Mister Sullivan.

"You all right, boy?" he said to his son. "They say you need some rest; well, I'll be off and back when they ring me. Really got to get some dry clothes." With that, he backed out of the booth and left.

Sophia stepped across the line by commenting on how inattentive Phillip seemed; the junior Sullivan nodded in agreement and told her that was how he'd always known him to be; limited with his words and more so with his feelings. Sophia suggested that Gordon now tried to rest and told him she would be looking in on him while he slept, which she did every half hour and as the night progressed every fifteen minutes, her smile becoming wider upon each visit, she couldn't explain why, but she felt drawn towards this man.

As Gordon awoke in the hospital bed, he felt a little sick, a little hungry, a lot of searing pain and for a couple of minutes, a little confused as to where he was and to what had happened; everything shot back into clarity upon the booth curtain being drawn and the entrance of his very own nightingale, nurse Sophia who bore the welcome gift of tea and toast and was wearing the most beautiful smile that quite melted his thoughts. He thanked her for the tea and everything she had done the night before, once more apologetic for his nuisance.

"Hush," said Sophia. "It's a pleasure to be able to help a gentleman."

"Well, thank you. I think you are an angel."

"That's sweet to say, anyway, here are your clothes, all dry after a few hours in the boiler room; the duty doctor will be here soon just to check you over and then you can go home."

"Nurse, I wish there were a way to thank you properly; maybe buy you dinner, perhaps?"

"Mister Sullivan, the very idea… sounds wonderful. Here, call me." She handed him a card that already had her phone number written on it from a few hours earlier when she herself thought she might be bold enough to ask him out on a date; she was happy she'd been beaten to the question.

Love blossomed between them over the following months; they spent as much time together as they could, much to the approval of Phillip, Gordon's Father. Sophia wrote home to her parents to say she had unexpectedly found love; upon learning that just like themselves, he was from a devout God-fearing Catholic upbringing, they wished her well and hoped they would soon meet him. Sophia really did love him; her desire to feel part of him overwhelmed her promise to the church to remain celibate and one night, following a romantic meal in a river view restaurant, the yearning passion ignited and they made passionate love with each other over and over, throughout the night. Just a few short weeks later, the couple learnt their fate was about to be sealed as Sophia discovered she was pregnant by the man she had known for a mere five months. Religion meant that abortion of the foetus was not an option; neither being an unmarried mother, the couple felt compelled to marry as soon as possible. Phillip Sullivan was a loyal member of his local church and, since the death of his wife had found solace there in each of his almost daily visits. His son had informed him of his situation, a disappointed father took matters into his own hands and arranged for a wedding ceremony to be performed at the earliest opportunity, just two weeks away. A hasty wedding was organised; Sophia's friends from the hospital rallied around and sourced everything she needed; a simple plain white gown, flowers, shoes and even a veil, all of it borrowed yet combined to make a glorious bride. The short notice meant that her parents could not attend the marriage of their only daughter, but suspecting the reason for the timing may perhaps be that she was indeed with child, gave them cause to not comment and wish them both well.

The reality and consequences of the whirlwind romance, wedding and all too soon birth of her son Macaulay did not truly become apparent to Sophia until several months into her new marriage. She had moved into Sullivan's home, which offered ample space for all of them but moreover was also the location for her husband's workshop, from where he used his extensive skills as a carpenter to craft bespoke items alongside solid pieces of furniture that were sold in a local department store. There was no denying the talent that Gordon possessed or the dedication he had to his work. Such dedication meant he spent more and more hours in his workshop after the baby was born. He hated being disturbed, saying it put him off his flow and insisted on solitude while working. He began to work earlier each morning and later each night, stopping only to eat and then return to his projects before joining his wife hours after nightfall. Sophia became very lonely and felt isolated and trapped in the house with the baby that her husband barely looked at, let alone helped her look after. Her father-in-law was no help either. In fact, apart from showing up for food, she barely saw him, which, with his silent stares and gruff responses to any question she may pose, was indeed quite the blessing.

Phillip passed away just a year after the hasty wedding, leaving the house and savings to his only son. Gordon would never talk about his feelings regarding his father, and even right after the return home from his funeral, he returned to the solace of the workshop. Sophia became desperately unhappy. She sat in front of the dressing table mirror one day and looked at herself. She wondered when was the last time she smiled. She pondered how the charming, handsome, kind man, she had fallen in love with, could have changed into this withdrawn, communicative, soulless man once a ring was on her finger. She was forbidden to work; she was told a wife's place was in the home and for five long years, apart from visits to the local supermarket, that was precisely where she remained. December came that year and the celebration of her little boy's fifth birthday, meaning he could begin school in January, Sophia was unsure how she would fill her time without the company of her son, who had pleasantly and completely occupied her life. She had grown to adore little Mack they had a special bond that filled her heart with joy in every second they were together. Gordon had begun to show a little interest in his boy and introduced him to the workshop, promising him he would teach him the skills of carpentry as he got older. The excited little boy who wanted nothing more than for his daddy to spend time with him squealed with the anticipation of sharing something with him. The department store that sold Gordon's furniture was due to close at the end of January, a casualty of the out-of-town shopping park full of National chain brands that the family-owned independent store simply couldn't compete with. This, of course, left Gordon without his steady source of income to support his family; luckily for him, however, an opportunity arose to teach his craft at the technical college in the next town; he jumped at the chance to take it, term time would leave him able to still work on bespoke projects during the many weeks' holidays, weekends and with the early daily finishes he could work in the evenings too. His interview went well. Well enough, in fact, to be offered the position and start free the February half-term break. His wife said she was pleased for him, yet inside, she felt desolate. Gordon may have ignored her most of the time, but at least he was on the premises, which offered a strange sense of comfort even though she couldn't see him. What on Earth was she to do?

In April, the phone rang; Sophia answered the call, which was made by the school. Mack had fallen and cut his leg. The panicked Mother slammed down the phone, grabbed her coat from the hook in the hall, slammed the door behind her and ran as fast as her legs and heart would allow the short distance to the Primary School. The receptionist recognised her and ushered her through the main office to the first aid room at the back, where her crying son sat with blood slowly flowing from the side of his knee down his leg into his sock. The dinner lady that sat with him said he had fallen onto broken glass that a passing youth had flung over the school wall; she'd brought him straight in here and stayed with him holding a wad of gauze onto the wound. Sophia spied the first aid box, grabbed it, and administered the required cleaning and dressing of her little boy's leg. Checking his tears had dried and given him the biggest of reassuring hugs; she left him to relax while she went to say her piece to the headmistress.

Sophia marched the short distance down the hall and knocked hard on the door but to no reply; she knocked again, then from behind her, she heard, "Mrs Sullivan, thank you so much for coming to see me; I wanted to express my sincere apologies for Mack's fall, I regret it was unavoidable as Mack was running as the bottle was thrown, the timing was simply unfortunate your boy tripped as the bottle smashed, I am so sorry. I was told you were here; I've just been to first aid to see you. I'm sorry I missed you."

The worry and rage from seeing her only born child hurt dissipated upon hearing Mrs O'Reilly's words. Instant realism set in; accidents happen, people get hurt, get patched up and get better; from her training, she knew this and was usually the calmest of people under emergency or pressure; it was just that seeing part of her damaged…

"Mrs Sullivan, may I comment on the excellent first aid you have administered. It looks very professional."

"Thank you. I was a nurse before I married and had Mack."

"Really."

"Yes, fully qualified just before I met his father."

"How interesting! Mrs Sullivan, would you consider reprising that role?"

"I'd love to, but my husband wouldn't like it."

"Ah, I understand; it happens more than you think around here; what if he wasn't to know?"

Sophia pondered this for a second. "How would that work exactly?"

The very last thing that Mrs Sophia Sullivan had expected when she awoke that morning was to be offered a job as a school nurse at the primary school and adjoining grammar school, which was headed by Mrs O'Reilly's husband. The headmistress declared she knew from rumour that Gordon was possibly not the most affectionate of husband, and also that he'd taken a teaching position at the technical college. She proposed that Sophia work between the two schools, which, of course, ran parallel term times so she would be off work at the same time as Gordon, start work after he left in the morning and be home with her boy before his return. "So, you see with a little discretion your husband would never know if you didn't want him too. Please, take tonight to think about it and let me know tomorrow."

A restless night of wonder and, for the first in a very long time, a glimmer of hope that life may be a little more liveable with something meaningful to do, although balancing those emotions with what she felt would be betraying her vows and her husband's wishes felt like a challenge too far. The morning came with its routine of preparing Gordon and young Macaulay their breakfast and packed lunches, washing the dishes, saying goodbye to her departing husband and wishing him a good day, to which, as every day, she received no reply, before taking the short walk with their son to school.

Mrs O'Reilly was waiting at the gates greeting her pupils. "Oh, Mrs Sullivan, do you have a minute?"

Sophia nodded her reply. As the bell rang, she bent to kiss Mack goodbye, asking him to be the best he could and to learn lots of exciting things. Once he had entered the doors, she approached the headmistress. "Good morning, Mrs O'Reilly. I trust you are well."

"Very well, thank you, as I trust you are? Do you have a minute? I wanted to continue our conversation from yesterday and also to apologise."

"Apologise?"

They began to walk towards the head's office. "Yes, apologise. I was chatting with my husband last night about you and how suitable I thought you might be for the joint school nurse role when it dawned upon me just how rude I must have seemed passing comment in respect of what may or may not happen between you and your husband, I am sincerely sorry, it has absolutely nothing to do with me."

"You don't have to worry. To be honest, I hadn't even noticed."

"Well, anyway, I am. It's just that, well, we do listen to our children here and young Mack has been overheard commenting on some of the differences between his home life in comparison to some other children. There's nothing to worry about, nothing at all; it's just that I know Gordon personally; my family lived in the house opposite yours and I know exactly what his dad was like as he grew up. Sorry. It really wasn't my place to make judgments or comment."

Sophia smiled, feeling cared about. "Honestly, please don't worry; it is good that you care about the families you work with."

"Anyway, about the job. Quite the coincidence, I must say, but then everything happens for a reason, I believe they say. We have been looking for someone to take the position for three months now; you saw the state of our first aid offering… a little lacking, to say the least."

Sophia agreed. "Well, a little, perhaps. Although, I cannot really see the need for a nurse, surely just someone who could administer decent first aid?"

"*Ah,* yes, this is true. However, the job is more than sticking plasters on grazes. We need a person who is able to talk and communicate with children and the young adults at the grammar school, to ease their minds and explain things properly, things outside the school, impacts of epidemics upon their lives, puberty questions and the like. This is where a practised bedside manner we feel will come in."

"Well, I am flattered by the offer, but Gordon wouldn't allow it."

"I meant what I said. We can keep full discretion; as an individual employee, this is automatically applied anyway. It's a none uniform position apart from inoculation periods where sanitation is required, so there's one barrier overcome; as for the stray word, Mack may say to his dad, we could perhaps say you are part of the parent volunteer scheme that Father O'Shea introduced, Gordon would never question a priest's suggestion... look, we need someone and I'm sure you could do with something constructive to do to occupy your time and mind. But it is, of course, entirely your decision. It's quite well paid, too, though, if that helps."

Money. Independence. Purpose. People. Conversation. Such words pulsed inside her head; Sophia suddenly realised who she used to be, the fun-loving, hard-working beauty that loved life, the girl who was going to travel the world. "I'll take it," she said.

—

"There's not a chance she would ever go back to him," Mack continued. "It took her till I came here to university to finally leave the miserable git. You know, he spoke with her so little that I don't think he ever discovered that her so-called 'volunteer' schoolwork was actually a well-paid job. Imagine her freedom, taking thirteen years of saved income and going home to the little vineyard her parents left to her brother. She won't divorce him, though; her belief in the sanctity of marriage would never allow it."

"Why not come back with me for Christmas? Nanna would love the extra company, and it would save me from the endless monotony of repeated village gossip, too!"

"Are you sure?"

"Hell, yes."

"Great, should I get a little something for your grandmother? It's my birthday next week, and Mum has sent me some money; I shouldn't turn up at Christmas empty-handed. It doesn't seem right."

"That's a nice idea, only something little, though. Knowing Nanna, she wouldn't appreciate anything extravagant. When is your birthday?"

"Third December, want to come out for a drink?"

"No, shit."

"What? I don't understand?"

"The third," replied Pip. "Mine is the fourth; shit, you're a day older than I am; wow, that's awesome, joint birthday party ahead, methinks!"

The young men did indeed celebrate their birthdays together, a full-on student night out which began relatively civilised with a 2-4-1 pub meal and a couple of happy hour pints, but that soon developed into a full-on celebration; by nine p.m., both had matched each other in drinking seven pints of strong lager, four shots and half a bottle of sparkling wine that they jokingly pretended was fine champagne. The night, of course, continued the alcohol consumption continued with it. The young men enjoyed the birthday outing, they laughed, sang bad karaoke and somehow managed to take over an hour to walk the short half mile to return to the university halls. Arm in supporting arm, they staggered to Pip's room where somehow, they managed to eat every snack that Pip had stashed away and manage to get into bed, which is where, mid-morning the following day, they would awaken.

Mack stirred first and his eyes opened to look upon the face of his very best friend. These last few months, he had become more than fond of this man. He knew his deepest, darkest feelings were surfacing, although it felt so scary to admit and in fear of losing the friendship, he knew he would never admit it, but Mack had already fallen head over heels in love with Pip. As he lay there, watching his sleeping desire, Mack allowed himself to fantasise. In a student room, the bed was narrow, which had thrust the drunken pair close together. Facing each other, Pip was lying on his friend's arm and, in his slumber, had his own hand upon his friend's neck. Mack had woken with a hard cock, which throbbed as it grew thicker and more solid. His breath began to become deeper, his body tingling with want; the need to kiss his friend, the desire to make him his lover, was near unbearable. Mack closed his eyes and tried to sleep, hoping the desires would be more manageable when he woke again, but sleep was not going to be an option; wanton desire was taking over. He steadied himself with controlled breath, cock still throbbing and now seeping warm pre cum. He thought he should maybe leave the bed and remove himself from temptation; he actually thought he could do it, but with a groan and a small shuffle, his bed partner moved closer to him, holding him with his strong arm. The urge to kiss this man was so strong; slowly, he pressed his shirtless torso closer to Pip's body. He did brush his stubbled chin against one of his hoped lovers; the feeling in his head was divine. Then he realised his wet cock had now escaped the restraint of his boxer shorts and was touching Pip's; no, wait, could it be? Oh, hell yes, his wet, pulsing head was touching the equally hard and wet head of Pip's well-endowed member. Mack took a chance; he had to; existence wouldn't be possible unless he tried, so using his free right arm, he stroked the back of Pip's neck and continued to feel his body through the tight white T-shirt that showed his growing muscles so well, moving his hand slowly yet firmly down his back to his naked backside. Mack couldn't believe his luck or the exquisite feeling beneath his touch; his drunken friend was wearing only the figure-hugging T-shirt from the night before and nothing else but the traces of musky aftershave he'd splashed on for the night out. Gently Mack stroked the firm globes of ass cheek and strong thigh whilst watching closely to see if there was a stirring in the face of his bedfellow; satisfied there was no waking movement, he continued to feel and explore, finally brave enough to reach and feel the girth and hardness of Pip's erect penis. Slowly Mack began to move his hand back and forth on the veined shaft; he moved his grip to the head where he connected it to his own; the feeling of heat on the head was like nothing he could ever have imagined, gentle movements of his gripping palm and fingers massaged the two heads together over and over until the raised body heat became near unbearable beneath the sheets, stopping at this point was no longer an option, his breathing became deeper, he felt the swell of both cock heads in his grip and sensed his friend's body begin to tighten, Mack moved his mouth closer to the parted lips of the man he wanted so much and gently brushed them with his own, the sensation caused overload, and cum blasted from him into his fist, the feeling was simply the greatest of his life then his joy grew more as he felt a second hot pulse of fluid shoot through his fingers from the other hard cock he held.

Wiping the contents of his fist on his shorts, Mack closed his eyes and drifted to sleep. Moments later, Pip opened just one eye to gaze upon the man who had given him his first sexual experience, one he'd wanted since the very first time his eyes had seen the face that now lay smiling in his bed. Pip had been awake for a while and kept his eyes gently closed through the whole thing. He wanted it so badly and dreamed of its night after night; through fear of it ending if he was seen to wake, Pip had fought his own yearning.

A couple of hours later, the young men woke once more, yawning and stretching with no comment of the morning encounter. Neither mentioned anything apart from just how bad they felt as the hangover set in. Classes that day were missed entirely, and in true student style, the hair of the dog and a cheap all-day breakfast eventually made them feel a little better.

The Christmas break was, of course, only a couple of weeks later and the boys travelled to the village on the Welsh border to spend the holiday in the little house where Pip's nanna had raised her ward. A buffet tea was laid out and enjoyed by all until Nanna insisted the young men go and explore the village and have some fun and leave here to clear away, a task she stressed she would enjoy doing as she somehow missed the motherly feeling that was given from caring for her household.

The local pub was filled with seasonal revellers, many of whom welcomed home one of their own and his friend with plenty of drinks and shots. The night was thoroughly enjoyed by all, and Mack was somewhat amazed at how good community spirit felt even when the entire pub began singing carols after someone lifted the lid of the piano and started tickling the ivories.

"I can't believe I'm drinking; I swore never again," Mack confessed as they staggered back to the house after quite a late lock-in. Arms across each other's shoulders, torsos pressed close side by side in an attempt to stay upright; Pip squeezed as he smiled and replied, "Yeah, same here, but staying drunk and sobering slowly has to be a much better option."

Mack squeezed back, which caused a stirring in his crotch. "Can I say something?" Pip looked up, eyebrows raised, to acknowledge and give permission. "It's just… well… thank you. You really are my best friend; I couldn't imagine not having you around."

"Aww, you're sweet; I must get you drunk more often," Pip jested. "But really, nice to hear; I must say I've never had a friend like you either."

With that, they chinked the cans together that some kindly partygoer insisted they take for the journey home and raised a toast. "To us," they said together.

Christmas Eve was a lazy day, and after a long walk where Pip showed Mack an old mill that he used to go to escape before wandering back and taking a much-needed early afternoon nap.

Pip's room was a decent size, containing all the usual belongings of a young man; double bed, wardrobe, chest of drawers and a desk, loaded bookshelves and scattered around the room stuffed toys and small items from throughout his life. Nanna had fetched the 'put you up' folding bed from her sewing room and made it with fresh linen alongside Pip's bed and put clean towels out for both of them; later in the afternoon, she shouted up the stairs that they should shower and freshen up before dinner, to which they looked at each other and giggled like little boys.

"I think that's an order rather than a suggestion," said Pip, and threw a towel to his friend and pointed to the wall at the head of the bed.

"You first, that way," he instructed. Mack obeyed the command, left showered and dressed in just a wrapped towel around his waist, and returned to the bedroom. Fifteen minutes later, Pip returned from his refreshing to see Mack, still in nothing more than the towel, bent over the bed, rummaging for something in his bag.

"Lost something?" Pip eventually asked after spending way too long admiring the navy towelling-clad body before him.

"Deodorant, I'm sure it's in here somewhere... Oh, here it is," responded Mack, who had completely staged the scene, wanting Pip to see him semi-naked, maybe even totally? Maybe walk up behind him, stand close, press his groin against him, stroke his back, straighten him upright, lean around and kiss his neck. Fulfil the very fantasy he had imagined the night before with his cock in his hand, he hoped and, in truth, longed to feel again.

He cleared his throat. "So, *erm,* dinner then," he said as he stood up, looking Pip straight in the eyes as he applied the roll to his armpits, hoping that if he kept Pip's gaze, then he wouldn't notice the semi-erectness of his cock that was displacing the towel it was poorly hidden behind. The trick didn't quite work. Pip was subconsciously touching his own member through his towel as he had been staring at Mack's behind; he wasn't sure if he had been seen or not as he felt his face redden. He wanted so much to grab his friend, push him to the bed and kiss him all over, from his lips to his groin; more than anything, he wanted to taste the cock of this man he had spent so much time with that he dreamed about at night, that he masturbated to over and over again, he wanted so much to tell him that he'd been awake throughout the birthday fondle and to tell him he wanted more.

"Yes. Dinner."

They both dressed, both casually catching glances of each other's bodies as they did so, before descending the stairs to the dining table where a Christmas feast was to be served. The meal was superb; Nanna had laid the biggest spread that could easily have fed six people; she informed them that they could take the bulk of the leftovers back with them, so at least for a day or two, she knew they would be fed. Nanna had taken a real shine to the handsome young Irishman; she considered him to be most charming and that was before he presented her with his Christmas gift, a vintage sewing box he had found in a charity shop near the University.

"I hope you don't mind that it isn't new, but it seemed to have so much character."

Nanna responded with a beaming smile. "Oh, dear boy; it is beautiful; look at the craftsmanship; it felt lined, too; I love it. I simply love it."

Mack smiled. "My dad is a joiner and taught me loads of things about carpentry as I was growing up, so I know what to look for when it comes to how things are made. All of the individual boxes slide really well both when opening and closing."

"Well, I think it is wonderful. Thank you. Goodness, I don't know if I should use it or just look at it."

The gifts were exchanged and opened, the table cleared, and the dishwasher loaded; Nanna suggested the boys take a stroll whilst she took a short nap. The air was still clear with little breeze, making the cold more than bearable, so the duo donned their coats and headed out. It wasn't long before Pip, with quite an absent mind, guided himself and his friend once more to the deserted old paper mill in the valley. This time, they sat in Pip's favourite thinking spot on the steps that led to the entrance doors and looked up the grassed valley to where the dam wall had once been; daylight was rapidly fading.

"I love it here," Pip said.

"I can see why; it's really calming here, pretty too."

"Yes. I've had all of my best ideas here. I think at one point I came every single day."

"Pip…"

"Yeah?"

"I got you another little gift. I wanted to give it to you alone, sort of something just between us. It's only a silly little thing, but… anyway, I hope you like it." With that, he handed a small box wrapped in red tartan printed gift paper and tied it with a red ribbon. Pip almost shook with a mixture of nerves and excitement.

"Thank you. Should I have gotten you something else?"

"Not at all. That wallet is a class piece; I will always treasure it."

"Good, I'm glad now. Remember, there is an American dollar bill in the card slot. I was told that a purse or wallet must always be given with money in it and then it will always have money coming into it. I used a dollar because you can't accidentally spend it."

"Thoughtful as well as generous. Now come on, open the bloody box!"

Pip pulled at the ribbon bow and slid his finger to release the tape holding the paper, revealing a navy-blue box, the kind you get at a jewellery shop. He opened it and took out its contents. A silver mouse. It was quite a remarkable yet simple piece, around five centimetres long, quite heavy, so he reckoned solid in the simple shape similar to the white chocolate mice one ate as a child in the mixed bags from the local store. Its tail trailed around on itself and re-joined the body before branching out once more, creating a sealed hoop so it could be attached to a key ring. On the mouse's flat underside was an engraved message. *"To my Squeak."*

"It's amazing," Pip said and stared into the eyes of his friend; without any more thought, he leaned forwards and kissed Mack square on the lips. He eased back the shortest of way and said, "Thank you. I love it." Before re-joining their lips. Mack had wanted this to happen for so long, and he felt his dreams had all come true. He kissed back. The young men carried on with their embrace, tongues lashing against each other, hands exploring the bodies that they had so desperately wanted to be connected with since the day they met.

An hour or so later, they thought they should head back and re-join Nanna. Neither spoke much on their return walk and spent the evening trying to look at each other as little as possible to avoid suspicion. Mack was petrified of being found out as gay. As much as he knew it was natural and true for him, he felt his father would surely kill him, or have him sent for electric shock treatment to rid him of the internal sin, let alone the Aids plague that his dad had ranted on about that it was justified and God's way of finally getting rid of the bloody faggots. It was these thoughts that hounded his mind daily. He knew deep down that women were really not an option for him. Not that he felt repulsed in any way, just that he felt no attraction whatsoever, no desire to spend time with women and certainly no lustful thoughts. Yet men, however, aroused him to the point of embarrassing hard-ons that showed so clearly through his trousers, his tracksuit, his shorts and the worse of all, his swimming trunks, where it was all he could do to keep the thick long shaft covered up at all, just the sight of a stubbled strong jaw, a tight torso, strong chest or solid thighs and ass would set him off.

Nanna took herself off to bed around 9.30, very early, but she explained that the afternoon nap wasn't enough to catch up with the five a.m., start she'd had that morning. She offered the pair a bottle of whisky and bid them good night, saying if they drank the lot, it wasn't a problem; it was Christmas, after all, and sometimes letting your hair down was the only thing that should be done. Pip fetched the glasses, and very heavy measures were poured.

It was Mack who broke the silence. "Earlier... *erm*... did you mean what happened to *erm*... will happen?"

Pip didn't speak, just nodded.

"I just wanted to say..." Pip looked at him with sheer dread as to what the end of Mack's sentence would be; thoughts of panic, mistake, hope and ultimately fear that he had destroyed the best friendship he had ever known scrambled in his mind; he felt a cold sweat encompass his body before Mack continued, "I wanted to say that I am really glad you kissed me, that we kissed even. I wanted to do it with you for ages."

Relief calmed Pip almost instantly. Serenity took over him. This man sat with him had become the absolute centre of his existence. The fear of rejection proved to himself that this was so. "I was hoping you would do it first because I wasn't brave enough. I was scared you would run away and never speak to me again or something, but when you gave me the mouse, I knew you must have thought of me more than a friend. You're the only one who has ever called me Squeak, you know."

"I know," Mack responded and leaned in to kiss him more. They sat until about one in the morning, chatting and laughing like they always did before Pip announced that perhaps they should get some sleep. They climbed the stairs and took turns to use the bathroom before going into Pip's childhood bedroom. Not knowing what they should do or say next, they went to their separate beds, Pip in the double and Mack in the foldaway. Just fifteen minutes passed, and it felt like hours of them lying on their backs staring at the ceiling in the moonlit room. Both of them were too nervous to say anything; nothing to be heard but the sound of each other breathing. It was Pip who broke the silence. He had agonised over what to say and must have thought of a thousand possibilities during those eternal seconds before he settled on something, he thought was innocent and polite to ask his house guest.

"Hey, M, are you warm enough?"

"No, not really; it's a bit cold in here."

"Yeah, sorry. Nanna turns the heating off at night; she says she sleeps better in the cold."

"Have you got another blanket?" Mack asked.

Pip knew exactly where the spare blankets were and that there were plenty but apologised, and said he didn't think so and instead offered an alternative source of heat.

"You could get in with me if you like. It'll be way warmer."

"Thought you would never ask," said Mack, and within a second, he had joined Pip. Mack decided not to be nervous or hesitant any longer; after all, he had known this guy inside and out since the birthday encounter and had fancied him since the very first-day meeting in the Halls corridor. He moved straight into an embrace and deeply kissed the man he was about to make his lover. Mack touched and stroked the warm body next to him, ran his fingers up and down the spine before caressing the cheeks of Pip's ass, fondling them, enjoying the feeling of the firm curves beneath his hands before bringing his hand to the front and taking his first ever touch of another man's balls. Mack loved the feeling of the ample set of globes in his palm; he loved holding them and more loved the sensation that he knew he was providing; he was surprised at how erotic and arousing it was to pleasure another man. Mack moved his hand upwards and around the shaft of Pip's cock; it was as hard as a rock, as hard as his own was, as hard as he'd felt before. As the two kissed and hugged, their two throbbing members rubbed against each other, it wasn't much longer before Pip's breathing became heavier. "I can't stop… I think, I'm gonna…" With a low deep growl, a suppressed scream Pip shot his load, pumping hot wet cum over his partner's cock and stomach, the feeling of it on Mack's hard knob was also too much to be able to hold back and he bit the pillow in a bid to be quiet as his own load joined the party. They lay holding each other, staring at each other. "That was awesome," said Mack.

"I wanted to go longer, though; sorry, you got me a bit excited."

"Don't worry about it. It's hot as hell to know I get you that wound up. I am sure the more we do it, the better-paced it will be. Mind you, if it feels like that, I really don't care how long it goes on for."

Pip smiled and moved to give the tightest embrace he had ever performed, kissed his new lover, and they both closed their eyes to sleep, yet the urges of fit young men meant they did not rest for long; in less than an hour Pip was hard and ready for more, he leaned into Mack's strong back and began to gently kiss down the length of his spine until he reached the crease of this handsome man's ass. Pip teased at the top of this beautiful place, kissing and stroking his chin; Mack groaned with approval and desire and pushed his back and ass closer.

17

With the Nachos nearly gone and the fine blended whisky starting to take effect, the pair began to relax a little more and remember just how damned good it was to be in each other's space once again.

Pip recalled how much he had missed his lover way back in the old days when they were split by their first jobs, Mack, a trainee sports teacher at a private girls' school in Hitchin, Hertfordshire and himself studying business as a second-degree. Their time together, however limited, was as precious as any amount of gold could be; they never quarrelled, just simply picked up where they had left off, usually in the bedroom. Sex had become a longer-lasting occurrence as those initial couple of years spanned. They knew every inch of each other's flesh and knew exactly how to please each other from the magical thing Pip could do with his tongue when he sucked his lover's cock that would make Mack explode his hot cum down his throat to the angle that Mack would fuck Pip, ticking his prostate with every pleasuring stroke.

Mack took a long sip of his drink. "Hey, remember when we went to see my mum from Uni?"

"How could I forget? It took me ten days to realise your Uncle Sep's name was short for Giuseppe, and Oh

My God, how much of his wine we drank? My liver didn't recover for weeks."

Mack giggled at his joke. "I've been there for a few years now; it's where I have left to be here."

"Oh."

"Yeah, after the disaster of the wedding, I left everywhere and everything, got a job in Dubai teaching the English kids sport. It was OK for a while, then one of the parents offered me a job in close personal protection with really good money, so I had a go at that for a few years. Travelled quite a bit with that one."

"You mean you were a bodyguard?"

"Yup, then back to Italy for the last seven years, first-year learning the wine business and the rest as a cop."

"Really? I didn't think an Irishman could join an Italian police force. Hey, did you get one of those super tight uniforms?"

"How did I know that would be a question? Yes, I did get the tight uniform, the nightstick and the gun and before you ask yes, I do still have all of the gear and a gun, but not the service issue; of course, everything is in a lock-up about ten miles away. In fact, my entire life is in that storage unit. I've had it for ages since Dad died; there's assorts of crap in there. Anyway, yes, an Irishman can become an Italian cop if he claims his dual nationality and gets his passport; Mum was a resident there, remember."

Pip listened intently. He had desperately longed for so many years to be reunited with this man and although happy he was there right then, he also wanted to be angry at the time lost that they could have spent together. "So, Mister Hot Cop. What happened?"

"When?"

"You know when. The wedding. How is Mrs Annabel, Lucy Sullivan?"

"That's why, I ran Pip. Ran away from it all. The marriage was over before we got off the plane on the honeymoon. I swear I thought I was going to pass out and die with the fear of telling her I didn't want to really be married, but I was saved from the strain as she said it to me first; she explained that she had gone ahead with it to please her parents but really just wanted to be single and go back to college to study journalism. She knew deep down that my father's power and control over me had forced the arrangement between the two families, he put me under so much pressure to 'finally become a man' and to 'stop running around with that Nancy boy'."

"Yes, I remember his 'fondness' of me," recalled Pip and gave a sarcastic grin.

"Well, Mum helped me get the whole thing annulled and very kindly gave Annabel a little money so she could go and follow her dream, but then I felt like I couldn't come back home. There was no way I wanted to face my dad. Can you imagine his reaction to his 'failed' son? I was too embarrassed to stay with Mum, having gone through with the ceremony in the first place, as she has always known about me being gay, and how I felt about you. She said it was as clear as day when she saw us together that summer and all she would ever want was for me to be happy and safe. But, Pip, I couldn't do it. I'd hurt you. Hurt my one true love, the only person who has ever had my heart, my soul even. I knew I had destroyed everything when you didn't show up for the wedding."

"Oh, I was there. I kept watching from a distance. Watching, waiting for you to turn around and change your mind, to come running into my arms, but to my dismay, that didn't happen. I watched as you left the church to the sound of bells under a shower of rice and into the car. I cried so much I could barely focus on the 'Just Married' sign as you drove away. That and the fact your ever-loving father had called me and advised it would be inappropriate for me to attend, the church didn't need infecting with my sort, or something along those lines. Mack, the night before the wedding, is the only argument we have ever had. I swear I was only trying to do what I thought was best for you. I'm sorry if it put more pressure on you. I was trying to help by not letting you go through with it."

"I know. You were right, of course. Hell, it was proven so not twenty-four hours later. Do you remember your last words to me?"

"I'll never forget; I was walking backwards towards the door after you said you had to go through with the wedding to save face. I said, 'Don't you realise how much I love you, that you are everything to me?' I meant every word."

"And that's why I couldn't come back. I thought I had royally fucked up, not only split up what we had but broken my Squeak's heart to boot. It was such a horrible time. I am so so sorry."

Mack leaned back in his seat and raised his arms above his head to stretch; as he did so, his shirtsleeve rode up his forearm to reveal the top outline of a confectionary mouse with a tail that looped upon itself. He saw Pip notice it and presented his arm for a proper look. "My Squeak," he said. "Forever with me."

At that moment, Jackie appeared. "There you are. I'm heading off now. The email is sent, and I think you'll like the new plan; anyway, don't worry. Charlotte says she is happy to lock up tonight; glad I've caught you; I think you might need these."

As she finished her jumbled sentence, she placed Pip's keys on the table. "He forgets them more times than I don't know what. Are you having a good catch-up?"

"Yes, Jacks, thanks, and don't worry, I will fill you in on all of the gossip tomorrow, and yes, I will bring the biscuits."

Jackie smiled and gave a comical over, enthusiastic wave as she left the bar. Mack looked at the bunch of keys and at the old battered silver mouse which hung from the ring by its tail. "Still my, Squeak," he said and smiled. "So sunshine, I've fessed up about what I've been up to, although in somewhat brief detail, what about you?"

"*Ah,* for that, I think we should walk and talk." And then whispered, "Walls have ears."

After donning pairs of rigger boots in the gym office, which Pip had courteously stocked up for guests and prospective buyers to wear when visiting the building site, the duo headed out towards the building. As they approached the first house, Mack said, "Crikey, that's impressive. Is that one yours?"

"Sort of. It's complicated. It does belong to me, yes, the whole thing does, the site, I mean, well, to my building company anyway, but I might be giving it away?"

"What? The whole site! Who the hell to?" enquired Mack.

"The house, and it's going to Marcus, *erm,* my, *erm* husband."

"Fuck. Sorry. Of course, if you're with someone, why wouldn't you be? Shit. Fuck. There's me with this notion of declaring my undying love to you and I don't know, maybe I was expecting violins to play as we ran into each other's arms, FUCK. Sorry. I knew I shouldn't have come. How the hell did I expect the most handsome hunk I have ever met to be available just because I decided we should be back together half a lifetime later? Shit. Sorry. I should go."

"Will you stop rambling? Shut up and listen," Pip said as he took his former lover by the shoulders and looked deep into those big brown eyes, he so adored to calm him down.

"It's not quite what it seems. Yes, I am married to Marcus, but he's nothing but a lying little robbing-stealing bastard. He seduced me, proposed, and suddenly we were married; you know what it's like? The date is set and bang, you're in. Hardly ever spent time with each other, rarely had sex, like less than ten times in a year, then I caught him 'mid-flight' with one of the gym instructors! The prick had the audacity to blame me for the affair because he said,

142

he thought I was old and ugly. Then like the end of a Scooby Doo show, he began telling me the rest of his little plan to take basically every penny profit out of this development and this house. Number One."

"Can't you just kick him out? Or do you love him?"

"I never loved him, fancied him, yes, the rest was a combination of the onset of middle-aged panic about being lonely in my latter years and... well... after what you and I had together, I thought that kind of feeling only comes your way once so I would make do with what was on offer as it was probably as good as it was going to get. As for kicking him out..."

Pip and Mack sat in the shell of Number One, the grandest of all of the projects and slightly changed the subject. "I was hoping this would be finished by Christmas, but there's a delay with the edging stones that will go around the roof line, so it looks like next February before expected completion."

"Sounds nice."

"It does Marcus's idea. Must admit he does have some good ideas when it comes to finishing touches; mind you, they do tend to cost a small fortune."

"I bet. So why are you with him if he's not the right one? If he's having affairs, surely that's grounds for divorce."

"Every way I turn, he has me over a barrel, I'm afraid, and not in the good way. Blackmail, I guess you would call it."

Pip explained about the jewellery, the stones, the selling of the smaller pieces, showed him the article from the newspaper on his phone and that he would questioned about bribing the planning office, the fake cruelty he was supposedly inflicting and that Chris, the only one that could support the truth was nowhere to be seen since it all kicked off.

"Jesus, Pip. Even with my police head on, I can't see how to get out of this one cleanly. What shall we do?"

"I don't know, I've tried to think of every scenario. Whatever I try to do, it seems he has a way of landing me either in jail or broke. Oh, and the latest is, he says, while we were in Manchester last year for a sports and leisure industry conference, he drove to the casino. Apart from losing nearly four grands, he got completely wasted and called me out of bed at three a.m., to go and fetch him and his precious bloody Range Rover. Like a gullible prat, I dressed and took an Uber. He was in the right state. Kept turning off the sat nav and playing with the air con and the controls; I drove around for ages until he stopped fiddling, and I could finally re-set the nav route and get back to the hotel. Anyway, now he says he wasn't actually drunk and had planned to mess around in the car to make sure I was seen by the city CCTV driving it. He claims that he hit a man with it and drove off and will turn me in as the offender."

"The calculating little fucker. We have to stop him."

"That twice you've said 'we'."

"Well, *erm,* I was hoping that maybe after what you said about not loving him, that maybe, you know, perhaps… Do you still fancy me?"

"What kind of question is that? Do you really think that you can casually stroll into my life after fifteen long, lonely years looking as youthful as ever with that olive tan, tousled hair, strong jaw, and a body that probably won Men's Heath cover model of the year for several years running, those big brown eyes that make me melt and don't think I haven't noticed the scent either, Amen Thierry Mugler, our scent, and think that I could not fancy you. Fuck me, you're the embodiment of perfection in my eyes. Hell, yes, I fancy you; hell, yes, I've missed you, and my God, I have never, could never, will never stop being head over heels in love with you."

The men lunged into each other's arms and kissed with enough lust to try and fill the void of missed passion from their time apart. The feelings they experienced were as exciting to their brains and bodies as it was the very first time they had touched. "You had me at 'hey, Squeak', by the way."

"So, together, what are we going to do to get that little shit out of our lives?"

"I wish I knew, M; I really wish I knew."

Pip led his true love around the development, explaining his plans. "So, they all face outwards?"

"Yes," Pip replied. "Not quite sure how I came up with the idea; it all began staring at the remaining footings of the old damn wall, which, if you were to see it from above, looks like it's part of a perfect circle, then I thought how cool, every ten degrees could be a plot. Thirty-six houses were the first plan, but then I thought of access for repairs and maintenance and all that, so I reduced the

145

builds to thirty-three and the other plots are access points. All of the rear gardens will have gates leading here."

At this point, they had reached the large stone monolith in the centre of the site.

"I'm going to put benches all around it and maybe some shelters. Thought it might be nice for this new little group of residents to have some shared space maybe form a new community. Oh yes, the facing outwards thing. It just seemed a nice idea to be able to see the views of the valley, that's all."

"Well, I think it's beautiful. You have certainly put thought into it."

"Thanks. Oh, and the roof tiles are those new solar power ones, so no one has to have those slabs strapped to the roof, although the real reason is, I thought as the sunlight reflected off them, it might shimmer like the water that once sat here may have done. Every house is leasehold with the tiniest of peppercorn ground rent; maintenance will be covered easily by the sale of the excess generated electricity."

"You're a bloody genius!" exclaimed Mack.

"Aw, shucks. Flattery will get you everywhere."

"I hope so."

18

Pip's phone rang at 5.45 the following morning. He grabbed it and hit the green button without noticing who the caller was. "Hello?"

"Pip, it's me, Jackie. Get dressed and get down here. Now. Emergency!"

Pip shot out of bed, threw on a t-shirt, grey jog pants and trainers and for once managed to remember not only his keys but also his phone and his wallet before bolting out of the apartment and bounding down the marble staircase and bursting through the heavy glass entrance doors of the gym to see Jackie stood holding two cups of steaming fresh ground coffee from the lounge upstairs.

"What's the emergency? Are you OK?"

"The coffee was getting cold."

"Jacks, is that what I've just given my heart a pounding for?"

"Oh, *shush*," Jackie said with a smile. "I had to get you here quickly for hot coffee, yes, but the real emergency is my need to know who that dishy man was that you were with last night. Whey Hey! The boy has remembered his wallet, good lad. Toddle off over the lobby and get the biscuits, then meet me in the office."

Pip took the deepest of breath in relief that there was nothing to really be concerned about, smiled to himself and obediently fetched the sinful snacks from the convenience store before returning and taking his seat behind the desk.

"Oh, Jackie. I don't know whether to laugh, cry or throw up. I'm so confused. Happy, angry, I just want to scream, maybe?"

"Jesus, whoever the mystery man is, he's certainly having an effect. Come on, tell me! I've been here since five; I can't wait any longer."

Pip sat back in his chair, took a sip of his coffee and began. He told her about everything he and Mack had gone through. It felt good to share it and even better to hear himself tell the tale in chronological order, which made it seem more real and not a distant memory that had no more substance than a remembered dream. Once he had completed sharing as much as he knew, he asked Jackie what she thought he should do.

"What about Marcus? The ink is still wet on the marriage licence, isn't it?"

"About him. Jackie, I have to tell you something." He spent the next half an hour telling her of the situation with his husband and all of his threats and how trapped he felt he was.

"Christ on a bike, I don't know what to suggest?" she said, having listened intently to her friend. "Right, for a start, we need to get these refilled." She gestured towards the coffee cups before lifting the phone, pressing the button connecting to the cafe and asking for refills to be sent down. "When will you be seeing Mack next?" she asked.

"About ten. He's coming here."

"OK, that gives me a little bit of time to think. Tell you what, when he gets here, we will go up to the fitness assessment room with the treadmills running outside; no one can possibly overhear us."

A tad bemused, Pip agreed before taking a spare outfit and wash bag from the office closet and heading towards the showers in the changing rooms.

Mack was far too keen to see his man again and was stood in reception at 9.30, wearing a smart but casual fine-knit jumper and chinos and the broadest of smiles that he simply couldn't hide. He asked Tina, the morning receptionist, if he could see Mr Scot and she buzzed his office to relay the request. Pip stole through the office door and thought he might faint seeing this almost perfect man standing there, confirming it was all real.

"Mr Sullivan, how kind of you to revisit us. Let us go straight up to the assessment room and get started, shall we?" he spoke as he offered a guiding arm to usher the handsome Adonis in the direction of the stairs, and Mack followed him to the room. Pip flicked on the light as he closed the door and twisted the cord to close the blind. They kissed with such heat that both knew they would be soaked through with pre cum. It was all they could do not to strip each other bare and throw themselves onto the desk to complete their desire. Before long, a double tap on the door and the lowering movement of the door handle urged the men back into some semblance of reality, and they disengaged their embrace and stood back from each other as Jackie entered, closed the door behind her and turned the toggle built into the door furniture to lock it.

"Really, boys. You didn't think to bolt the door?"

Pip knew his face was reddening. All three of them smiled. Mack offered his hand. "Jackie, isn't it? Nice to meet you properly."

"You, too," she replied. "Now. Both of you sit down. Mack, Pippy Longstockings here has brought me up to speed about you and everything that little fucking wanker he's married to has done; forgive my French, but I'm so fucking angry; I mean, it's not even like he's trying to blame someone else or a rough childhood or something he's just bloody greedy. Oh, I could..." Jackie took a deep inhale of air and held it for a couple of seconds to calm herself. "Sorry. Right then. To start with, I suggested meeting up here partly so we can't be heard. Secondly, if it's mentioned that we are seen, then it's nothing more than a fitness test for a new member, OK?"

"Seems a bit over the top, a bit cloak and dagger, but whatever you say, Jacks."

"Pip, my darling, the way that little fucker is playing games, there is no way we are taking any chances. I was privy to all of my late husband's cases and the one thing that always is needed is discretion."

Both the men nodded in agreement before Jackie continued, "Now. Firstly, is there any way that Marcus could know who Mack is? Any old photos he might have seen?"

"Erm, I don't think so. No can't have done. All my old pictures are in two shoe boxes on the shelf in the office

150

closet. I've been there since I had to live in it to save money. Every time I thought about taking them upstairs, I thought that I should scan them and make them digital so left them there. I must get round to doing that one day."

"Well, lucky for you, you didn't. I'll take them home later to be doubly sure. I don't think there are any limits as to where Marcus would take anything. He cannot know who Mack is, who he is, where he's been or anything. I'm going to help you as much as I can, but it's not going to be easy keeping you two under wraps."

Pip shot his hand in the air like a schoolboy and eagerly said, "Wait, I have an idea!"

"Very well, Philip, you may continue..." Jackie said in her best school teacher voice as she looked at Mack and both of them shook their heads, mocking disbelief that he had put his hand up. Pip reddened again. "Oh, shut up, both of you. Anyway, I'll sign you up as a gym member for a start, don't worry, you won't have to pay, and then what about if I gave you a foreman's job on the building site, then we would have to have loads of legitimate meetings."

Jackie joined in, "You know that's not a bad idea; it would cover you if you were seen in a bar or pretty much anywhere. What do you think, Mack? Have you any skills you could blag?"

"Yes," Mack replied. "The only thing my dad ever taught me was carpentry and joinery, so I'd always have a skill to fall back on. Pip, if it means I'm near you, I'll do anything."

His lover smiled at the words. "I think this might work, at least until I can work out what to do about this mess."

Mack chimed in, "Until you and I can sort it, you mean."

"Wrong again. It's until WE can sort a solution," Jackie confirmed they would indeed be a trio through this problem-solving activity. "Now, Mack, where are you staying?"

"I've got one of the rooms they let out above the old post office, but only for one more night. They said that they are all booked up accommodating the builders. Oh my God, Pip, your project will make me homeless!"

"Yeah, yeah, very funny. Actually, I have another idea."

"Careful, Pip dear, that's two today; we don't want to be risking a stroke with all this brain activity."

"Jackie, go and fuck yourself; you're just not funny, either of you for that matter; oh, dear, I can see between the pair of you I'm in for ribbing for the rest of my life. My superb and flawless idea is this. Beneath the big old staircase is what I presume to be the original caretaker quarters; I'll show you in a bit; it stretches right to the back of the building, a bit dark as the back wall has the only windows from the corridor that joins the shops delivery bays and the apartments storage cages but it's a good size overall, loads of features in there two, the ironwork that supports the steps is brilliant, and there's a mezzanine that could be used as a bedroom. I had planned on it being an office. There's a little en suite and a small kitchen that I had put in; you just need a few sticks of furniture."

Mack's eyes lit up. "Pip, that's a wicked idea; I've got everything I need in that lock up, including that deco sofa and chairs that Dad had, you know, the ones with the arms that look like the wheel arches of a vintage car, I had them reupholstered in walnut leather. I can't believe I'll be in the same building as you. I can't wait to tell Mum I'm not going home."

Pip nodded, smiled and took advantage to mock. "OK, I think we have the beginnings of a plan, although fuck knows what the end of it will be. Moreover though, Mack, did you just say 'wicked'."

"Might have done."

"Thought so! Are you stuck in 1995 or something?"

Leaping to Mack's defence and joining the banter and fun, Jackie commented, "1995, what a year, the same one when his husband was born. Now, who on earth mentioned reupholstered sofas before they've even seen a place? Oh yes, the Gays."

Mack laughed; he hadn't enjoyed conversation like this since, well, since his original involvement with Pip. "Funny, both of you. Pip, husband, 1995, hilarious."

"Oh, *shush*, it's only a 'slight' age gap."

"Slight. Yeah, it's a slight number of decades. Cradle snatcher."

With that, the first meeting came to a close. Jackie headed out first to go down to the office to sort the gym membership and employment paperwork for the ruse. Pip pushed the door closed and looked directly into Mack's eyes. "Seems so unreal. So quick, too. I love you, M, and always have. Can't believe you're here. It's like a piece was missing without you around. It is real, isn't it? You won't go again?"

"Pip, I swear it. I love you and I'll be at your side no matter what. Listen, I can take you away from all this if you want?"

"I don't understand. How?"

"Well, I saved a heck of a lot of money, especially from the bodyguard stuff and on top of that, there's the vineyard."

"Your uncle's place?"

"My uncle and his sister's place, it's been handed down from my great-grandparents to my grandparents and then to Uncle Guiseppe and my mum, which was quite the surprise for her as she thought it was all going to her brother with him being, one, a male and two, having stayed there and run it. He and his wife couldn't have kids, so their half is mine as well as Mum's. I get the lot, land, house, vines, wineries even any cash they have. I really can take you away from it all."

"I could cry, that's amazing, but I have to fight for what I've worked so hard to build. I can't walk away; it's not just me; imagine what would happen to the members of the gym, the tenants, the staff. I can't let them down."

"Your wish is my command."

"Wait, does it mean you will have to go and run the vineyard?"

"Pip. Stop it. I'm not going anywhere. We have managers in place. You and I can pop over whenever we feel like it together. Mister, I'm not letting you out of my sight; there's no way I can lose you a second time. Mad as it might sound, I started imagining I could see you in a crowd a few years ago. You've never been out of my head."

"Saw me? Where? When?"

Mack took out his phone and scrolled through the photos until he found what he was searching for and presented the image.

"Look, this guy. Looks just like you. Nearly fell off the police bike when I saw him. Didn't breathe for a minute. I got the image off my police chest camera. I rode back around the square but couldn't see him; then I remembered he had a suitcase and a bit of a tan, so he may be travelling home. I raced to the airport and flashed my badge to get access to the passenger lists on all of the UK flights, but your name wasn't there. It was just my mind wishing. Didn't help that it was at that little coffee house where…"

"Where we first kissed in public. It's not something we could have comfortably done over here back then. Wow, how the world has changed. You took that photo three years and three months ago. I think you will find."

"I guess around then, how did you work that out?"

"Because dickhead, it was me. My third and final visit. The first time I went was about ten years ago; I got so lost trying to find your uncle's place I couldn't remember the name or location, and after a week, I had to come home. I went out again two years after that, and that time, I found that little coffee house, but just like the last time, I never found the vineyard again; I wish I'd had paid more attention whilst clinging to you on the back of that scooter. I had this romantic notion of seeing you, our eyes locking and running into each other's arms, but each time I came home disappointed that I hadn't found you and that I was a sad ageing git that was living in the past."

"Oh, baby. It was you. I knew in my heart it had to be but it was so surreal and sort of proved it wasn't when I couldn't find your name at the airport. You know I'd even planned to arrest you if I found you so I could get you off the plane."

"Mack, you wouldn't have found me on the UK flight manifest because I flew to Paris to meet Jackie; she had gone back to where her late husband had proposed. It would have been a big anniversary for them, and she didn't want to be alone."

"Well, at least we are together now."

19

A whole week had passed since Mack had burst into Pip's life and he had bared all feelings to his best friend. Today was move-in day for Mack into the caretaker's flat. During the week, Pip had George, the retired odd job man who helped around the gym, give the place a fresh coat of paint and pull a couple of the builders from the site to move the entrance door from the left side to the right so it was opposite the glass wall of the gym which happened to be in line with the gym office door behind reception, which Mack pointed out and jokingly accused his lover of being an obsessive stalker. Pip had agreed that he was, totally and completely, in fact, considering having secret cameras installed into the flat so he could keep watch and make sure that Mack couldn't run away from him again; he suggested electronic devices that would give deep shocks if the boundaries were crossed to prevent escape and even some kind of tracking device installed under his skin in case that failed. The men had spent hour upon hour in each other's company joking, chatting, filling in everything from the missing years and re-establishing their attraction to each other's bodies. It was as if every time they made sensual love or fucked hard and fast, their connection became stronger than it ever had been before. They openly discussed this and concluded that it must be down to maturity and having a clearer mind to assess and realise what true feelings were and to embrace them. Jackie had been an absolute rock, as always, and given Mack use of her spare room while the flat was refreshed and the removal company sorted.

Pip lay in bed the morning of the move, the early sun beating through the window onto his face. Mack appeared at the bedside, completely naked and wet from the shower. Pip admired his beloved body, still with a strong tan. The dark hair that covered his skin was like a dust of shadow that looked as if it was there just to further enhance the defined lines of strong muscle that was his body. Mack's legs and ass were firm and full and felt perfect beneath his hands as he reached out and grabbed them, pulling Mack towards him in bed with the intention of taking his cock deep in his throat. Music played loudly; Pip recognised the tune immediately as the theme from James Bond. Suddenly, Mack was standing before him, silhouetted by the sunlight and white drapes from the full-height window. He was dressed in a tuxedo, standing a quarter turn towards him, adjusting his cuff links. Large casino chips were falling from nowhere around him, then Mack had turned away just a little more to reveal a fresh stance with a silencer-clad revolver gripped and raised to the sky with both hands.

"Well, hello, Mister Bo..." Pip sat upright and reached for his phone to cancel the alarm, giggling about his dream; he couldn't wait to tell Mack about it, especially since he was convinced, he had spoken out loud the welcome. Deciding this must be what being deliriously happy was, he smiled and headed towards the shower.

It really was move-in day and as Pip descended the stairs, he saw Mack was instructing the removal men where to unpack some of the boxes and which ones to leave for him to do.

He spotted Pip instantly and met him halfway up the first flight of steps; he whispered, "Morning baby." And offered the happiest of smiles before saying in a much stronger and louder voice. "Mister Scot! Brilliant timing; I hope I don't cause too much chaos in the lobby; it shouldn't be that long, to be honest. I'm hoping to have it all in by ten; the new telly and fridge will be here by nine. I've just had a call and the upholstery service says they're round the corner with the suite. Bedrooms did, though." Mack winked as he said the last part, making Pip smile at the suggestive cheek of sharing the information.

Loud enough to be heard he responded, "Oh hey, don't worry, I'm amazed you have all of this done already, it's only just after eight. Do you need a hand with anything?"

"Possibly this afternoon. Can you spare an hour? Oh, and you mentioned there might be some storage space I can use. The guys will be bringing in some of my deep storage stuff, Dad's old tools and some boxes of pictures and things from his house, not massive amounts, you know, the kind of thing, stuff you just can't seem to throw away."

"Oh yes, of course; sorry, I meant to show you where that was when I showed you the flat last week. The keys should be on the ring Jackie gave you."

Pip knew his face was reddening once more. He had fully intended to show the storage room, but once the pair had entered the flat and the door shut behind them, being passionately stripped bare and fucked hard and deep had somehow distracted him.

Mack had stayed away from the Mill building since the meeting in the fitness testing room the previous week under the advice of Jackie, who suggested that they should take the time to calm down from the excitement of reconciliation and changes so as to not rush the prospective plan to sort out the growing problem that was Marcus. Staying with Jackie had been quite nice. She was clearly a very intelligent woman as well as being kind and extremely witty in a style he and Pip had always enjoyed, teasing and having banter; he had always felt that this kind of communication proved the strength of a connection. They hit it off right away; talking to her was like talking to his long-lost lover; it felt like coming home. The cover-up plan of Mack taking the foreman's role, or 'Site Manager' as the employment contract said, seemed plausible. The position had been filled as part of the proposal and schedule by the architects building division, but the gentleman who had agreed to take the role was called abroad for 'family business' and never actually started or even saw where he was to work.

Marcus had an idea. He had been with Jackie for a day or two, over breakfast, which she had cooked a full English version for him; he began, "This is amazing, Jackie, thank you. Christ, it's lucky Pip owns a gym and the flat will be ready soon, or otherwise, I'll be the size of a house. Do you miss looking after your husband?"

"For the food, you are welcome and for the rest, well, yes and no. It's nice to have a guest to fuss over, but it's not every day; mind you I've had your other half to fill that gap. My husband was a good man. I loved him dearly, but at the same time, I did so much for him that sometimes 'me' time just didn't exist, so I don't know, I really don't."

Mack had admired her natural organisation skills and felt grateful that Pip had her in his life. She was one of those people who catalogued information and could recall facts instantly; he bet she knew every gym member and business transaction that happened there and could offer an answer to a question far quicker than any computer.

"I can't believe what that little toad is doing to Pip," she said as she swerved the conversation away from her lost husband. "Moreover, I can't believe he didn't tell me!"

"He was scared, Jackie, really scared. Afraid you might storm in and have it out with Marcus, that it would become the catalyst of the threats becoming reality. It's hard to see another way, a way out, when you're living with the constant reminder of fear."

"I know, and I forgive him; I'm a bit mad with myself, too, if I'm honest. I knew he looked down this last couple of months; I assumed it was the pressure of the new building site."

"Jackie, please don't beat yourself up over it. You and I know now, we are here, now. We will help him. By the way, I've had a thought."

"So, have I," she replied. "You first, though, mister lover man, let's see if we are on the same lines."

"OK," Mack said with an expression of intrigue on his face, wondering what this fine lady meant by her phrase.

He continued, "The chap that was going to take the job I'll be fronting. Do you have all of his details? National Insurance number, bank details and all that."

"Yes, of course. I even had his name badge and swipe card for the porta cabin site office door ready for collection. It will be in his file."

"OK, good. *Erm*... what if he still took the job?"

"How?" Jackie questioned. "He's in Outer Mongolia somewhere, sick family or something."

"It's a bit out there, but what if I was him? Pretended to be him. The only ones who know who he really is and what he looks like are probably the architect firm; I could maybe work it so there's no one else around when I meet with them. Would that work?"

"Well, aren't you the devious dark horse! I'm impressed."

"Thanks. I've had to play the role of others before. There have been several times my old boss was too scared to attend a meeting in certain parts of the world and I'd have to pretend to be him with an earpiece for communication. I was like a big kid; it was like being a spy, I loved it. Never gave a thought to the fact that some of the deals were really dodgy and I could have been shot;

I treated it as a role-playing game. Paid very well, but there might be the odd country I won't revisit."

"I'm looking forward to learning more about your clandestine life, dear heart; how fascinating! I thought I would have the best criminal tales to tell from the law firm, but that sounds like so much more fun. So, how do you envisage the pretence being an advantage in blocking the blackmail? More tea?"

"Please, yes." He handed her his mug with the slogan 'Actually you do have to be mad to work here' printed in American type on the side; she refilled it with Earl Grey from a traditional earthenware pot and dropped it in a slice of lemon. "I thought perhaps that if the guy…"

"Jonathan Glass, oh, and the architect doesn't know him personally; their usual team are delayed on a build in Birmingham; they drafted in Jon from an agency, excellent references; Pip was impressed, at least."

"OK. Even better. Mister Jonathan Glass takes up his position a little later than planned due to circumstances and simply does his job; it covers me seeing Pip completely."

"Why, though?"

"Right, well. You got me thinking when you said it might be better that Marcus didn't find out who I was or how we were connected so he can't even further screw over Pip with extramarital affair grounds for divorce. We would have to pay the real Jon; he will never know why; of course, he will just have free money every month, which he is bound to see as a clerical error; he might report it back to us, well you, he might be cheeky and keep it hoping no one will notice, I'm sort of relying on the latter but reckon even if he does own up to the free cash we could claim accounts and payroll error and keep him on the books for three or four months. I'll keep a low profile around the site and the mill, use the gym at quiet periods, have shopping delivered and all that. Maybe we have enough info to set Jon up a new account so he/I could pay for stuff?"

"Whoa there, Neddy! No. No bank account. Not so much the fraud side of things, although impersonating someone and being paid for it does cross a few lines…"

"Technically, I'd be standing in for him while he attends to his family, and if he is getting paid, then I'm a volunteer."

"OK, for the purposes of the conversation, I'll go with that, but why wouldn't you use your own cards to pay for shopping?"

Mack paused before answering the question, looking deeply and observant into Jackie's face, trying to read her, but to no avail; she had spent far too long in the company of lawyers and clients to let a twitch give away her emotions. He surrendered to his need to share.

"I won't be here."

"No! It will kill him if you leave now; he's only just got you back; you can't."

"Oh, *shush.* Jon will be here, well, me as Jon. Macaulay Sullivan will be at his family residence, his vineyard in Italy."

"And how will you achieve that?" Even Jackie's face was now giving way to intrigue.

"I have dual citizenship. Two passports. I also have a return ticket booked with my British passport back to Italy for this coming Saturday. I booked a return trip in case I couldn't find Pip or worse if he didn't want to have me back. So… I thought that I could be seen to travel home and then come straight back on my other passport, or well, more likely come back without using it if I can."

"Oh really? Friends in low places?"

"Joys of being connected through the Italian Police, let's just say an ocean voyage on a very nice yacht might be happening."

Jackie nodded and stood up, raising her hands slightly as she paced the dining kitchen, clearly thinking through this part of the plan, wondering what advantages it may bring to solve the situation. She began to put in her suggestions, "Right, so you will be here as Jon, the site at least will be in safe hands and hopefully move on a bit quicker at least; oh, you can use the gym after it closes at ten if you want. I'll get you a key, actually; Pip likes to work out after closing, too; anyway, that's an easy one; deliveries concern me; we can't open an account; it would shatter the illusion of accidental payments as it would trace right here."

"Oh fuck, of course. Bollocks, I should have seen that one."

Jackie shook her head. "Don't worry, that's why two heads are better than one; cover the silly mistakes. Oh, how stupid am I? It's easy. All of Pip's accounts, the bank and the credit cards are registered to the Mill building; the delivery address is the gym, as there's not often anyone upstairs to receive things. Anything you need or want; we will simply put it onto his account and take it that way. Trust me, with the amount of crap his soon-to-be ex-husband has delivered on Pip's cards; no one will ever spot anything extra. You know, I think your anonymity is achievable. You will be hidden in plain sight, although it's quite an elaborate deception. Do you really think it is needed?"

"I hope not, but that creep seems to have lots of tricks up his sleeve, and I fear there's more to come. I feel somewhere deep down that I need to be prepared to do whatever it takes to help my man."

"I concur," agreed Jackie, and with that, quite formally, the deal was set with a handshake.

20

"So, if you would care to follow me?" Pip said to Mack as he guided him to the left side of the grand staircase to the access door. "Sorry, you will have to use your key; I've left mine in the apartment. It's the silver-coloured one with a thousand teeth, one of those high-security jobs."

Mack smiled. "Don't ever change," he said and smiled as he unlocked the door. They went through passing the freshly painted wall in the narrow corridor that a few days ago was home to the original entrance door to the caretakers flat. "Why did you have that moved?"

"Oh, didn't I say? It really is so I can stalk you live from my office."

"Funny. Sick, creepy and I feel like Julia Roberts and I've suddenly an urge to straighten the towels to keep the peace, but mainly funny."

"Is because of this corridor. Either from here or from the delivery bay are the only two access points to the storage cages behind the gym. I had them put in for the top-floor apartments to maximise space up there; it's entirely unnecessary. They're all huge properties, but it seemed like a good idea. There's a further two, one for the gym stuff and one for the coffee shop. That's the one you can use; they don't need it any more since I put it back inside the gym. All yours."

"Yes, fine, but why move the door?"

"Oh, sorry, you know I'm not usually this vague. It's your fault I get distracted by very rude thoughts when I see you." They passed through the connecting corridor behind the caretaker's flat; Mack saw the high windows built with these glass bricks that were his light source from the same style windows on the outer wall, and they passed to the storage areas. Mack saw the largest one was spotlessly clean with a polished tile floor, custom racking and neatly labelled storage boxes, all perfectly matching in shape, size and colour. He pointed as he looked at Pip.

"Erm…"

"Welcome to the reason I moved the door," Pip said. "Marcus's domain, the storage facility. He's bloody obsessed with it. In there, defined by an organisation system, most reference libraries would envy an absolute ton of shit that he's collected. Note the gentle warmth; he keeps it bloody heated! God, there's assorted stuff in there; he's like a super neat hoarder. There are bags, wallets, designer clothes galore, game consoles, and heck knows what other gadgets. There's even an entire blue and white dinner service, enough for eight people, in there somewhere; we only had it for a week before he got bored and changed it; that's what he's like; if you look, you will find socks that cost a stupid amount of money that are still in the packet, well, boxes actually, little flat boxes, who the fuck buys boxed socks? And don't even try to estimate how much underwear he has. It's ridiculous."

"Amazingly well organised, though, I'll give him that."

"Obsessed more like. I think he comes down here daily and must spend more time with his stuff than he does with anything or anyone else; that's why I moved the entrance door, so you're not bumping into him; he's already asked me why it's been done and I told him it was so the CCTV would cover the door, don't know if believes it or not, don't really care either, it seemed a bit odd though for him to not kick up a fuss just for the sake of it. Mind you, knowing the care of his precious hoard, he probably thinks it's better out of your way."

"Maybe so."

"So here you go, one lockable cage for all your worldly goods."

"Why thank you, sir, it will do nicely; room for my bike too, brilliant."

"Very, very welcome. And over there is the gym's washing machine and dryer; there isn't one in the flat; we haven't used it since the first floor went in as there's a laundry room up there, so I guess this is your new utility room."

Mack took in the simple Victorian elegance that was offered by the original tiled walls and supporting arches of the high corridor; the building really was impressive, it seemed, in every aspect. The men completed their tour and re-joined the removal men who had now completed their tasks in the flat and were waiting for directions to put the shabby tea chests used for storage that were older than their owner. Pip choked open the door and gave instructions as Mack received his reupholstered furniture.

Less than forty minutes later, all deliveries, including those from the electronic store, were complete and the lobby was back to normal, apart from the man finishing the installation of the TV after adding it to the Gym office Wi-Fi and apart from a few kitchen boxes to have homes found for their contents one would have thought that the flat had been occupied for quite some time. The delivery guy finished and left the couple who re-entered and Mack turned the key in the door; Pip approached behind him, pressed him up against the wood and kissed his neck, making them both erect and intent on some hot sexual action.

"Let's Christen the bed," Pip suggested.

"Too far to walk," Mack said as he turned round to face his lover and kissed him before swapping positions, pinning Pip's back to the door. Mack dropped to his knees and began pulling at the belt buckle of his tight blue jeans, ready to expose the thick hard cock that looked as if it was trying to escape its trapping. Before he had mastered the buckle, both men jumped, slightly startled by the knocking on the door. Mack shot up to a standing position, and Pip leapt into action to get to the sofa as quickly as possible where he sat, crossing his legs to hide his erection. Mack adjusted his untucked denim shirt to hide his and he unlocked and opened the door.

"Jackie! Hi," Mack said, greeting his first guest with kisses to either cheek. "Welcome."

"Hi, boys. Mum's been to Iceland."

"OK… when? I saw you this morning at your house," Mack was confused.

Looking just as befuddled before it clicked, Jackie smiled. "Of course, you wouldn't get the reference, would you? I bet they don't run the adverts in Italy."

"I wouldn't know. I barely watched TV there; I've only bought that one to catch up with old box sets. I thought it might be nice to do whilst snuggled together. What adverts?"

"Oh, it's a silly slogan from a frozen food company; everything food-wise is sorted because 'Mum's been to Iceland' actually, I suppose it could be a bit sexist, really, indicating that Mum is there to sort out the shopping."

Pip piped up, "Or that dads aren't capable."

Mack was still a little confused until he saw the huge pile of shopping bags behind Jackie.

"I did your first shop; Pip, I've seen your fridge. I'm going with most men can't shop. Mack, happy new home, I popped into M&S on the way in and got a few things to set the kitchen up, there's champagne too so you two can celebrate, dawned on me that I was shopping underneath your initials, made me smile. Anyway, are you helping bringing these in or what?"

The men, now with calmer bodies, fetched the shopping bags and took them to the kitchenette underneath the mezzanine and began to unpack them into the cupboards under Mack's instruction of what should go where. Jackie found the cups and kettle, made them all tea, and stood on the lounge side of the tall counter that separated the area from the living room.

"Gentlemen, I have been thinking," Jackie began. "When the firm was still open, we used to use a chap to assist in finding evidence for certain cases, you know, dirt to be found for exchange in negotiation or to prove an affair in a divorce case and all that. I have dug out his number. He's retired now, but I'm sure he would take on a project for me; he owes me a few favours. I thought we could start to build up a case to undermine Marcus. Try and destroy his character; try and get him out of here without it costing everything you own and have worked so hard for."

Mack smiled; he liked the thought a lot. "I say make the call, do it. I'll pay anything to get that jerk out of here."

"Oh, you don't have to worry about money sweetie, as I said, a few favours are owed, this one will be a freebie I assure you." She drained her mug. "Right then, business to run. Pip, you are off for the whole day, cross that hall and there will be hell to pay, understood?"

"Erm, but... Yes, ma'am," Pip obediently replied to his best friend. Sometimes, it was better to take a step back and do as you are told when people are attempting to help you, and right now, the stress he was feeling was building to a crescendo that he felt would erupt inside his brain with the force of Mount Vesuvius on the day it covered Pompeii with molten lava. He knew she was worried about him; she was always worried about him, to be honest, but since he had told her about Marcus, he could see she needed a way to help and make it right.

21

"Harbridge."

"Highness."

"Have lunch sent to the glass house and meet me there if you would be so kind. Two o'clock say?"

"Yes, sir." James left Albert and went to the kitchens to complete his task. He had been hoping for this meeting for three days, but Prince Albert had been ridiculously busy, and there hadn't been a second to spare to discuss the under-dam development. The day passed, and James greeted his friend in the Glasshouse and poured tea for him; they sat in the winged chairs, ready for discussion.

"James, how are you? I've been so busy; I was wondering if we would get the chance to speak candidly at all this week."

"I am well, sir, very well. The widow I employed has now taken the basement flat under my house and takes care of me incredibly well. She has been a God, to be honest, running around the city, making new contacts and organising the extra things for the build; time has been limited for me too; Mrs Silver makes sure I have food when I need it and happily takes messages for me."

"Sounds like you may have your own version of yourself! So, how is my project?"

Six months had passed since it all began and the build had come on in leaps and bounds. James had astonished himself at how adept he was to make sure the building ran to maximum effect; he'd even organised an extra shift so the operation ran for a full twenty-four hours.

"I've altered the tunnel plan," he said to the prince.

"Really, how?"

The tunnel, of course, was a dead end, just a place for discreet alighting from the train for the Royal family should they need it. "I've added a turntable for the train engines. It seemed that being a dead end was just a little obvious, overkill in fact, so I considered the position of it and how much space was between that end of the bridge and the tunnel mouth, and there isn't room to install one there so it gives the space a false purpose."

"I like the idea! And the elevators? Are they running well?"

"Yes, brilliantly, they are used all of the time; I'd say they have saved thousands of hours transporting deliveries down the hillside. I am excited for you to see everything; it is quite an achievement."

"I am indeed looking forward to seeing it. However, it will have to wait until closer to completion. Also, I wish for you to take the wheel table from my quarters in the big house and have it put in my section of the unit."

Moving one of the four wheels meant that this new place would be used a lot by Albert. James was highly honoured to own the third one he looked at and stroked its golden stripes every day he was in his London house, curiosity however took hold of him. "Albert," he asked. "Where is the fourth table located?"

"Downing Street. I gave it to the accommodation there when Peel was in charge, thought it a poignant move, you know, tie the palace to the office even more, mind the queen was not at all amused that I had given a gift without her prior knowledge."

"Ah, I see." James's body felt warmer with a contentment of acceptance within him, that simple gift really was a symbol of trust and extreme gratitude.

In London, the following week, James attended the Gentlemen's club he'd joined under the prince's advisement when first moving into the City. The thick clouds of cigar smoke and grumbling voices of what seemed a room full of grumpy old men was not his ideal situation. However, it was an appropriate venue to meet with building company owners and designers. He had quite become accustomed to the facade of being the wealthy son of an American tycoon and considered himself to play the part well. He sat alone near the fire this one particular day, thinking of how well the project was going and how rapidly it would completed way before the original schedule; despite enjoying being in charge of it, he was also very tired from the combination of it with his royal duties. He ordered brandy and sat staring into the flickering flames, mindlessly swilling the fluid around the oversized goblet.

A man approached him and indicated to the matching chair at the other side of the fireplace.

"May I?" he asked James.

"Of course, it isn't taken," responded James, straightening his position in the chair, his body and mind readying to be alert to perform once more.

The stranger raised his hand a little to gain the attention of the waiter, who came immediately to take an order. "Ah, Billy, good lad, go get me a scotch, would you?" The man sat and looked at James. "Billy, story chap; I've changed my mind; I'll take a brandy, a large one, be so good as to fetch one for this fine gent too if you would be so kind."

"A pleasure, sir," replied the waiter, who promptly left to perform the request.

The man introduced himself. "Billingham, Edward Billingham at your service, kind sir."

"It's a free chair, you know. More than entitled to be sat there, just like all of the other members."

"Well, I think it is only polite to offer a chap a drink and request permission to invade his space and private time, do you not?"

"I guess so," James replied. "To be honest, the company is rather welcome, a distraction from the exhaustion of the day, although I really shouldn't take another drink; this is my second one already."

"Don't be absurd; a couple more will not hurt a man. I didn't catch your name, old chap."

"Sorry, how rude of me. I'm James Ha…" He forced a cough to try and hide his near mistake and broke out into a small sweat that his deception may unfurl at his own doing. The split second of a thousand combined thoughts of panic passed, and he cleared his throat, ready to correct himself. "I do apologise; I fear the smoke in here gets to me somewhat; I'm James Percival."

"I thought you were about to say something beginning with an H for a second."

Harbridge had become rather good at quick thinking. "Possible, my dear friend, so used to saying one's full name, James Harvey Percival, separates me from my father, also James. He used to add 'the second' to my name, but I never liked the thought of it; it is like you are never prepared to win and do not even start to mention my feelings about the other option."

"Other option?"

"Junior."

"I see. Well, I am very pleased to meet you, sir." Billy returned with the drinks, and so began an afternoon that ran into a late evening, the two men swapping tales of the past and plans for the future. James had become so used to his make-believe life that he could easily reel off the same set of rehearsed and practised set of fabricated stories despite the state of intoxication he was nearing. Little did he know, however, that his new acquaintance Teddy Billingham was capable of doing exactly the same...

22

Edward 'Teddy' Billingham was actually Russian-born who was given at birth the name of Gleb Sokolov by the family that had found him left in the middle of a village square wrapped in a clean tablecloth and lain in a box that had once held fruit. The Sokolov family had attempted to raise him as their own and managed to hide the fact that he wasn't theirs for almost eighteen months, at which time the authorities came crashing through the door of the humble home and took the infant from them. The child was taken to a military facility where he would spend the next fourteen years unknowingly being trained to become an agent on behalf of the Russian Government.

It was a time of suspicion across the world, country upon country secretly set and prepared to undermine the power of each other and it was not unheard of for unwanted children to be raised to become infiltrators to provide valuable information. Teddy had been raised with four other similar-aged boys in secret, being taught how to fight the greatness of Russian history, and then each of them had three days per week being taught the language and history of a selected country by natural speakers from the assigned places to authenticate the accents. The teachings lasted until the boys' mid-teens, followed by a short two-year army service and then between three and five years living incognito in the selected country before being allowed to begin infiltration.

Teddy had been informed almost a year ago that this newcomer, Percival, had arrived on the scene and was building a construction to be used as a vault for his father's wealth. This was all very well. However, the sources reported to the spy that this man was trying so very hard to fit in but was sticking out somewhat; however, this was assumably due to his American heritage. Teddy thought it might be worth a look; who knows what kind of valuable information could be obtained. He spent three months watching James Percival travel to and from his Chelsea house to an assortment of places around the city. He noted that James was usually alone but would then be out of the city for days on end after taking the short train ride that terminated in Windsor. Following further, he discovered that the repeated journey always took the same format and always led to the castle that was known to be the home of the royal family away from Buck House. Whomever James Percival was, he had to be a good connection to have; surely there aren't many who would have a key to a discreet door within the castle's outer wall and presumably access to Queen Victoria. Teddy had become curious, even excited that he may be the one who could supply the information that could be used to upset the powers that be here and give chance for his home country to expand their empire, so he had made a report to his secret service contact and was under instruction by reply, to obtain as much intelligence as possible by any means necessary.

"Another?" Teddy chinked his ring a couple of times to the side of the brandy goblet, which summoned Billy to replenish the glasses. "I really shouldn't, old bean."

"Ah, shush, how often does one have the opportunity to make a new friend in this smokey old city? Seems to me if one hasn't been around for years, they are rarely accepted. Have you found that?"

"I guess a little, maybe; most people are polite, I find, but then some of the more senior gentlemen can perhaps be a tad gruff."

Teddy was pleased with how he had twisted the conversation his way into finding a common ground between them. They finished their last drink and gave young Billy a large tip once he had helped them into their coats and hailed a cab, which they shared, delivering firstly James to his door before Teddy rode home.

"Rest well, James," Teddy called to him as he reached his front door. "I shall call upon you soon. We will have fun, maybe take in a show. Driver. Onwards." James found the right key to the door and let himself in. The effects of the unknown number of pours of brandy had taken him once he had been in the cool night air. As he stood in the hallway, he felt the room sway and just managed to get to the front room chaise, where he threw himself and passed out until the following day.

He had never been much of a drinker and, with his dedication to serving the crown, had not had so much opportunity to create a large circle of friends either. When in the city, he missed the brief and rare occasions when the staff would sit together below stairs and share food and stories of them upstairs. He was now at a point of missing such contact, tiny morsels being the good old days, as his time was now divided between London and Windsor and although there is no huge distance between the two, the image he was meant to portray meant he couldn't commute as much as he wished. He loved the new house; it was really beautiful and ordinarily far out of reach for a man of his merger means, but there were days when he wondered what it would be like if he hadn't accepted this challenging task. As the day progressed and the hangover began to fade, James ate a late lunch of beef pie that Mrs Silver had cooked the night before with a small glass of red wine, which he had tried not to have, but his housekeeper insisted that the hair of the dog that bit you would have great effects, he had to admit it did seem to work. As he drained the glass, he heard a knock at his front door. Mrs Silver told him to remain still and she would attend to it; she did wonder if he would ever appoint a butler to do these tasks as she could never quite grasp the concept of modern living of fewer people to run around for you. She returned to the dining room and announced to the caller, "Mr Edward Billingham to see you. Shall I show him to the drawing-room?"

James had to take a second to fathom out who on Earth this Billingham was, then through the cloud the hangover had firmly swamped his brain with, he remembered the name. "Teddy! Yes, please, please bring us tea; I shall be there momentarily."

Mrs Silver bowed her head slightly to confirm the instruction and excuse herself to do as requested. James stood and checked that he looked at least half-civilised in the mirror above the mantelpiece before greeting his new pal.

"Teddy, hello. I didn't expect to see you quite so soon. I have to be honest with you, old chap; I am still suffering from the effects of the brandy we consumed."

"James you really need to exercise that drinking arm of yours, do not fear my good fellow, I will assist. Anyway, I had an idea and was about to pen a note when I thought 'dash it' I shall visit in person. Smashing place you have here; I do like these new white-walled buildings; gives the area a much-needed touch of style; you must show me around."

James politely agreed to his visitors request and offered the man a tour of the still undecorated house including the front bedroom he had been using as an office. Teddy seemed to like this room most of all and took great interest in it including the wheel looking side table next to the reading chair. "How delightfully unusual," he commented as he sat in the chair and casually stroked the piece of furniture.

"Thank you; it was a gift to welcome me to the house." Teddy looked at him with an expression that insisted on more information. James suddenly realised that in all this time Teddy was his first visitor who wasn't related to the building project, he was unpractised in small talk and hadn't rehearsed any details about the personal version of him, the relaxed James at home. Without any deep thought.

He continued, "It was given to me as a source of inspiration. Something to look at and marvel over until a new idea takes form." He was on a roll now and carried on, "It was one of four, built by a coachbuilder; he made four to represent the four wheels on a carriage as a gift for…" James stopped himself; this was exactly the conversation he was not supposed to have.

The few seconds of silence prompted Teddy to enquire, "One of four, as a gift that is quite an impressive amount of work, who would be worthy of such craftsmanship? Certainly nobility. Who was kind enough to split the set and give one to you?"

"Oh, I am not the only person to have received one; Robert Peel has one in Downing Street, thanks for the Peelers and all that." James wanted to slap his own face for spewing out the words; he couldn't believe how giving of detail he had been. Teddy was wise in ways of alleviating information; it was indeed what he had been trained to do throughout his entire life. He read the face of the man before him and saw it was time to halt this line of questions to allay any suspicion. He stood up and walked over to the bookcase, finding the most random of objects to pick up and change the subject. "And this, such lovely carving," he said as he studied the bookend in his hands shaped like a knight from a chessboard. "Simple but elegant taste my friend, I am mightily impressed, rather puts my flat to shame I must say."

James was automatically relieved that the chat about the table was over and calmed himself, thinking that this man was just overly inquisitive. Teddy, however, had decided to play a longer game to extract all he could.

"Why the visit? You didn't say," James asked.

"Tickets! I have tickets for that new play at The Haymarket for tomorrow evening, I wondered if you would join me? I'm rather at a loose end otherwise I fear?"

"I would like that very much, thank you."

For the following two hours, the men chatted. James was enjoying the company and thought that he should indeed take the friendship that was clearly being offered. They shared more tea and cake brought in by Mrs Silver before Teddy announced he should be on his way and headed home. Mrs Silver also excused herself, and James was left alone once more with nothing but his thoughts for company.

Teddy was pleased with his work. His plan to befriend this non-practised socialite meant he thought it would be easy to cement a relationship and got off to a favourable first twenty-four hours. He spent the evening creating notes in a newly purchased leather-bound writing book. His writings were done so in his native language to hide the initial discovery of the content should a non-authorised reader should happen upon it; in addition, the sentences were constructed using a simple code taught to himself and his fellow students as they were growing up.

Before London, Teddy was assigned to Paris purely as an observer in the initial instance to become nothing more than an active member in the higher echelons of French society to report upon gossip and rumour originating within their government for a man who had grown in the confines of specialist military training camps; the Parisian nightlife was more than one of the wonders of the world to him. Night after night, he would visit venues offering the best in food, wine and entertainment, the kind he never knew existed, especially the attention he gained from the ladies of the night. One such evening, Teddy had wandered the city streets and came upon a grand-looking building with a pair of burly men stood at the entrance wearing smart suits; he approached the doorway and offered a simple nod to the pair, who gave acknowledgement of the greeting and one of them stood aside to allow access. Teddy had discovered the art of nonverbal gestures, which gave him an air of knowledge. Combined with his fine clothing and excellent military fit, strong-framed body, he felt he was accepted in nearly all circles. He entered the property to find a large, ornate reception room with lavish patterned wallpaper and rich velvet furniture occupied by several clearly wealthy men being entertained by women wearing what he could only consider as their underclothes. A beautiful woman with ample curves and a smile that made him feel wanted to approach him and led him to a large winged chair; he sat and, in his broken French, introduced himself as Edward. The woman sat in his lap, smiling more, draped an arm around his neck and leaned backwards, clicking her fingers as she did so to gain the attention of one of the other girls who was carrying a silver tray holding several full glasses of champagne. She took two of them, handed one to her guest and sipped from the other. For nearly an hour, the two laughed and drank; Teddy was becoming quite intoxicated, not only from the alcohol but also from the human contact of this fine woman who had stroked his body as they sat. The woman gave her name as Chantelle. She leaned and whispered into his ear a suggestion that he may wish to be entertained further in her private room, to which, without realising he was a guest in an upmarket brothel, he agreed and allowed his to be led to the second floor. Chantelle sat him on the edge of the bed and kissed him deeply, undoing and removing his clothes as she did so. Teddy felt an excited heat surge through his body; the woman began to lift her skirts and pushed him flat on his back and sat on his hard and throbbing cock. The prostitute's money was easily earned as Teddy burst his load inside her within less than a minute; he groaned as he did so; this was the greatest feeling his body had experienced. Not that he would admit it, but this was the first time he had had sex with a woman; quite simply, he'd never had the opportunity to be raised and groomed for his adult task, which was devoid of female company. The teenage urges were, of course, there during those times and if the powders his trainers gave him didn't subside them, then he and the other young men would occasionally experiment with each other. He had one favourite out of his fellow students, Vladimir, who was eventually willing to crouch on all fours and take Teddy in his backside, enjoying being filled by him; however enjoyable those times were, it always felt like something his body had to do rather than want to.

Chantelle removed herself from her seat and offered Teddy a cloth to wipe himself. She politely told him his account should be settled with Madame Ottessa at the end of the evening and he should stay in the lounge for as long as he wished and enjoy his evening. Following the implied indication that he should dress, he did so and removed himself from the room and went to the big reception room. Here was a small bar in the corner with high stools in front; he approached and, once more, in his limited French, asked the gentleman sat there if he may join.

The charming chap welcomed the company and instantly took a shine to this sturdy and handsome looking fellow requesting a seat, recognising an English accent speaking poor French, he smiled and used words the man should understand. "But, of course, my friend, please sit and share the evening, I respect your attempts to speak my mother voice but I detect my English is better than your French?"

"Indeed, that may be so; I do apologise," said Teddy, who was quietly pleased with the fact he'd been identified as an Englishman in the first instance. "My name is Edward. However, I find people tend to call me Teddy, must say at first, I was not all too keen on the nickname, but over the years it has become acceptable to me."

"Well Teddy, it has a certain charm about it, matches that smile of yours. So, tell me, apart from the obvious joys and delights on offer here what brings a gentleman to Paris?"

"Just a trip to see the sights; I thought it may provide content for conversation for when I move to London."

"To London?"

"Yes. Yes. I am from a small town near Bristol, but now my apprenticeship is complete and all further training is done. I have a new engineering job to go to when I return to England."

"Engineering Eh? Do you specialise in anything in particular? Oh, I didn't catch your last name, by the way."

Teddy was really feeling very relaxed from his sexual encounter and the bubbles from the ever-refilled glasses of champagne. He was not at all used to this quantity of alcohol and had never before drunk anything sparkling. It had lowered his guard and he unknowingly was giving away far too much of his fabricated history, breaking all of the rules of short and simple conversation so as to never be suspected.

"Didn't I? I thought I did, I am an engineer, no wait that wasn't the question, was it?" Teddy giggled a little before continuing, "Billingham! That's what you asked me. Yes, that is my name, I am sorry I do not seem to be making a lot of sense."

Laughing in agreement, the man leaned in and gave a reassuring grip and squeeze to Teddy's shoulder. "You're doing splendidly, have no fears. It is the bubbles; they make you drunk; let us swap to a cognac." He gestured to the waiter that service was needed and ordered the drinks; once poured, he offered one of the glasses to his new chum. "Enjoy my friend."

"Thank you. Did you tell me your name? I am really sorry if I have forgotten. You must think me rude."

"Not at all. Actually, I am not sure if I did; how funny. Anyway, I am Pascale Abreo; I am an architect. I work

188

hard a lot of the time in London, as it happens, which is probably why my English is as good as my work and my reputation. I have little time for a wife, so places such as these fulfil my needs adequately, all the fun, none of the pain and I am sure a lot less money than marriage would cost."

Despite the haze in his head, the penny finally dropped for Teddy and he realised he had been 'entertained' in a brothel, it dawned on him that the account he should settle at the end of the evening was not just for the drinks. He consoled himself and justified his experience in his head and decided to not linger on the thoughts but to accept and carry on regardless talking to his new acquaintance Pascale.

"Elevators."

"Pardon?"

"Elevators, I design and build elevators; you asked if I specialised in anything."

"Oh, right, yes, of course." Pascale was equally beginning to feel the effects of the night. "You know I think I might have a project for you, I have been commissioned to design an underground chamber of large proportion that will have a very discreet entrance and only one point of access, by elevator! How perfect we should bump into each other!"

The thought of having to provide genuine designs had quite a sobering effect on Teddy. He had the engineer back story ingrained into his mind for years until he almost believed it himself. It was presumed that an elevator engineer would be one of the most random career choices and should defer any real interest; just how many people could find interest in such a thing by way of small talk? Teddy thought it bizarre that the very first time he had used this cover story, he could be caught out by it. Dawning on him came to the thought that it really didn't matter as it was highly unlikely that he would ever meet this gentleman again; tomorrow was a new day, and his move to England was planned for the following week, that was until Pascale continued, "We must meet up in London! I know the city well. I can show you around, it will be great fun. Perhaps, in exchange, you could work on this underground project for me. The pay is handsome; it is as if money grows on trees for my client, who says he is the son of a wealthy American investor who is going to use the structure as a vault with a whole living floor above it. Odd though, James Percival says his name, but nobody at the clubs ever heard of him until a few weeks ago; he says he is American, but he doesn't sound even slightly that way, with an accent and comes across as a bit too reserved and too shy to have that much money, his manner doesn't connect comfortably with a wealthy background if you know what I mean, I swear sometimes he acts as my butler does, you know, waits to be spoken to, always there with the drinks, always a step behind, I don't know, you will see for yourself if you meet him, gosh am I rambling about work, sorry I do tend to."

Something sparked in Teddy's mind about the tale of this client. Being an expert in deception, he felt compelled to learn more about someone who sounded as if he wasn't very good at hiding a false identity.

"Please continue, the man sounds fascinating I should like to meet him, perhaps he is simply a little shy of being in new surroundings and this project of yours is quite intriguing too! I could never imagine wanting to live underground." He took his turn in ordering drinks. "Make them large pours, my man." Teddy knew this Pascale fellow clearly had a loose tongue. Information was about to flow.

"Well, I shouldn't really speak about clients, but seeing as you, and do more than presume here, will work for me, it cannot hurt. This Percival fellow wants the whole thing to be self-sustaining and very well hidden. In fact, it is not only underground but also underwater! He wants a reservoir on top of it, the water from it is to feed a paper factory. Well, I have done some investigation work to make sure I get paid; it is a huge project, after all, and it turns out that one of the cheques sent as a deposit traces back to an account that is regularly deposited with funds from no less than Queen Victoria herself! So, I think that it is all a cover story. I have come to conclude that the paper mill is for printing money and the vault is to store it, hence the secrecy and security. What do you think of my conclusion?"

Teddy was now rapidly sobering; this was precisely the kind of information he was hoping to discover. If this conclusion of Pascale was anywhere near true, his government would be able to wreak havoc. He quickly thought of solutions to the engineering problem; he decided he would hire an additional company to do the design and the construction, paying them well to have his name adorn the plans. Should anyone question who the workers were, he would tell everyone they were a trusted commissioned firm. In fact, he felt that this opportunity might open many doors and could connect him extremely well within many of the circles he could only ever have hoped to be part of.

"Monsieur, may I say I am grateful for our meeting each other this evening? I could listen to your stories for hours, and I am simply fascinated by your skill in unusual building; I would adore to be part of it. I cannot wait to see your work. May I request your details so we can continue our talk tomorrow, perhaps?"

"But, of course, it would be a delight; we can then sort meeting up in London and, of course, plan the trip to the borderline of Wales and England to assess the building progress so you can evaluate your requirements."

The men ended the evening armed with contact information, much lighter wallets after paying the Madame and a sense of accomplishment, one of them thinking he had solved an architectural problem, the other thinking he had an opportunity to serve his country. What a spanner in the works of the Great British economy if he could put a dent in money printing, harm to the Bank of England, perhaps?

Before the trip to London, Teddy spent as much time as possible with his new friend to learn as much as possible about the client under the facade of being employed to do a job. Pascale was not due to return to England for several weeks, far too long a wait to get the initial meeting underway, so armed with the knowledge of James Percival's favourite drinks and the club he frequented, he decided to break bread himself and befriend the man, in a similar way to how he had accidentally met Pascale.

23

Pip sat down on the sofa in Mack's new abode and looked around the place, now filled with furniture and the belongings of what he considered his lifelong soul mate. The flat had come together really well and didn't seem at all as dark as he had feared with the limited light from the glass brick wall at the back of the mezzanine where Mack was finishing putting away the last of his clothing before making up the bed, he had excused himself to Pip and denied his offer of help telling him to sit and relax, a thing that Pip had to force himself to do. He shouted up to his lover.

"Are we mad doing all this so soon?"

"No, I told you, I don't think so. Feels like we were never apart. Can you pour me a drink, please? I will be down in a minute."

Pip happily obliged the request, took the beverage, and placed it on the side table; as he turned around, readying to sit, a smile broadened across his face as he saw Mack stood in front of him wearing the tightest Italian Police uniform that he could have ever imagined.

"Told you I still had it," he said and flexed the muscles in his arms, back and chest, stretching the fabric to the point of tearing, showing the beauty of the curves and lines of his body. "So, you like?"

Pip responded by kissing him deeply and not stopping apart from once again to stand back and observe. Pip felt his breath become a little more rapid and heard his own heartbeat accelerate as his body pumped additional blood into his hardening cock. He studied his lover; the thick, defined thighs beneath the taut fabric, Mack's ass beautifully displayed, round, strong and firm, then back to simply staring at his lover rock hard dick, the trousers so tight that he could see the definition of the rippled shaft and head. Pip almost groaned with desire and had to bite on his lower lip as he relieved Mack of the outfit he had only just put on; starting at the top, he slowly undid each button before sliding the shirt over his shoulders and down his back, pausing at the point where it trapped Mack's arms behind him so he could not resist having his belt being undone and his trousers lowered over his rock-hard erection.

Pip pulled the trousers off Mack's feet one by one, his face and opened mouth in line with the rock-hard erect penis throbbing before him; he reached behind his lover's back and grabbed the fabric of the shirt still holding his lover's arms and twisted it in his fist making sure escape was not possible. With his other hand, he used his middle finger to trace the shape of the balls in the sac before him with the lightest of delicate touches and with his mouth moved close so he could gently blow on the head of the now throbbing tool. Mack was breathing hard and moaning, desperate for this act of love to begin fully; he tried so hard to be still but could not control squeezing his ass cheeks together, making his cock bounce in a bid to make his man begin. Pip took his hand to the sack once more but this time took it and its contents in his fist and, with a gentle tug, pulled on them as his tongue lapped the beads of sweet precum from the head before taking it and the veined shaft slowly and fully into his mouth and throat. Mack felt his legs physically shake in response to the sensation. His mind could see only explosions of colour as the connection thrust sensation through every cell in his body; all at once, he needed to feel more; his nipples needed touch, squeeze, kisses, his flesh demanded stroking, gripping, holding, the muscles in his legs were insisting in helping his ass thrust forwards and shoot the load of hot cum. Sweat beaded on his back and his chest as somehow he controlled himself. His man withdrew from his act of torturous pleasure and released the grip on the shirt, allowing Mack to shake his arms free. Taking Pip's face in his hands, he joined him on his knees and leant in to kiss him. Both men were now more excited than either could have considered imaginable, the surge of ecstatic endorphins to their brains as the kissing became deeper, tongues lashing each other's, mouths desperate to feel closer than possible, a need of passion so strong that each was almost trying to kiss the very air their love combined in a way to absorb their lover.

The men continued to express their mutual desire by sharing passionate lovemaking. Mack took Pip into his throat and sucked and licked his shaft before lowering his mouth so his tongue could tease the crease in the flesh atop the thigh as he lowered him back by raising this beautiful man's legs high to give access to his sweet hole. Mack lapped at it and probed it with his tongue over and over until the only words he heard above the sighs and groans of pleasure were. "Please."

Mack took the cue and positioned himself, placing his head at the entrance point of his desire. Resting Pip's legs on his shoulders, Mack gently pushed his wet cock against the muscle he could feel pulsing, begging to be entered. He pushed harder. The feeling of heat in his cock as it edged inside the tight hole, he'd moistened with his tongue was unbelievable. A little further, and he felt the head pop inside; Pip lay desperately wanting all of it, wanted to pin down his lover and ride him, but somehow managed to refrain by holding grip around the head that had just teased him with delight. Mack pushed deeper, not stopping or withdrawing, simply moving deeper until every last possible part of him was inside. He held there for a few long seconds before moving back, pulling out all but the head. Pip felt the long shaft fill him over and over, the pace becoming faster; he grabbed at his own cock and began to stroke it with a tight grip in time with the rhythm of being fucked. Breathing in unison, they stared into each other's eyes and simultaneously shot their loads. Pip pulsed ropes of thick white strings that landed on himself and his lover as he felt the pulse of the encased member inside him leave its contents, its owner's contorted face uttering guttural sounds as it did so.

In only a few moments after holding each other and kissing again, the boys began once more, spending nearly two solid hours fucking each other right there on the new bed, the new rug, on the stairs, in the kitchen and finally, the sofa which following repeated powerful climax they collapsed, naked, hot and short of breath into each other's arms.

Through gasps of intake of air, Pip said, "My God, I love you."

Mack smiled; those are the words he would never tire of hearing. "You know something, I've fantasised about fucking with you on this sofa so many times over the years; I can't believe we have just done that. I don't know why you had it re-covered, but I'm very glad you did, but more wipe clean than before…"

"It's a soft thing, really and to be fair, a bit of a cheesy line, but I kept it because of how much you admired the Deco style of it all those years ago on your trips to Ireland with me, that and I find a little comfort and warmth remembering squeezing in at the side of Mum in one of the armchairs, we would read together or occasionally watch the TV. Crazy, really, but I also had the notion I may give it to you as a gift, you know, to perhaps rekindle old times."

"I don't think you are daft at all; you are sweet, the sweetest man I have ever known."

"Good, I am glad." Mack smiled; he felt that finally the universe could allow him to be complete and happy; he'd had an interesting career so far, which was to inherit wealth, land and a business and now he had his soul mate back to share it with. There was just one nagging little problem yet to sort. "Babe, not sure if I mentioned it, but I have to go to Italy this weekend."

"Oh, am I losing you again? Already?"

"Not at all! Besides, all my stuff is here now. No, it's just that I want to see my mother and tell her all about you and how we are back together. I've also had a meeting with the lawyers over there regarding the vineyard; it seems I may be owning it sooner than expected to evade an inheritance tax, buy it for a Euro or something. Sep has it all worked out. Anyway, I will be back by Tuesday."

"Oh. OK. I'll miss you though."

"Well, it is said that absence makes the heart grow fonder."

"That is true but, my dear, it has been years in between our encounters; how fond does that make us?"

"I'm going with eternal love bordering on the lines of total obsession," Mack replied.

He knew he hadn't mentioned the Italian trip to him as he wanted to leave his mark by moving in to ease any fears his beau may have had about being abandoned once more. He felt content that his plan was running as he and Jackie had devised; using the return trip would put him out of the country and away from any suspicious eyes, on return, he would begin work at the building site, having only essential minimal contact with any crew who would assume he was the original site manager. In Italy, he genuinely had arranged the transfer meeting with his mother, uncle and the lawyers firmly placing him there should the need ever arise. An in-depth conversation with Uncle Sep away from the ears of his mother had also taken place regarding exactly how he was to be coming back to England.

The weekend came and Mack made his trip; he did indeed inform his family of his newfound happiness with the love of his life. Sophia was overjoyed that her little boy was finally settling with someone and Sep was equally happy. They discussed the future and how Mack would maintain and operate the vineyard, although he would be the legal owner of it in just a few days. Sep was going to continue to run it until he felt it was time to retire. Mack assured them that he would keep a regular eye on the place by visiting and be in constant communication with the managers and growers via the Internet when the time came for him to have total responsibility.

Following a celebratory feast and a shared FaceTime between his Italian family and his English lover, Mack sat alone with Uncle Sep, his aunt and his mom, retiring to their beds.

"So, my boy," Sep began. "Finally happy, we are all relieved to see the day come. Now, about our 'other' conversation, what do you intend to do with this Marcus fellow? He sounds like a nasty piece of work from what you say."

"I have to discredit him somehow, or Pip will never be free, which means, ultimately, I can never have him. I'm worried for him, Uncle; his friend told me he was near full mental collapse just a few years ago. I couldn't bear to see him suffer. I wonder now that we are together and the power of the love between us if part of the strain was my fault. I have to sort this out for us. That is why I thought by going back either on my other passport or smuggling myself back in somehow; the world would think I was here and if the little creep ever discovered the history Pip and I share, he would be unable to connect the dots and use it against us, I just do not want to give any unnecessary ammunition."

"Oh, I fully agree. Love conquers all. I only wish your mother had left that father of yours and found happiness herself instead of sticking to her vows. I still cannot believe she never sought a divorce and stayed married until he made her a widow even after all those years apart."

Sep shuffled his chair closer to Mack and continued speaking at a level just above a whisper, "Now about the travelling, I have called a favour from an associate of mine in Sicily. You will ferry across there; I have a train ticket booked in another friend's name for you to cross the island to a marina where you will board my friend's yacht, The Riviera; now, for added security, the name of the boat is false, you do not need to know its real identity nor that of the man who will captain the craft. He has been instructed to take you to a remote bay; he has a choice all depends on which is the most deserted-looking. Then, you will be dropped off to find your own way home. Just be careful and use this if you need to."

Sep reached into the pocket of his jacket, withdrew a British passport and handed it to Mack. "It is not traceable back to anyone here, so do not worry, but only use it if necessary."

Mack opened the passport to see his own face staring back at him, but named Benjamin Hughes. For a second,

200

he was dumbfounded; he looked at his uncle. "But how? Who?"

"My boy, one does not grow and live in business around here without gaining contacts. It is not a thing one uses often and of course, with yourself serving in the Police, I had to keep things even more secret; imagine your mother's face if it was you that found out about... well anyway... but now this is needed. You will find the passport to be a copy of the finest detail and that is all you need to know. You are a fine man and I am proud to have you as my successor; I love you as the son I did not have, family first, my boy, no matter what. Now, with that little task done, I shall join my wife. Good night, Macauley. Remember, I love you as if you were my own."

24

The journey went without a hitch. Mack was still stunned at the reach his uncle had; he would never in a million years thought that he could provide such things as forged passports and covert travel and at the same time quite in awe of him for exactly the same things. Mack had packed the bright red camping rucksack that he'd been instructed to use with a sleeping bag, a couple of changes of clothing and the contents of the shoebox that was hidden in the floor via a loosened board underneath his bed, a mixture of several thousand Euro and a smaller amount of Sterling, a ring left to him by his grandfather that he thought he would give to Pip and his revolver and three full boxes of ammunition. He was not sure what he would ever do with the weapon but felt that seeing he had undetectable transport, he may as well take it with him. He tested the passport in Sicily upon his arrival and just before his departure at two different currency exchanges, managing to swap all but five hundred euros into Great British Pounds. It was late afternoon when he took his position next to the kayak rental hut as per his instructions; only a few minutes passed before he was approached by a sea-tanned old man who had recognised the rucksack.

"Do you think the grape harvest will be good this year?" the man asked.

"Yes, I believe it will be a particularly good yield," answered Mack, who had been told the question and answer were to be said to prove he was the correct passenger. The old man indicated which boat to go to.

"Then, Mister Benjamin, please climb aboard; there is food below deck, you will also find bedding; my only request is you please wear the disposable gloves for your time here." He handed Mack a box of medical latex gloves, who took them, donned a pair and boarded the large and well-appointed ocean-going yacht.

It was more than comfortable aboard the boat that must have been owned by someone extremely wealthy, this had to be a million-euro craft at least. Mack explored the many rooms over no less than four decks; this place had everything one would expect in a five-star hotel and then even more. He decided that he should perhaps just keep to the one room for the trip to avoid trying to find clues to identify the boat owner.

Curiosity killed the cat, he thought to himself as he entered his quarters with a plan to rest as much as he could over the next three days, the time he spent reflecting his life, his circumstances and the sheer joy of the future he was set to have with the only person he had ever really had any connection with. It was deeper than any kind of love that they shared, almost indescribable, the feeling of being complete whenever they were near each other, knowing each other's needs, wants, desires, thoughts and opinions without words needing to be said. The time apart from each other had not affected anything at all except his desire to protect his partner at all costs. The Marcus situation made Mack angry; he really didn't think there was a line he wouldn't cross to sort it out, releasing Pip from entrapment, freeing him so they could finally live the destiny they had always been set to have, to at last, be confident in his choices and able to be content and happy.

Day four of the journey came soon.

The knock at his cabin door was firm and heavy; Mack opened it with his obediently gloved hand to see the old man holding a wet suit, life jacket and two clear bags, the type that have a plastic valve enabling the air to be taken out by a vacuum cleaner to make them compact.

"You'll be needing these. Be on the lower rear deck in twenty minutes, put your belongings into these bags and roll them tube-like before getting the air out; there is a vacuum cleaner in the corridor cupboard you can use. Don't forget to put your rucksack in there. I guess you'll be needing that at the other end."

Mack took the items. "I guess we are there then? Why do I need a wet suit?"

"End of the line, as they say. Yes, we are near England, I reckon, just in her waters. That's as far as I go; the rest is up to you and those gym arms of yours; there's a canoe for the rest of the way; split your belongings evenly, then stow a bag in each end. You've got about three miles to get into Torquay; there is a little bay you can get to if you aim in a straight line. The sun is just coming up, so by the time you're close to the beach, you should have come across quite a few other people on the water; it is a really popular place in the mornings. Just go with the flow, don't panic, don't rush, just head towards the beach, haul the canoe as if you were collecting it later, take your things to the toilet block, get changed, pack your bag and hike up the hill. Do not take the funicular. We don't want anyone wondering why you haven't got a return ticket. Then head into the centre. I would get the first train if I were you, but my job is done; your choices from then on in."

It was the most the man had spoken since this leg of the journey began. Mack donned the wetsuit and followed the instructions he was given in the letter. He wrapped the weapon he'd bought with him in a heavy jumper and the ammunition into the pockets of the rucksack before putting everything into the clear sacks and removing the air. The shapes were unusual that the vacuums had created; one looked like a distant mountain range, and the other was more difficult to identify, but as he turned it, he decided it resembled a section of a very large rope with its curves ever-revolving. Of course, these thoughts were nothing more of a distraction from the small amount of fear mixed with excitement he was feeling about going home to his new life and the change of being caught by the coastguard with an unregistered firearm, a fake passport and several thousand pounds in cash all stuffed in watertight packages stowed away in a canoe which he had absolutely no idea how to control. He feared this plan had more holes to it than a mole-infested lawn and as the seconds ticked away, he wondered if it would be a good idea or not to mention to the old sailor that despite the buff looks and tough guy employment when it came to water that wasn't contained in a building with changing rooms and showers and that could be seen through to the touchable bottom, could reduce him to a quivering wreck, he hated the sea.

Standing on the slightly rocking deck next to his neatly prepared next section of his journey, Mack felt a rising urge to vomit. Nerves were getting to him. He checked once more the straps of the life jacket as he followed the indicative arm gesture of his captain into the vessel. Paddle handed to him, he braced himself for the tiny shove that launched him off the lower deck boards that were designed for easy access to small shore-going boats. The whole three centimetres from deck to sea may as well have been a thousand miles as time stood still and eternity passed until the joining of H2O and fibreglass. Mack inhaled the deepest of breath and opened his eyes; he thought that he might not breathe again until this was all over. He used every part of his experience and training to focus on the image of a white chocolate mouse and considered its every detail in a bid to allay fear as he dipped the oar into the water for its first stroke. The second stroke on his left side was too heavy to perform and Mack realised he was reaching too far forwards and back with his body; he sat a little more firmly and thought about the required arm movements and began once more. The sea was thankfully calm, with the waves only gently bobbing him up and down. Although a hated task, with the right mindset in play, his fears subsided a little and rapid progress in reaching shore was obtained. In his mind, he decided upon a new gift for his love; he would have a golden version of the mouse made perhaps with diamonds as eyes or perhaps a glass one or maybe carved wood or all of the above for anniversaries. Yes, that is what he would do. Glass first, it wasn't as if he couldn't afford the jewelled version; moreover, his sudden realisation that anything bejewelled right now may seem a little insensitive. Forward gift plan complete. Mack noticed several other people on the water and had neared a small group of three. One of them shouted to him, "Hey, you OK? Looks like you were way too far out."

"All good, no worries," replied Mack. "Got a little carried away thinking about stuff. Good exercise, though."

"I bet where you come from, we didn't see your head out from here. Are you lost?"

Mack had to think quickly. He knew that this bay was called Oddicombe, but that was his entire knowledge of the area; he prayed that his bluff would pass muster and replied, "Next bay down, West. I'll have to get a cab to fetch the car, had enough today; I need to get out and stretch."

"Know what you mean?" the man responded. "Hey, if you leave the canoe at the back of the cafe, it will be safe till you get back."

"Thanks for the heads up. Nice meeting you." Mack raised his fingers slightly off the oar and moved them a little in a partial waving motion before retightening his grip and resuming a fast and strong row, not stopping until he hit the beach. *The early morning was surprisingly busy,* he thought, *for a British beach.* There were several early risers out with dogs and around twenty people taking a morning swim. Mack hauled the craft far up the beach next to a sandy cliff face that looked as if it had collapsed some years before. He checked his surroundings before removing the sealed bags and quickly opened the one containing the red rucksack. He pulled it clear and shook it, watching it unfurl as air reoccupied the fabric; quickly, he stuffed the remaining sack contents and the sealed one inside and zipped it tight before casually putting his arm through one of the straps and pulling it to his shoulder. Mack stowed the canoe upside down next to another one that looked abandoned and strolled down the beach calmly and deliberately slowly to try and look as if he did this on a daily basis. He entered the toilet block and was relieved that the recent construction had shower facilities. Using the prepaid card his uncle had given to him, to tap against the pay machine, he paid the small fee that opened the cubicle door containing a bench, a coat hook and nothing more than a shower head and push button hot water tap. Mack unzipped his wet suit, eased the top half around his waist and then folded it down to his knees before sitting on the bench and removing it completely. Sat naked, he afforded himself a moment or two of reflection as it dawned upon him the value of being with someone that, no matter what happened, he would always be a part of, that despite a lifetime of independence, he only now felt complete, felt strong. He knew that financially; he was set for life; there was a tidy sum from working abroad combined with his father's house sale and now he would have regular income from the profit of the vineyard. Mack had never regarded himself as poor by any means but now he realised he was actually quite wealthy but none of it meant a thing without Pip, being with him again had set a fire inside him giving an eternal warmth, he smiled to himself and sang in the shower, washing away the journey, then dressing for the last leg to see his man.

Mack walked up the winding road that snaked its way to the top of the incredibly steep hill; he wondered if the instruction to not take the funicular was actually somebody's idea of fun. The hill was no easy feat, even for a strong, healthy and fit man such as him. Reaching the top, he saw a taxi rank with available cars; by waving an arm, Mack caught the attention of the driver of the first one, who started the engine as Mack climbed into the back seat. "Can you take me to the nearest big supermarket, please?"

"Of course, Tesco, do you?"

"Any, I'm starving. Had an early start."

With that, they drove just a couple of miles to the store; Mack paid the driver and gave him a tip, an amount he considered not too mean and not too extravagant, with the intention that he would not be remembered. He pulled his cap down a little further before entering the store and collecting a shopping basket. Mack filled the basket with a magazine, a couple of pre-packed sandwiches, and some fruit before walking over to the phone section and speaking to the young sales assistant.

"Hi, can I have three pay-as-you-go phones, please?"

"Sorry, sir, did you say three?"

It hadn't occurred to Mack that this would be an obstacle; simply, he wanted to call Pip and whilst he was at it, he thought he would get one for him and another for Jackie so they could communicate without using their regular phones should they be conversing about getting Marcus gone from his picture of happiness. He needed to think quickly.

"Yes. Three. My nieces, twins, it their eighth birthday and I sort of promised, which will, of course, make me my favourite uncle but least favourite brother; their mum said they couldn't have phones until they were ten, so guess who will be in the dog house?"

The assistant smiled and giggled a little. Mack continued, he was on a roll with developing his all-new imaginary sibling and her children. "The other one is for little Jimbo; God, my sister hates me calling him that; he will be seven next month and I don't think I will get down to see him so he can have his present early."

"I wish I had an uncle like you! Good plan, though; if they all get one, there won't be any jealous fighting or sulking. I used to hate it when my sister had something and I didn't."

Mack smiled and selected the phones from the ones available; three smartphones, a mid-range that he thought would be suitable for his faux family; he reached into his rucksack for his wallet from the inside pocket and removed 'Benjamin's' pre-paid credit card and moved to hand it to the young woman, then suddenly pulled it away. "No, wait, sorry, I'll pay cash. Just thought, I got cash out to put in the girl's cards before remembering my little underhand promise to them; I'll use that."

Mack dove into the red bag once more, feeling for the shoe that he had placed the wad of exchanged money in a sock to keep it together after the rubber band he was originally using had snapped. He felt the webbed band of the bright striped 'Happy Sock' and began to remove it; as it began to exit its temporary home of the shoe, Mack adjusted his grip, then abruptly ceased his movement. His face was still. He had to use every technique of self-control and concealment to hide his personal terror that the sock package was not the one containing money but the one from his other shoe containing his gun. Being so used to having a weapon hanging from his belt as a policeman and beforehand a holstered one beneath his jacket, Mack thought nothing of owning one, but he was now in the UK and self-protection was very different; carrying arms was a big no-no. The scenario of the assistant catching a glimpse of the pistol and the chaos that would follow with inadequately trained security guards, a panic alarm, screaming customers and the inevitable surrounding of the store by rapid response Police followed soon by the armed squad and probably a helicopter to boot flashed through his mind, he prayed that the cold sweat he could feel drench his body was internal and not visible.

"Wrong pocket, can't pay with shower gel! Or can I?"

The girl laughed. "Terribly sorry, sir, we only take cash, card or vouchers, although I can ask if the soap could be returned and used as credit towards the sale. That is, of course, if it has not been used and you have the proof of purchase."

Mack smiled at her cheeky reply and held her eye contact as he rectified his mission of retrieving cash; he pulled several random notes from the pile, roughly £400 and paid for the phones and his food, the change from the sale he stuffed into his pocket as he kindly thanked the woman for her service and for making him smile, reusable carrier bag in hand, he exited the store, walked for a while and then asked a passer-by for direction to the train station.

The walk cleared his head. This game of deceit seemed extravagant for what should be a simple task of getting his lover out of a bad relationship, but Jackie and Pip had convinced him that Marcus would destroy Pip just for fun and was the type of nasty character that would not stop until his narcissistic greed had been fulfilled. Moreover, Jackie had privately told Mack during one of the evenings at her house the depth of depression Pip had suffered previously and that she could see hints of signs that he was still struggling. There was no way Mack could let his love be harmed either physically or mentally. With a deep breath and a rucksack-correcting heave, he marched on, having decided that a complete cloak and dagger was the only way forward; he would do whatever it took.

Arriving at the train station, Mack used the ATM to check the remainder of the pre-paid card funds, then purchased a ticket to finally get him back in the arms of his love; it was three hours before the train was due at the station so he settled himself in the corner of a coffee shop, ordered a large black coffee and began to unpack and charge the mobile phones from the power points below the seats, once the battery levels were adequate Mack then split the card balance as phone credit across them, not long after he called Pip's gym and spoke with Jackie, telling her he would be home soon and to please ensure that Pip had no appointments pending, she agreed and told of her relief that he was on his way and an outline of a conversation shed had with Pip a few days before.

25

"Jacks, why hasn't he been in touch? I knew it was too good to be true; he's gone, hasn't he? Again! Why do I let myself get hurt all of the time? Can't do it, Jacks. It's all too much. Those fucking houses, that Twat I'm married to. It's wrong. I've had it. Too tired for a mess like this. So tired. Feel like everything is slipping away. Even tried last night to be brave and get Marcus gone and ready for Mack to return; that went wrong, of course. What is the point?"

Jackie had been very conscious of her best friend's mental health in recent months; she knew he struggled with depression, but to hear him speak so negatively rang very loud alarm bells.

"Pip, *shush*." He looked at her, not sure if he was going to cry or run away. Right now, though, Jackie was all he had that he was able to talk to and respond to. He resisted his urges to walk out of the gym office and sat on the small sofa facing the desk.

"Now look, my darling, I know just how hard it is sometimes; I know that things can get on top of us, but listen to me. I know that everything will work out. I can feel it. Between us, we will sort out Marcus. I promise you we will find a solution and I promise that Mack is coming home to you; otherwise, he wouldn't have sent these…" Her words said in her calmest of voice settled him a little;

he sat back, placed his hands on his thighs and closed his eyes whilst taking deep breaths in and out to the count of ten. As he was performing his calming exercise, Jackie reached into her handbag and retrieved an envelope that she placed in his lap on his last intake of air. Pip opened his eyes and looked down at the brown paper.

"Open it," she instructed. Pip unfolded the seal on the envelope and shook out the contents into his hand; two passports, one UK and one Italian and a white piece of cardboard about the size of a credit card; on it were the words *I love you* and an outline of a chocolate mousse.

"See, he is coming back to you and before you ask, no, I don't know. I don't think I want to know how he will get here without those. However, he must have gone to great lengths to get those to you; I found them in a case of wine that was delivered from Sicily to my house. I thought I'd won something at first, but then I found a simple note that said, *'The envelope must squeak.'* I knew right away what it meant."

"Wow, I wonder what is going on? Oh, Jackie, I'm sorry, but some days are such a struggle. The last row with Marcus really rocked me; if only there was a reason for him punishing me like this."

Jackie sat beside him and stroked his arm. "Pip, look, it's OK to not be OK, it's OK to wobble, get stressed, cry, scream, shout, whatever; I will always be here and so will Mack. Like I said just, we will not let that little creep get what he wants or hurt you in any way. This building, this land, business and the new development are yours, not his and that is how it will stay. I've watched you build all of

214

this and see how the stress has gotten to you. Please believe me, I don't care what I have to do; I will protect you. OK?"

Pip gave a deep sigh and nodded.

"Good now. What was this last clash about?"

"Oh, that. I tried to confront him, tried to say he hadn't the nerve to go through with blackmailing me and that he should hand back the trinket box and leave me alone; I offered to give him a third of the development if he would stop the nonsense. No joy, though. He actually laughed and called me the world's biggest loser, said there was no way he was backing down until his demands were met, then announced he needed £10,000 for a skiing trip after Christmas, meeting up for a couple of weeks in Monte Carlo with some Uni Chums before off to Val d'Isere to one of their Chalets, wants the money to be flash in the casino and in dire need of new gear for the slopes! I tried to tell him no way, that I hadn't got it, that any ready cash was tied up in the development, but of course, he knows there's contingency money, so he yelled that at me, called me fucking stupid and laughed as he went to his room and slammed the door behind him. Seconds later, he airdropped a bunch of pictures of the jewellery, the box and what looked like a typed statement of some sort and a DVD; God knows what is on there."

"Show me the pictures," Jackie said as she passed him his iPad from the desk. Pip pressed the home button, selected the photos icon and showed her what had been sent. Jackie flipped through them several times zooming in and out, studying every inch. "This one of the boxes closed... looks like it was taken inside an open safe, see, just there the door frame on the left, that is definitely steel and the way it is built, it has to be safe."

"So?"

"So, knowing the way that little shit works, I reckon he has that box stashed in the safe you had put in the storage unit. Just go and get it; I bet it's there."

"Jacks, I would if I knew what on Earth you were on about. I don't have a safe other than the floor one in this office and trust me, there's no lost gems in there."

"Yes, you do; I signed it off myself; it was your name on the order and your credit card number on the invoice; the guys came while you were on a honeymoon; they had quite detailed instructions of where to locate it inside the storage cage allocated to the apartment."

"Jackie. I didn't order anything; I don't know anything about this." He stood up and headed towards the door of the office, left the gym and headed to the far side of the giant staircase and entered the corridor that led behind it to the storage areas, he smiled as he glanced across to Mack's section and noticed a small pile of unattended laundry, resisting the urge to grab it and smell it, he turned towards his own cage that Marcus kept in impeccable condition to contain his belongings.

"Third shelf, third section," Jackie said as she walked to the position where the strong box had been installed. Pip joined her as she moved one of the neat, black plastic-lidded boxes to expose it.

"Oh my..." Pip whispered as he drew his hand across the door of the foot square box that was clearly heavily bolted to the wall of his sturdy old building. The strong steel door, despite being relatively small, had an electronic keypad and two keyholes. "It is in here, isn't it? Has to be; Marcus never leaves his goodies far from sight; he is too paranoid. This has to be it! Jackie, if I can get inside this thing, I can make it go away!" A rush of relief and joy swept through him, making him feel several stone lighter. The headache that had been hanging around lifted, the room seemed somehow brighter. For the first time in a long time, Pip had a glimmer of hope again, just the one small problem; how to get inside it?

26

Albert paced back and forth in the glasshouse; he was unsettled and restlessness encapsulated him.

"Are you all right? You look troubled," questioned his loyal servant confidante and friend. Albert spoke quietly, "Oh, I'm sorry, old chum, it is just that the Palace has once more informed me of yet more threats to end the life of my beloved Victoria. I must protect her. I have offered to take her abroad, but she refuses to leave her throne unattended. How goes my little project? It is imperative that it is ready soon; I want to move the family into it for a short time at least."

"Ahead of schedule! That new chap I met has sorted the problems we had with the lifts, stronger cables have been installed and larger counterweights, added extra light and ventilation shafts too."

"Really, how? Where?"

"Along the bridge supports. We have added mirror-lined channels brick tubes, if you will imagine. Highly decorative. Discrete and useful."

"Splendid, well done, so how soon?"

"Just two weeks, all I have to do is employ a housekeeper for you; however, to initially stock up, I shall have my own compile the orders; I can trust her."

"Excellent news! Organise a train, a good standard but not royal; no attention must be gathered."

"Of course."

"Two weeks this coming Friday, I may have to be a little devious to get her there, but once in situ, I have every confidence Her Majesty will agree on the necessity of safety."

Harbridge left the glasshouse and strode towards the castle boundary; he felt a little rushed and stressed; Albert had unnerved him; there was genuine fear in his voice and an agitated look upon his deeply furrowed brow; whatever these latest threats were, they must have been of magnitude to stir the effervescent prince. James thought it best not to converse with his fellow staff; he knew the damage that castle gossip could cause; the slightest slip of the tongue had the potential to escalate and subsequently destroy the efforts of maintaining the secrecy of the plan. He walked into the town and down the high street to a tea room and took a table near the back, as far as possible from the windows. Before his train journey back to the city, he felt he needed to calm himself and collect his thoughts.

A few minutes later, as the waitress placed a small collection of fancies in front of him to accompany his tea, he heard a voice that instantly made him smile.

"Percival! What luck! Brilliant, oh how this wonderful world of coincidence can give us gifts like this."

The voice was of his newest and rapidly becoming closest friend, Teddy; he looked up with genuine surprise and also a little happiness; a friendly face was what he needed right now.

"Teddy! What in heaven's name are you doing here?"

"Dear heart, I thought I may explore; you do mention how much you favour Windsor, so much so that one considered it essential to see these streets with one's own eyes. That is on top of the fact that I have signed off the project alterations as complete, travelled back to London, visited your house to find you missing and your wonderful Mrs Silver as the only occupant. After feeding me sandwiches and a freshly baked cake, she said you had come here for a meeting or something, So I thought, *Why not?* And here I am!"

With a thankful sigh, James looked into the face of his friend. "Well, this is the best surprise. I cannot express how much I am in need of good company. You know what? Dash the day! Let us wander around; I can show you the sights and introduce you to some people."

Teddy did not want this. Not at all. He knew he should remain in character, but he also knew the risk of shattering the illusion of his identity if too many unnecessary people could recognise his face and connect him to James. He wanted to get them both back to London. James had unknowingly given titbits of information as their friendship had bloomed over the last few months. Teddy had taken full advantage of the minor elevator problem at the project site, which he made sure became a potential disaster upon his very first visit, firmly placing his supposed engineering skills in need. Being raised to do nothing but perform required tasks and to be conditioned to survive alone, Teddy had genuinely enjoyed befriending James; he knew he loved him in some way, the brother he'd never had. The best friend he'd never had? Or maybe the lover and partner he recently discovered he needed in his life, the sudden exposure to society, clubs, restaurants and theatres had stirred man's natural need for closeness being an essential element of existence. He knew he might never be allowed to feel like this again and took advantage of every second he could. The fact that his mission required the need to follow James and gather information was a bonus, yet he made his personal rules of limited contact and the company orders to leave no evidence and termination of those who could identify you as a conflict of interest. This morning, he had indeed travelled to London from the Welsh border and had taken a handsome cab to James's Chelsea home, eaten the dreadfully sweet cake he'd been offered as part of his coercion of the loyal housekeeper to give Percival's whereabouts. A short journey into Windsor gave him exactly the suspected knowledge he had been trying to confirm all along. James Percival was connected to Windsor Castle and from the friendly and light-hearted conversation he witnessed between him and the security men at the castle gates when he entered the Bailey wall, it was clear the connection was strong. This man was now of major importance. This man had access to the ultimate target. This man could help him gain access to the queen.

"Old boy, as much as I would love to wander these streets in your company, I rather think it is a little late in the day and having been here for a few hours now, I think I may have already absorbed the offerings of this quaint little town. Let us travel back to London and dine. We can perhaps return here together at another time?"

Eager to please his friend and so keen to not be alone, James felt he would agree to anything. "But of course, forgive me, I had not considered your travels today; let's go now." He rose from the table, leaving his payment and a generous tip for his waitress who had brought him his hat and coat, he thanked her. Seeing the large tip made the young woman smile.

"Oh, thank you, Mr Harbridge; I shall add this to my learning fund. I will make sure Mama cooks you something special next time you're back at the big house."

James cringed and closed his eyes for a second, being so preoccupied with the instructions to welcome the Royal Family to the emergency abode he had completely not recognised Penelope, a girl he had known since her birth, the daughter of Milly, a senior cook, and, Will, the stable master. Flustered by the reveal of his real name and a rapid succession of thoughts, James could do nothing more than nod his head and smile as he turned towards the door, Teddy at his side.

The men were back in the city and in a cab en route to James's house before Teddy mentioned the girl in the tea rooms.

"James, may I impose on your generosity?"

"What do you need, my friend?"

"Well, two things, actually. I shall be leaving the rooms I have rented rather soon, I wondered if a chap may beg use of a room to rest his weary head whilst finding more suitable accommodation?"

The idea of the company other than that of his housekeeper excited James immensely. He thought that being able to converse with a readily available companion would be most advantageous. Being brought up to serve meant years of standing still by a door in silence, he had himself become accustomed to having company. The two men may have been from very different worlds, yet their unbeknown similarities were forging an undeniable bond.

They had arrived at the house by now and were standing by the fireplace, very large measures of brandy in crystal glassware being swirled in their hands.

"What a splendid idea!" he almost shouted in his excited response. "In fact, it is an excellent idea; you are welcome to stay, my friend; it would be a pure delight to have company; please, come stay for as long as you like. Open invitation. Yes. Yes. I will have the top rooms made up for you. What was the other thing?"

"Thank you, James; I think I am going to enjoy sharing. The other thing is of less magnitude; I wondered if I may borrow an evening suit for dinner; I feel a little tired and travelling across town to fetch mine seems like a bore."

James giggled and agreed to the request. "Let us make tonight a celebration. The project is near as damn it finished, and our friendship is in growth; champagne this evening, I insist."

"Whatever you say, Mr Hargridge."

"Pardon?" A flit of panic shot across James's face; the untrained eye would never have spotted it, but Teddy was far from being that and despite his ever-more becoming split of loyalty between friend and role, this was a conjecture not to be missed. "The girl in the tea room, she called you Mr Hargridge, Hardridge, Harridge? Something like that."

Teddy knew that James would loosen his tongue far too easily after even a small amount of liquor and had topped up his glass from the decanter kept in the intricately glazed cabinet near the window; he gestured a toast, forcing him to take a gulp of the warming fluid which like clockwork he did, Teddy took the smallest of sip from his own glass before continuing.

"Come on, old boy, spill the beans. Are you some kind of secret agent working for the government with special missions?" He smiled with what was meant to be an obvious tease, although James simply took it as discovery.

He gripped his glass tightly and sat in one of the studded leather chairs that sat aside his prized wheel table. "Teddy. You are my trusted friend, aren't you?"

"The very best of friends. What is it that ails you? My comment was only in jest; I do hope I have not offended you. It would certainly not be my intention."

"I'm not offended. Not at all. In fact, it's quite the polar opposite. As your friend, I feel I must be honest with you as you have been with me, helping with the project and every time, you have listened to my rambling stories, never once interrupting until I had finished. Please do not hate me for my dishonesty. I can only apologise and hope you will understand once my secret is learnt."

Teddy fetched the decanter and once more added liquid to James' glass.

"James, my friend. I do not think there is anything I could not forgive you for; you've been thou…"

Teddy's words were cut short by a firmly said word. "Harbridge."

"Pardon?"

"Harbridge. My name, my real name is Harbridge. That is what you heard said by the waitress. I was going to tell you that she must have been mistaken and called it to me in error, but alas, no, in fact, I have known her and her parents for many, many years."

"Oh. Please continue. I am a little confused."

"My name is James Harbridge; I am a personal assistant to His Majesty, the Prince Consort, Albert, husband of Queen Victoria, ruler of Great Britain and the Empire."

"No way! That's amazing! Really? Do I really know someone that works for the queen?"

"Yes, you do?"

"So, your father isn't a rich American?"

"No, my father was in service to the throne just as I. My riches are fantasy, although I have been well rewarded with a lifetime income and this house. Also, the furniture, a few trinkets and a wardrobe that one might say is fit for a king."

"But why the facade?" Teddy had him exactly where he wanted him, willingly giving up priceless information that, once relayed to Russia, would offer him a great reward.

"Because of the project. Albert is almost paranoid that his wife and children will be harmed or even killed; there have been several assassinations attempted on her life. He holds such love for her. The subterranean structure is a stronghold, somewhere safe and unknown in which the family can be safe."

"So, the dam is not to provide water to the paper mill? I thought it was there to print money or bonds or something."

"No, the mill is only there as a front; it produces nothing more than fancy writing paper. The dam is to hide the safe house. Albert was quite clever with the whole illusion, even the train track which could safely take them there and the lifts you were involved in that take them down from the secret tunnel. The whole thing is a ruse. One big masquerade. I am so sorry, I lied. The prince gave me the identity so I could carry out the mission. I'm nothing more than a loyal valet who is out of his depth; I've had to learn so much so quickly."

"Well, all I can say is…"

James had the look of a scorned puppy begging for forgiveness as he listened with hope to the resulting response.

"Wow! I am so proud of you! Well done for stepping up to the plate and serving the throne like that. I think you must be the best citizen that England has ever known. Of course, there are no apologies necessary, and if it is my forgiveness you seek, then, my dear, dear friend, you have all of the forgiveness you want and need! How amazing. So, when I bumped into you today in Windsor, were you relaying secret messages? Sorry, I bet I shouldn't ask; it's none of my business. By the way, your secrets are safe with me. I would never betray confidence."

The relief that washed over James was immense. Enough indeed to prompt a tear from his eye. He knew deep inside that he was safe and protected by Teddy; he would trust him with anything, which is why he freely gave the details of the planned trip to escort the Royal Family in a couple of weeks. Teddy not only reassured the trust he was holding but also offered to assist in the planning of the journey as payment for friendship.

"My dearest friend… I don't know how to thank you for being here for me." as James spoke the words whilst they stood facing each other in front of the grandiose fireplace, he felt a sudden rush of emotion towards what, in truth, was the only adult he had ever bonded with outside of Royal Court. He stepped forwards without thought to what he may be doing and kissed Teddy lightly on the lips. In response, Teddy simply smiled. This was not a piece of his espionage he had considered he may take, yet simultaneously, alongside the fact he was trained to do whatever for his mission, he felt warmed by the sentiment, as a glowing ember inside had flickered into full flame.

Following the night of celebration, Teddy returned to his own apartment. As he lay, he allowed his mind to think openly. Having now been released to perform his duties alone, it had been quite a shock to the system to experience joy, friendship, laughter, comradeship and actual connection, all things denied to him by his country and his mission. Now, he pondered his future, his friend James had trusted him. Enough to bare all and sealed it with a kiss?

What was that? An English custom or something more? The thought remained in his head and triggered memories of the young man with whom he released the teenage tension years before then wondered more about what the feeling would be like if James's kiss had been longer. He decided that if the need was there, he would, indeed, follow through with any act required for the mission. He could not risk rejection at this crucial point in time. With his eyes closed, he began to think in detail of how such a scenario would play, realising he had been stroking his hard member throughout the whole process

James retired to his bed a few miles away in Chelsea; the relief he felt having shared the burden of such a secret was unlike anything he'd ever known; he felt lighter, somehow freshened, renewed. His friend being around had enforced him with hope and strength. As he lay, he wondered what life would be like once this plan was concluded; the prince had offered him release from employment with ample reward to retire if he so desired by way of gratitude. Lying there, he wondered what it would be like to travel, perhaps with his friend as a companion. Trying to ignore his body's response to these thoughts was not easy and eventually, he succumbed to grabbing his cock and beating it rapidly until it spewed hot milk over his sheets. Relieved, he sank back to his pillows and drifted to sleep, thinking of how he would have to hide his smile when he saw Teddy's face the next day and suppress his mind's image of his ejaculation upon his face.

For one of them, perhaps both dreams and plans were coming true.

27

The morning was warm. Pip had lain awake since it was dark, thinking and waiting for the day to begin and his lover to wake and be the company he needed. Mack was a loving and giving man even in his sleep; never a minute resting went by without some part of his flesh touching Pip's body, an arm, a leg, perhaps just the back of his strong hand. It was as if he was always in a protective mode. That was fine with Pip; it felt good, made him feel wanted, made him feel loved.

As the light began to seep through the high glass bricks and began to illuminate the mezzanine bedroom of the under stairs caretaker flat, a new dawn was breaking too in Pip's mind.

He found it so difficult to explain how he felt. He knew that his depression was a battle to behold, but right now, when things were supposedly going to fall into place, it befuddled him to feel more alone, frightened and irrational than he ever had before. Mack lay next to him. This beautiful, strong, honed, wonderful man who had reciprocated his love for so many lost years was right where he should be, lay in the same bed, on his back, thigh pressed against his own, breathing calmly in his state of slumber. Pip watched in awe, his lover's strong, toned chest rise and fall, and listened to his light murmur as he shifted slightly to raise his right knee, propping his leg up and out of the bedclothes. Pip stared at his beau's limb and sank back to his thoughts. He desperately wanted Mack to be awake. As the days and weeks had passed since his return from Italy, Pip had found he needed Mack more greatly. Pip wondered if this was actually falling deeper in love but, at the same time, recognised that his needs were rooted far deeper in his mind than he wanted to admit. Pip knew that for him to have this unfaltering support would help to ease the depression a great deal, but he also knew that even the best things in life could also be difficult to cope with.

Pip was by far not a stupid man. Despite the suffering of the years battling with his own head, he could see exactly what the causes of feelings of loneliness and uselessness were, yet recognition was nowhere near the solution. Pip wanted to switch it off, but that was one lever he could never find to flick. He felt that having a woken Mack was an easier distraction from facing his internal darkness; it was so easy to feel 'normal' in that man's company, just to look at his eyes; his smile helped to close doors in internal corridors, putting a feeling in a room and locking it out. Pip thought more deeply. He decided that the dark, daring, destructive feelings should no longer be around to affect this state of happiness but were so because of that exact same state. Finally, being looked after, loved, adored, safe in strong arms was the very cause of what he hoped was a sort of final release, yet feared greatly the effect of the magnitude of emotion he may face. This was a time to deal with things and not hide behind work and stress in a subconscious attempt to avoid processing and helping his own mind.

Pip made a decision. He was going to get help. He was ready. It had taken such a long time to get to this point and he suspected that dealing with whatever issues caused his mind to be this way may be hard to do yet the challenge had to be one he surely must partake in. He owed this to Mack, he owed it to Jackie, he realised that he owed it to himself.

Jackie had previously offered to help him set up counselling appointments and naturally had said she would be his support whether that meant being around to listen or if he wanted, to keep away. He reached over for his phone and text his best friend. He simply typed 'Head stuff, it's time, I'm ready'.

Jackie was just waking up when she heard the blip on her phone, she reached to the bedside cabinet and picked it up as well as her glasses, after placing those on her head she read the phone screen, however, it was blank. Her waking fogginess meant it took a further long second to remember the trio's group phones and leant over to the other side of the bed where she had placed that one to charge overnight. Unlocking the phone and reading the message made her smile as so patiently she had waited for these words to allow her to help a friend that she genuinely loved so much that tears had been shed in concern for his mental health. Being the super organised and caring person, she had a plan for this exact circumstance, it had been hatched a long time ago following in depth discussions with private therapists. By the end of the morning, Pip would be booked into a thrice weekly session with a wonderful man who had helped her husband years before when he broke down after discovering one of his biggest clients was not only guilty of the money laundering they had been accused of but moreover the sums had been generated from a child trafficking ring that had run for over ten years. She even discussed with Pip the possibility of him going away for a week in the near future for a fully supported respite, of course, with full reassurance that herself and Mack would have everything sorted in his absence. Jackie made herself a promise right there and then. Enough was enough. No matter the lengths she may have to reach to, the matter of Marcus was going to be sorted, Jackie planned to use every resource and as much money as it took to discredit this evil being and expose him for the vile little con artist he was and oust him from their lives.

28

"Hi, Jacks, are you OK?" Mack answered the phone after the shortest of rings later that morning and explained what she had done following the text. She apologised for speaking behind his back but wondered if, as part of the therapy, Mack would mind setting up a break for his lover. "I just want him to take a break. Therapy is great, but it can be exhausting. I wondered if perhaps in a few weeks we make him take a break?" Mack supported the idea wholeheartedly and considered just what this break would mean for himself to somehow sort the stress that was the somewhat evil man that had entrapped his man.

Mack, used the landline in the office to call his mother in Italy; he requested his room to be made up in readiness for a guest, explained some of the pressure that Pip was under and asked if she would watch over him for a week or perhaps two. Sophia agreed without question; she had always had more than a soft spot for Pip, regardless of whether he was the love of her son's life or not.

—

Babe?

Why are you sitting there? I really wondered where you had gone; you were so quiet last night and this morning. To be honest, I am a little worried; have I done something to upset you? Is there anything I can do?

No, it's not you; you are the most brilliant thing I have now and have ever had in my life; it's just that, well, God, why is, it so hard to explain?

Pip was sat on the wall of the bridge at the rear of the site, looking over the rapidly completing structures below and looking up at the old paper mill that he'd worked so hard for. Mack had been looking for him for some time, then saw him, joined him and wanted to do nothing more than make this man happy, make himself happy, make dreams come true and nightmares go away.

He held out his hand. "Hey, sweet, *erm,* would you mind just coming off the ledge, not that I think you're going to jump or anything, but you know I can stand and lean at the wall, but I will be sick with fear if I sit next to you, I've been in scuffles and even disarmed a man but heights... nah."

Pip complied with the request and a smile unexpectedly appeared on his face. This big, muscular, healthy, handsome guy whom most would look at and think he was invincible was the same as everyone else; he had his own fears and he was humble enough to honestly accept them. They stood side by side, an arm around each other's waist and both looked down the valley. Mac sensed that he should do nothing but stand there and support his man; it was exactly the right thing to do as well. Pip squeezed him a little tighter and very gently began to speak.

"I can't always explain it…" he began. "I… how do I begin…?" Pip paused. Mac leaned in a little closer, maximising the contact of their bodies just to let his love know he was there. Pip tried to continue, but he cleared his throat and took a deep breath. "How do I explain to you, my love, the one being on the planet I have been in love with for oh so many years, the man I want to touch, hold, strip, fuck, look at, talk to, simply adore that I can feel like… like."

"Breathe baby, nice and slow, speak when you want to; I am ALWAYS here."

Pip did as he was told and took three deep, controlled breaths before he started again, this time with his eyes closed. "I love you, you know that; I have everything a man could ever need; money should be all right for a long, long time, I'm with someone who will never hurt me, I have the best of friends in Jacks, and those things should be enough, surely, but, it's like, well, almost that… I will sound crazy, but… OK, it's like all of the struggle, the madness of fighting to get everything going, from the day I bought the mill, the re-build, the tenants, the planning for the houses, the gaining of funding, Christ, even getting married to that little fuck, running the gym, everything has been a chaotic and hectic distraction. Now I guess that my whole world is nearly in order, that I can finally see the light at the end of the tunnel. I am scared of the emptiness, frightened that I will have the time and space to face myself, and even then, I am not alone, I have you, I have Jacks. This is nonsense; maybe I just needed to say it all out loud."

"Baby, look at me." Pip turned to face Mack, who took his hands as they looked into each other's eyes. Mack smiled. "Babe… I know what your headspace can be like; depression takes many forms and can confuse the hell out of simple things. You, my beautiful man, have gone through a personal hell alone. Nothing you say is nonsense; I get it, it's OK; however, saying things aloud does, help, even if you are alone; by speaking aloud, you form sentences that you respond to far too quickly if you only think them. I am always here. I will always listen and I will never judge."

With a tear in his eye, Pip, whose head had dropped to stare at the ground while he listened to the support being given to him, tightened the grip of the hand holding, took a deep breath and regained the mutual gaze. Pip smiled. It felt to him like the most natural and happy smile that had ever crept upon his face; he genuinely felt happy; yes, the pure ecstasy of Mack being not just back in his life but actually his very own forever was a wonderful feeling, but it came with fear. Fear of losing him and everything else to Marcus. For this very moment, all of the fears had subsided. Pip was far from stupid; he knew that depression takes such a lot of work to get through, but he felt that at least he had the hope and the desire to get through. He felt for the first time in years, indeed since the very man in front of him had gone away, that he was not alone. The relief was priceless.

Mack had had his own thoughts during the embrace. He loved this man, always had. Had regretted having to leave him before, thought of him every single day and knew that his own existence had only become worthy now he was back in Pip's arms. Mack knew that he would do anything it took to keep his man safe from vulnerability the best he could. He knew there and then, Marcus had to be taken care of.

—

The men strolled together towards the old blocked-up tunnel; Mack asked, "What is this for? Where does it go? Did you ever see the plans?"

Pip had, of course, investigated over the years. "Oh this, I love this, the tunnel in the hill that goes nowhere; as a child, I imagined it was a magical gateway to parallel universes or time travel. However, in truth, it's just a storage area; the plans have it as a dispatch station for the goods from the mill. There are elevators apparently that go down to the base of what was the dam wall and a path to the storage sheds at the side of the Mill; that end is bricked up, too, for safety reasons, I guess; it would be, quite the drop from here to there."

"Oh, makes sense, I guess." By this time, they had reached the wall mentioned in conversation; Mack turned his lover and leant him against it and kissed him long and slowly. "I got you," he whispered.

Marcus, from birth, had needs more than a needy child who craved attention. This child instinctively collected everything around him as soon as he was capable of moving it. His parents at first thought this was a cute little nuance, yet by the time the boy had reached his third birthday; it became quite apparent that the wanting and collecting items might well become a problem. Like some of them collect teapots as a hobby, this child wanted to collect everything. His mother denied it for far too long; it was his father who pointed out the rising problem, having been tipped off by the employee nanny. Blazing arguments would then ensue between the couple, the mother claiming it was from the father's impoverished upbringing that simply showed a life denied of niceties and the father claiming that his wife had not known just how spoiled she had been being born into vast inherited wealth.

Marcus was naturally quite bright and the private schooling supported, his academic side rather well. However, his mother still bowed to his every demand, even more so after the twins were born; rather than cradle her new horns, she handed them to the nanny and turned all attention to her firstborn, her special boy, her son. She missed him dearly when he was at school, and her lunchtime gin intake became earlier and greater as a way of passing the time.

His Father was indeed raised in a working-class environment, not as poor as his mama would make out; they had a nice three-bedroom semi-detached on a relatively new housing estate, and he drove a car never less than four years old, so he'd been raised knowing the value of money. This had meant that his dealings with simple investment and a side-line of flipping houses had amassed a tidy sum of seven million personally saved for retirement, separate from anything his wife's parents had left her. The man worked hard in housing planning and development, leading to his position within government where he, to his cleverness, had managed to contribute so much to housing shortages and homelessness by compulsory purchase and dwelling conversion of deserted department stores and offices left abandoned due to the economic forces the modern world had offered. Praise from the state was rewarded with a beautiful yet unusual side table that resembled an elaborate cartwheel with ebony spokes and a glass top held up by a pedestal leg. Told that this piece was once gifted by Queen Victoria to the Prime Minister; it had sat in the private rooms of Downing Street until Churchill had it put into storage. In fact, legend said that the famed portrait of Churchill sat next to a table with a cigar was originally showing the one that looked like a wheel, but he had insisted it be painted over with the brown cloth-covered square table that most would recognise to this day.

In the years following their retirement, Marcus had adopted the table as his own whilst using the apartment above the garages and gifted it to his husband at their wedding. He told his new husband some of the history of the table that became positioned in the penthouse hallway to hold a small leather tray in which keys could be placed as one walked through the door. Closer to the truth, however, a couple of years before, in a state of drunkenness, Marcus had fallen upon the table, forcing a mechanical click which opened the bulbous section of its pedestal, exposing a velvet-lined purpose-built chamber. Upon sobering, he examined the piece to find one of the brass lion's claw feet fully twisted to face upwards; it didn't take him long to fathom this was the release within the secret compartment. Giving the item as a gift ensured it would be kept pride of place and could never be over to store or given away and that little hidey hole could come in handy.

29

Pip's plan.

The pressure continued to build in his mind; every second of every waking moment seemed to take an eternity to pass, and each slither of time contained deepening distress and a sense of strengthening anxiety. Where most would usually be able to find some shred of hope and a chance to muddle through, the depression he suffered had taken hold with a vice-like grip and was not about to ease its grasp on his mind. Pip could see no way out; running away from the situation was an option; just pack a bag and go, maybe by a tent, and just live on that; he felt he may as well just disappear after all that good was; he to anyone? A sad, ugly middle-aged man loans to pay, and Marcus is on his case for more and more money. Should he surrender? Go to the Police and admit all? Tell the world he had used ill-gotten gains from selling stolen gems to finance his business. Shit, the jewels belonged to the crown, fuck! That's treason! Oh, Lord. This was impossible; what if they pin that guy's death on him, the hit and run? Shit, shit, shit. What else has Marcus tucked up his sleeve?

All Pip could envision was a light at the end of the blackest of tunnels; nothing could be seen and only a constant white noise to be heard as he tried so damned hard to reach that light, but as much the increased effort he made to fight his way forward that little light became smaller and smaller until it disappeared like the dot on an old TV when you turned it off leaving nothing, just blackness.

Pip passed out.

As he came round after a couple of hours of the forced rest, his body and mind had thrust upon him as a saving measure, he had to take a minute to work out where he was and quite what he was doing there. His mind slowly awoke; he could not instantly remember everything he had been thinking or feeling, and in this shrouded mental state, recognition of things he knew were clearing before him. It was his sofa, his living area, his apartment. Pip glanced around; knowing where he'd awoken was one thing; making sure he wasn't dreaming was another. Pip focused on a cushion that Jackie had bought him for his birthday a couple of years ago, a sackcloth fabric with a large blue circle embroidered on it that mimicked the blue plaques one finds mounted upon buildings in recognition of a famous person who had once been in residence. This one declared around the outer-edge that it was issued by the borough of gorgeousness, declaring that 'over-educated, handsome gentlemen live here'. Novelty items were rarely his thing, but Jacks had made an effort to hunt this down following a fitness conference they had taken in Manchester and had seen the original in a gift shop and found it amusing. Those, of course, were the days when things seemed simpler, the time when building a gym as a business and completing the apartments were priorities, the days before he had even met the Devil he had been duped into marriage with.

As he raised himself into a sitting position so he could clearly see the view of the valley and the nearly complete thirty-three houses with the sun bouncing off the solar panels that were built into the roof tiles, a flash of pride at the accomplishment encompassed him, Pip very nearly considered that all would be OK, Mack would be there; he could find a way out of the marriage, even Marcus would have a price to leave other than the several million pounds he had demanded? The thoughts from before he had slept flooded back. Pip closed his eyes and silently prayed to an unknown force for it all to go away.

"Oh, so the sleeping beauty doth awaken. Although I say that as more of a humorous reference rather than a precise description, we wouldn't want the darling husband of mind to become delusional now, would we?"

Marcus was part leaning part standing against the large dining table behind him with a bottle of white wine in one hand and a glass in the other. Pip had no idea how long he had been watched for, but the bottle looked like there may be one small serving remaining; the glass had only a sip that was gently being swirled around. The estimate of a small portion was proven to be correct as Pip watched the content poured into the glass. Pip pondered the math; one bottle of ice-cold New Zealand Sauvignon Blanc, one man, mid-afternoon must surely equal an hour of time. No, wait, this is Marcus, who was more than well-practised in the fine art of afternoon drinkies; if one factored that point into the equation and the dregs of the bottle still to go, the real passing of time could more accurately be estimated at just over twenty minutes. Pip remained silent. Marcus did not.

"Afternoon naps, *eh?* Sign of old age that." Marcus chuckled to himself as he spoke. He walked the short distance to the kitchen area and relieved the glass-fronted wine fridge of another of its contents. "You know, some connoisseurs still will not touch a bottle unless it has a cork, despite the screw cap being a much tighter seal, but over and above that, the ease of opening surely supersedes any quibble of a cork!" Without relieving himself of his glass, Marcus had gripped the fresh bottle between his arm and stomach and removed the cap; he glanced at the remaining content of the vessel and realised it still had the remnants of the previous bottle; he drained it before refilling and returning to his leaning post. "So, my dear heart, that silly little housing estate of yours is nearly finished; it won't be long before all the money will be in the bank. Time for Daddy to pay up, don't you think? Before you start wittering on, please remember that your beautiful husband, being full of moral fibre, is still more than prepared to betray his love for the sake of justice. That poor man, imagine him bleeding out, left all alone after being hit by that reckless driver… he must have suffered so. Tell me, do you think I should wear one of the Navy suits for the court? The TV press is bound to be there, especially with the family connections. Anyway, I cannot bear to share the air with you any longer, making me feel quite sick." With his little monologue performed, Marcus walked across to his bedroom, marched through the door and slammed it shut.

Pip sat, silent and a little numb. This constant roller coaster of emotion was day by day becoming harder to deal with. Pip felt so negative about everything; he knew that deep inside the blackness was building. This was worse than he had ever felt before. Depression had its claws in him for a few years, but now the noose it held around his neck was tightening. This was bizarre. Just a few months ago, he thought that everything would work out; the 'loss' of lying, cheating and blackmailing husband had been replaced with the original and only true love of his life, his building plans were being achieved, his business expanded and going strong, but now... Now, he was to be left not only penniless but in debt, everything would go. Then, of course, Mack would leave this disaster of a man and his best friend. Surely, there would be nothing to keep her around, either.

Pip got up and left the apartment, taking the fire escape to the ground floor and the little path that took him to the development. He climbed the stairs and stood on the bridge, leaning over the side and looking at the thirty-three houses from above as he did most days since the dream began. He ran his finger over the fake brass monkeys on the shoulder of his favourite blend of scotch that he'd grabbed from his kitchen as he left home before removing the cork top and taking a hefty swig of the warming liquid. He smiled to himself, thinking that life had finally got him, broken him, making him drink alone in the middle of an afternoon. "Fuck it, you win," he said aloud to no one and took a further three consecutive mouthfuls.

The swirling thoughts in his mind became darker and darker until Pip could see only one exit from this torture he felt. It had to end. He gulped another two large swigs and once again spoke to the air, 'fucking have the lot, you bastard, take it, fucking spend it, go shag some other fucking staff while you're at it, you fucking scum, I tell you if you were fucking stood here I swear I'd throw you off this fucking bridge right onto those houses you're so desperate to get your bloody hands on. SCUM! Fucking scum' he drank another gulp and lowered himself back against the brickwork and hugged his knees, and began to cry. "Yeah, like you'd have the balls to kill that bastard, not your scene, Pip; you know you would chicken out. Fucking chicken shit, fucking pathetic chicken shit loser, you don't deserve any of it, above your station, useless. Be good if he was dead, though; leave me alone then, wouldn't ya? Fucking cunt. Why me? Why not pick on a really rich guy? CUNT!"

With one last sip, Pip made his final plan; he knew there was no legal way he was going to escape this. His depressed and drunken mind concluded that the death of one of them was the answer. He hadn't the balls to kill Marcus; there was no way he could beg help from anyone; he would hate to have them involved; besides, that would only open up more possible routes of blackmail. No. Only one way to end the suffering. It had been half-assed and considered once before, but his heavy heart now knew this was the final decision. He would quietly grab a rope from the builder's supply sheds, wander alone to the woods on the other side of the hill and end his life.

"Enough… I have had enough. Sorry to let you down, Mack. I love you… but… I just can't."

With this whispered sentence, Pip inhaled the deepest breath of his life, straightening his back and throwing his head back, smacking it hard on the bridge wall and for the second time today, he passed out.

30

"First thing we did, they can supply both of the keys, but they have to be sent out separately with six weeks in between dispatch, but... only if I can access the online account. However, even if I knew the username and password he had set up, I still do not know the keypad code. That apparently is up to eight digits long, and if it is attempted more than three times, it sends a security alert to the owner and deadlocks the keypad."

"Oh, easy then..." Mack joked.

"We are at a loss for ideas on this one; the only thing I can think, though, is that for such extreme security, the contents surely must be the box and the jewels; maybe we can get into it whilst he is away? That reminds me, I need to sort money for him."

"He wants more! Christ, he never lets up."

"Oh, I know. I asked him what was on the disc in the picture. He replied that it is a copy of the dash cam footage of that poor chap being run over, and the paper is a statement placing me in the car and him elsewhere."

Mack nodded as he listened. "The little bastard. Look, I have hard cash we can use; just give it to him and get him out of the way for a while. Tell you what, tomorrow I'll rig up some discrete cameras to see if I can get him using the keypad, then all we will need are the keys. Come on, guys, let's be positive. Let's get the little runt out of our lives forever. I tell you, if I'm ever left alone with him, he will feel the wrath of a very angry Italian cop."

"Well, my darling," a very relaxed Phillip announced. "You will get the chance; Marcus has insisted on a private meeting with you."

"What!"

"Well, with John, the site manager to be precise, some muttering about the loft space of the big house, but to be honest, I didn't really hear what he was on about, designer storage or something, I don't know. I couldn't concentrate without you around. Mad, isn't it? Coped forever, well, sort of, without you, then once you're here, I can't seem to exist without you."

"I know the feeling; I guess once you feel whole, you notice if bits are missing."

"Like a portion cut from a wheel of cheese, it rots away once split."

"Has to come back to something mouse-related with you, doesn't it? My baby Squeak."

"Ha bloody ha. Very funny." Pip pulled a face showing a pretend yawn to mock the line he had heard; his lover smiled contentedly.

The following morning, Mack did his rounds of the building site; he had to admit he'd impressed himself with how well he had masqueraded as the site manager even though he had kept deliberately away from as many workmen close contact as possible to lessen recognition in the future when he could hopefully reveal and live in his own true identity openly with the man he loved.

Recognition chances were, of course, slight as the building teams had been brought in from all over the country by the architects.

The site was beginning to take real shape. Not only were all footings and plots in place but there were only seven houses that were without a roof and windows at the back of the site at the shallowest ground level. The central communal circular garden had been planted, and all surrounding gates that led to all thirty-three wedge-shaped gardens were installed, and bushes, trees and a mixture of climbing roses and assorted leaves of ivy were in position to quickly become established over the coming seasons. Benches and arches were too already placed in a circle all around the mysterious central monolith that Pip never found the true meaning of and had settled on that it must have been put there to remember the lives lost the day the dam gave way.

Mack climbed to the summit of one of the three hills that together walled this developing, beautiful lot of properties. He stood and looked across and became excited at what he saw. The winter sun beamed through a clear, crisp sky and reflected upon the solar tiles used to protect and fuel each house with free shared electricity. He took out the burner phone and made a short panoramic video, which he sent to his lover and their mutual best friend. The short silent film showed light bouncing from the ridges of each tile; as one looked at them and moved, the light seemed to move; it was as Pip had hoped for, an illusion of rippling water. Mack walked down the hill until he was level with the rooflines and took pictures with the phone.

From this angle, the hollow centre of the roof lines could not be seen, making it look as if it were a solid body that could easily be mistaken as water. There and then, he decided that an evening picnic right here on this hillside would be where he would propose to Pip using the ring, he had bought with him from his other home at the Italian vineyard, providing, of course, that he could somehow get Marcus out of the frame and their marriage dissolved without Pip's state of mind being hurt any deeper. The worry he and Jackie had about him was growing daily. They could see that depression was building inside Pip, yes, he was happy, yes, he felt safer than ever before, yes – without Marcus's demands – he was financially comfortable, yes, he had the love of his life and yes, a lot of people would be able to enjoy the moment and to hell with the rest but once it takes hold depression does not allow contentment. It allows a hollow smile to be displayed, even a laugh to support the image, but underneath the disguise, it eats away at your existence, taking away light and leaving shadows of darkness, taking away its victim's ability to think properly and rationally, to move energetically and day by day reducing normal functions and the want to perform them.

31

Mack walked around the building site and took in some of the details of the houses. All were similar in design, yet each had a little character of its own and although some of the plans had been repeated, no two designs were next to each other, the fact that each frontage offered views of nothing but natural greenery or of the impressive Victorian Mill was truly remarkable and unlike anything he had seen before, his love and admiration for his life partner he thought was already unrivalled however to now stand and see in brick and mortar what Pip had imagined added the strongest sense of pride to the list of emotions he felt.

Pip approached the most prominent of buildings, the one meant for Pip and Marcus. Larger than all of the others and taking a slither section of each adjacent plot to accommodate the sizeable floor plan right in the centre of the valley facing part of the circle. In his short absence, the house had been completed by teams working around the clock to satisfy the demands of Marcus, who apparently insisted it must be ready before his winter holiday; he opened the newly installed front door and stepped inside; the teams had done a remarkable job of finishing, the plasterwork was impeccable as was every last micro millimetre of cornice around this beautiful entrance hall that was bathed in natural light from the skylight directly above the centre of this quite remarkable space, the sun amplified the beauty of the black and white tiled floor, the centre of which was an ornate monochromatic mosaic showing images of Roman Gods the images contained by the most classic of chequerboard.

"You must be John," a voice spoke behind Mack as he crossed the front of the double doors that led to what would be a dining room. It took a very long two seconds for him to recognise it was he that was being spoken to and to remember the facade and put his brain into gear. The owner of the voice thrust out his hand to shake that of Mack's; he proceeded to vigorously pump his arm with a grip far too tight to be casual or friendly, an overly firm hold that any body language student would say described a need for dominance and power, verging perhaps on narcissism. Mack, of course, had been aware that this moment may arise and had anticipated his actions of response well in advance; in fact, Jacks had made him repeat a script et right at this moment in time, all of which had one out of the window. The rehearsals meant nothing because since that little plan was devised, more things had been revealed, more extortion made, and more torture given to the mind of his one and only by this creature that was holding his hand. Marcus.

Mack had to fight the urge to crush the hand that was gripping his, resist yanking it down, twisting it and breaking the arm it was attached to as he threw it up his back before grabbing the back of his neck and swiping his legs from beneath him as he forced the man's head hard into the ground. From his uniformed training, he knew he easily had the knowledge, skill and power to overthrow this man, to maim him, and make him feel pain, but he also knew the power of the threats he had over Pip. What if he actually could provide evidence from the dash cam that the hit-and-run was done that might? What if he could prove the history of those rocks? The lightning speed of thought gave the rapid conclusion that no action could be taken right now; this was a game to be played out a little longer. Whatever the solution was going to be, it had to be rock solid, with no stray avenues, no possible stone unturned and absolutely no trackback to himself, his lover or their friend. Mack resisted once more a tight bone, breaking soul, satisfying return grip and instead gently held on. "I'm sorry, sir, should I know you?"

Marcus let go of the hand. "Well, now I guess you should know who your boss is, but then I have noticed from passing by that you deal a lot with my other half, and I bet he has hardly mentioned me. I'm Marcus, the brains behind this build; this one here is my new house." He gestured towards the larger building. "In fact, dear man, I introduce myself now because I require a little favour."

32

Mack yawned, stretched and turned to face the empty side of the bed. He wondered where his lover was, not overly concerned knowing what Pip was like to leave phones and keys around, but it did seem strange that there hadn't been any contact since yesterday morning and that not one of his messages was showing as being read. Mack couldn't help but ponder about the man he'd loved for decades. He wished he could whisk them both away to a small tropical island and they could live out their days strolling along white sand beaches next to clear blue water, but he knew that anything more than a holiday would result in boredom for two men who had to keep active. A holiday, though…

Mack dropped the little capsule into the machine, pressed the button and let it pour his espresso into the little Gryffindor cup and sat at the kitchen island to drink whilst flicking through pictures on his tablet, the result of a Google search for the most beautiful beaches. The cup was a small gift from Jacks as a little housewarming token; she said it was in reference to the apartment being basically a giant cupboard under the stairs, which yes it was, but then most cupboards are only of a size to house a vacuum and not twenty feet wide. He liked this unusual space, though for what it represented, the final union of him and his beau.

He grabbed a short-sleeved-shirt and a pair of denim shorts that were possibly a little tighter than polite etiquette would suggest, shuffled his feet into his boots, ruffled his hair in the mirror by the door and crossed the short passage to the gym entrance.

"Well, hello, early bird, I'll put the kettle on" were the welcoming words from the mouth of one of the most amazing people he'd ever met.

"Morning, Jacks, did you get the short straw to open up? I thought that fingerprint access was up and running. Is there something wrong with it? Should I take a look?"

Jacks looked at the clock. It was only 05.47 and she'd been there for a while.

"Couldn't sleep, been awake since four, the house is clean, washing done, Mack some mornings I get so bored, I thought I might as well come and organise something, but I seem to be several months ahead of things to do here too! I'll get coffee; shall we go up to the lounge?"

The pair ascended the internal stairwell and settled by the glass wall that overlooked the grand entrance of the mill. "You know it's far too grand for a factory building," Mack said as he gestured to the opulent area.

"Oh, I agree, but then it's such a pleasant place to be; I think as I like it so much that I might take one of the houses on the plot; after all, my boys are here, work is here. Pip mentioned a big discount, but I neither need nor want it. Do not tell him, by the way, I will know it's you, you're the only one that knows, well, you and the sales agent…"

"Sal… agent? You dark horse! Why didn't you say?"

"Well, I was going to buy one anyway, thought I could rent it out perhaps, not really as a business concern; I really don't need the income, to be completely honest. I was only going to buy one to support you two, one less property to sell, etc., but now I think about it, the convenience is there; I'd be even closer to looking after my favourite couple."

Mack knew that this would actually be a lot of fun, although he knew being 'looked after' would seriously not be good for his waistline, but then his other half did own the gym… "That will be perfect, Jacks" – he looked again at the lobby – "a building fit for a king." He picked up his phone to see a blank screen, no notifications, no missed calls. "Have you seen Pip?" he asked.

"No, honey, not since yesterday; I presumed he was with you. Is he not in your place? With it still being so early, I thought you may have left him to lie in."

"No, sweetie, he isn't at mine. Perhaps, he is up in the penthouse; I am sure I saw Marcus's car, so maybe he's up there avoiding suspicion. I just hate that I haven't heard from him."

"I'm sure our little soldier is fine; he is quite the grown-up when he wants to be, although I have to say he has been a little more preoccupied than I have seen in a long while. Quiet one might say, I know with you around, I'm not going to see as much of him as I used to, and that, of course, is how it should be, but there does seem something more with him, deeper maybe?"

"Jacks, I need to tell you something. I am worried about him. Just a few days ago, I found him on the bridge; I mean, we all know it is his contemplation spot, but

Jack… there was something so very, very wrong. The things he was saying, that it was all too much, that he could no longer cope, that it was all falling away from around him. He said he wasn't deserving of any of it, your friendship, the gym, the mill, the development, even me."

"Oh Mack, no, please tell me this isn't true. Look, I probably shouldn't tell you this, but you're his partner, so I don't feel like I am betraying him. Before that scum ball Marcus, well going way back to not long after I met him, he had a patch of 'the blues' I think the thing that triggered it was money the fitting out of a modern gym isn't cheap and I know he had overstretched the borrowing, and I could see t was grinding him down with worry of how to repay it all. As a friend, I offered him a loan, even offered money as a gift, but he is such a stubborn creature at times he flatly refused; what you men get out of struggling through pride is bloody beyond me, I swear! Anyway, the one thing he would let me do was to organise a bit of a marketing plan; I told him to trust me and that I had some contacts from my husband's old firm, which is true, the contacts part anyway, but as far as knowing what I was going to do to fill this place with new cash-rich members, well, perhaps I had stretched that bit, just a little. Anyway, and I will castrate you if you ever let this slip, one of our old clients, Julio, one of your lot as it happens, owns a marketing company; he had used us to oversee a takeover of another local firm. Anyway, I dug out his number and gave him a call."

Mack lifted his hand to motion a pause. "One of our lot? Jacks that doesn't seem like a phrase I'd hear from your lips; I didn't think you categorised the Gays."

"I don't, how could I? *Oooooh,* the you lot thing? Funny, no, darling, I meant it as in hot Italian! Good grief, that man could melt your knickers away with one of his smouldering looks from those deep brown eyes and oh boy, the hair, the body hair…"

Mack chuckled.

"Anyway, I contacted the hot Julio and paid him for a full launch campaign, radio, socials, press, even hired sales teams for shopping centres, the whole shebang! That is the part that Pip must never know, that I paid for it, not cheap, but it worked, and members flocked in; it gave the foundation for what he has here today."

"Wow, Jackie, you really are the best friend a man could have; I'm truly blessed to know you."

Jacks cleared her throat. "Now listen, Philip and now you mean the absolute world to me. From the second I met him, I saw a spark I had not seen since I met my husband, the only difference being I fancied that one, but Pip I see as special; he has a beautiful core, a soul that wants nothing but for others to benefit, that is why he is my friend, that is why I would happily give him everything I own without hesitation, I love you, boys. There isn't anything I would not do to protect you."

"Like a fairy God Mother or rather a God Mother to the Fairies!" They both laughed at Mack's one-liner before fetching more coffee and continuing the conversation.

Mack stirred his coffee and began, "What do I do about Marcus though, Jacks? The threats, the blackmail, I know that is what is bringing Pip down; as much as I hate to say it, I am really worried as to what he might try and do to himself. I know he suffers and the courses I took in the force prepared me for things like this. When depression takes hold, rational thought can be out of the window. Jack, I'm scared."

"I know you are, honey; I have an idea or two; let's finish these, then you go find your man and I will go and find a couple of numbers. We can reconvene later."

33

Mack stood outside the mill and waved to Jacks as she drove away; he wondered what trick she may have up her sleeve, but right now, his priority was his boyfriend, Pip; where are you? He took out his phone and checked it once more, then it dawned on him to try the 'find my friend' feature, he did and to his surprise the little dot was located straight ahead of him at what must have been the bridge, of course, the one place Pip would go to think, Mack marched strong and true and climbed the steps to find the hunched over, bloody mess of the man he adored, 'PIP!' He yelled to his lover as he ran as fast as his strong thighs could take him and with tears in his eyes dropped to his knees to cradle this sweet man. Instinctively, he checked for a pulse and was relieved to find a steady one still pounding blood through the body in his arms. The blood was from a cut at the back of Pip's head and as Mack parted the sticky, matted hair, he could see bruising shining through. "Oh, my baby, who did this to you? Oh, my poor baby, how do I make this right?"

"Mack?" The single word filled his heart; the voice was quiet, gravelly, questioning, "Mack, is that you? My head hurts." The second Pip ended his sentence, he lurched forwards and violently threw up several times; it didn't take a genius to work out that the vomit was the result of the bottle cast aside near them, combined with a little concussion. Pip wiped his mouth on his sleeve, opened his eyes fully and faced Mack.

'I'm sorry' were the only words Pip felt he could say; sorry for what, he wasn't sure, but he felt the need to apologise. Pip burst into tears as Mack drew him in to hold his body close, to make his man feel safe, to feel loved. The two men sat in that embrace until Mack hinted, they should go and get cleaned up before they were spotted together; the last thing either needed right now was to supply more fuel to Marcus's fire.

Mack put the groggy Pip to bed in the big cupboard under the stairs and gave him the Elder wand to hold. "Now remember when you gave it to me, you told me only the strongest could master that wand, but for now, my strong boy it is your turn to hold it safe. Now get some sleep; I'm going to leave you here quietly. Don't worry, I won't be far away."

"OK, I won't move unless Hogwarts delivers an invite." Pip flicked the wand at him, rested his head on the pillow and tried to concentrate on the fun, childish side they shared; it was as if even after all of the years wasted apart, they could still share some of the youthful things they would have done if it had of been possible for them to have grown together.

Jacks entered through the main doors of the mill to see Mack sitting on the marble stairs. Wordlessly, their eyes locked as Mack pointed to the bar with his left hand; he met her at one of the more discrete tables with a bottle of Malbec and two glasses he had bought on his way in; he sat and placed his bottle down next to the exact same one that Jacks had bought. "Great minds think alike," she said to him. "I guess we could cap one and take it home?" A smile broadened across her face; she knew tonight would be a taxi ride for her; the chance of seeing flying monkeys was more probable than either of them using one of those useless inventions called a wine stopper. "How is he? Can I see him?"

The strong Irish-Italian hunk dressed in jeans and a loose-knit white jumper pushed up his sleeves and rested his elbows on the table to support the head that wore an expression of despair. His saddened eyes kept locked with those of his guest as he slowly shook his head.

Of course, once Pip was cleaned up and checked over and almost forcibly put to bed, Mack had phoned Jacks to fill her in on the state he had found him in. The hungover mumblings that had been heard through the tears during the stumble back to the mill were now being relayed face to face, causing tears to well in the eyes of both at the table.

"Jacks, he has really had enough; I am really, really scared that he will do something stupid; all he kept saying was how he couldn't take it any more, that Marcus had won, let him have it, that it would be over soon and that was all that mattered, what do I do Jacks? I've been so blessed to get him back after all those years; I cannot lose him. It will destroy me to not have him, or worse, to not be able to save him. God, I hate Marcus for doing this to him, to anyone. How can somebody be so fucking cruel? I could kill the bastard, I swear!"

"Join the queue! Oh, if only I'd have known that boy was such a little scoundrel, I would have seen him off well before his feet were under the table. I feel so guilty!"

Mack reached across the table and held her hand; with a soft squeeze, he said his supporting words. "Darling, never feel dismayed; we can all say, what if? What we really need to say is, what next? How do we solve this?" He checked his phone and opened an app that allowed him to view a selection of site cameras, one of which he had put in his own flat to keep an eye on Pip; it felt a little creepy to do it, but worry had long taken over morality, he presented the screen to his friend. "Looks like someone is asleep; we should continue talking at mine." The pair collected the bottles and left the bar one by one to re-join at the door of Mack's flat. They sat and poured fresh drinks, both knowing that a conclusion to this whole mess could wait no longer; it must be drawn to a close, a plan set tonight.

34

Pip lay still asleep, clutching at the wand. His dreams took him to a place he did not recognise, but there was a person there he thought was familiar; it was one of those dreams that had layers, stories within stories, the kind where you make mental notes ready for exploration the following waking day. He let out an audible sigh, which made both Jackie and Macaulay jump to attention. After they had both checked on their charge, they settled in the vintage armchairs, freshly topped up with glasses in hand.

"Oh," Mack began. "Guess which low-life scum bag cunt I met?" He relayed the short event of the meeting in house number one the previous day.

"And you didn't think to tell me?"

"Kinda didn't jump to the front of the mind, to be honest, had to stop me from strangling the fucker there and then; I tell you something if it had been today, I'd have met him after finding Pip in that state, I'd probably have punched him over and over until his twisted brains fell out."

"Oh, you should pop upstairs and start that little mission; I'll get the bleach and a mop and be up in five."

"Don't tempt me, Jacks… mind you, I think Christian Bale had the right idea in that film where he just killed everybody; he covered everything in plastic first, then got a chainsaw out."

"American Psycho."

"Huh?"

"The film! That's what it was called. I didn't really get it, but I did watch the shower scene a few times." Jackie chuckled. "But seriously, we do need a plan; a chainsaw is far too noisy, forget the blood splatter. What about injecting air? Causes heart attacks, I think?"

"Nope, he's too fit and healthy; the post-mortem would reveal the puncture site."

"Poison?"

"Jackie, we are plotting this far too easily; I mean, with the Police and the private stuff, I've done some things, but…"

"Mack with a lawyer husband, I've been in some kinds of situations and involved in some sticky cover-ups…"

"What are we saying, Jacks?"

"I'm saying it's time to open that other bottle. Now tell me the rest of your encounter with you know who."

Mack relayed the content and instructions he had been given by the one man who, through pure greed, was causing more pain than anyone would think possible. The anguish that was destroying such a lovely man's mind was derived from this calculated narcissist. Marcus wanted John to personally install a safe in the loft space of the new house on the instruction, apparently of this man's husband Philip. The safe itself had been removed from its original place and was ready to be installed at the very earliest opportunity. Marcus said he would assist with the task and oversee the job so the chance of one of the workmen knowing of its existence would be minimal to reduce the risk of attempted theft. Mack had kept very quiet through this whole instructive one-sided conversation and noted the extremity of false details that Marcus was providing, including elaborate detail of the contents being deeds to the Mill and this very house, a space to contain very old mariners watch that had been passed down through his family, somewhere for passports and vintage photographs and a whole bunch of other crap that usually a client would never tell, or invent. *You builder, me boss, sticking this box to the wall, a hiding place,* was pretty much what the task instruction should have been and nothing more. John, the foreman, nodded and agreed to help with the installation the very next day; Mack, the scorned, carried on listening, deducing Marcus's tell of overselling an idea in the attempt of disguise and wondering how this could be of advantage. The men then ascended the builders' ladder into the loft space, which, despite the footprint of the building, was compromised by not only the intricate shape of the roof but the frame of the light well that illuminated the hall. Marcus said he would have a firm install a proper access ladder before moving in, as there was no way he was using a regular ladder to store his things. It was as if the man was short of an off switch for his mouth; he was rabbiting about a whole lot of irrelevant nonsense for which the possible reason didn't become clear until they were both stood, very slightly hunched aside the chimney on the gable wall. Mack smelled it straight away; this guy was half cut; he had clearly partaken in a liquid lunch and not a dieter's portion, either.

Marcus indicated where he thought would be the ideal position for his strong box and offered to hold the end of the tape measure in Mack's hand; measurements recorded, he continued to hold the little clip at the tape end as it retracted into its casing. Mack held his breath as he could see exactly where this was leading.

"John." Marcus cleared his throat. "I have seen you around and noticed you have a fine body on you, one that I really want to play with." He stroked the back of the hand that held the 10 m tape measure then gently held Mack's wrist and began to pull it closer to his groin.

"Fuck fuck fuckity fuck, What the? Shit, *erm*... FUCK," was the only thing that Mack could form in his mind; how he had physically kept silent and not hit this fucker, knocking him out cold, he did not know. Against every instinct, Mack somehow managed to rapidly collect his thoughts and come up with something. There was no way he would ever connect with this despicable being regardless of who they were both attached to; this man was nothing but the lowest form of evolved humanity to exist! 'Think, think, think!'"

"I'm flattered, truly," he said after what seemed like an hour.

"So, you should be; it isn't often I choose to fuck with someone as old as you; it's only because your body is tight that we are going to have some fun." As he heard the words, Mack discovered it was possible to actually taste hatred. The arrogance of it all, why was it all so god damned frustrating? "You know you want me, who wouldn't? You really are a lucky man."

THINK.

"Honestly, really, I am flattered but…" Mack began to speak as Marcus released the hold on his wrist and took a step back. "I mean, I really could possibly get caught up in the moment and don't get me wrong it is a hell of a compliment to be offered a good time by someone as good looking as you, but, well." Thinking quickly once more, something triggered and reminded him of the cover-up of him seeing Pip. "I'm straight. Sorry, I have a wife and my girls back home; I mean, it's tempting to try and I'm not saying I haven't wondered maybe a very long time ago, but I'm just not into it. Sorry."

"Ah, no sweat, your loss, mister. Anyway, are we doing this little job tomorrow? Be here at ten. The unit is in my car; I hope you're feeling strong. It's bloody heavy."

Fascinated by how easily this creature could disregard rejection and flick without comment to another topic, Mack simply replied, "Yes. At ten."

35

"So, let me get this straight, please excuse the pun." Jacks smiled at her own little joke. "Tomorrow, you are installing a safe in Pip's house."

"Yes."

"The very same safe that has been removed from the storage area."

"Yes."

"That is currently in that wanker's car?"

"I think so, yes."

"Then let's steal the car."

"Slight problem Jackie, my darling," Mack swiped his phone open. "I repositioned more than one site camera, Dickhead drove off an hour ago."

"Well, I guess it was too easy; I don't suppose he has left it full of all the things we need; what was I thinking? Who would leave precious stuff in a safe that some random builder is about to install? Even he would never slip up to that extreme."

"Random builder? I will let you know that John, THE SITE MANAGER, was offered the job because of his professionalism and clearly acquired skills; thank you."

Jacks smiled once more. "Darling, you do realise you aren't really John, the site manager?"

Mack smirked. "I'm not? Oh."

"No, dear, you're not, you are… wait… You, the real you, you're not here. Didn't you say your trip to the homeland was on your Italian passport or your British one? Either way, it does matter you came back covertly so little wanker couldn't track you if he ever suspected anything; Mack Sullivan is in Italy."

Mack rose from his chair, crouched down and lifted the back of it. The low-to-ground frame of the deco three-piece suit had conveniently concealed a wooden box, which Mack shifted with his foot; he lowered the chair and bent to lift the box onto the chest he used as a coffee table. Opening it exposed its wares. Jackie observed the contents; two large bundles of cash, Sterling and Euro, his passports, a revolver and a box of ammunition. "Mister Sullivan may indeed still be in Italy, so there is no way he can be connected to the man who smuggled these things or himself into the UK."

Mack lifted the gun. "I think it is time to scare that little shit and get him out of our lives for good."

Jackie nodded. "Great minds, my friend; I may have dug out a little black book from back in the day myself; my suggestion was also to give the little fucker a taste of his own medicine; I may have already made a couple of phone calls. Nobody is going to get away with hurting my loved ones, and Pip has worked too hard to have it all taken away; I will not let it happen."

The pair sat and waited for the taxi they'd ordered to take the beautiful, strong force, that was Jackie, home. As they knew the following day would be a testing one. Mack checked on Pip, who looked like he had barely moved; he retrieved the portable security camera and took it to charge up. He and his friend had decided that they would take advantage of the safe installation, and Mack would rig the camera so that hopefully they would finally see what the contents were and the passcode to open it once and for all, being able to remove the items and remove the threat held over the much loved Philip Scot. Jacks had mentioned that her contacts might be able to provide an eye witness if required to the alleged hit and run incident, which she knew in her heart that the scum ball had done; the more she thought of it, the more convinced she was that Marcus had deliberately run that poor fellow down as a premeditated plot for blackmail. The pair had chinked glasses. This mess was going to be sorted.

Pip sighed. The sigh was of dismay. The joys of an open plan living space meant that sound carried. It was Jack's voice that had stirred him, or rather her laugh; it was one of those that, when heard, it was near impossible not to smile. He had lain and heard every word of the plotting conversation. The words filled his head and mixed with his own resurfacing thoughts from his time on the bridge. "My mess, my problem, my duty to fix it. They don't know what he's like, though; there's no way he will disappear unless it's with a concrete block and he's dropped into a lake. I can't let those two be involved with this. No. I won't have it. Come on, Pip squeak, be a man, not a fucking mouse. Protect them, sort this." With thoughts ordering themselves in his mind of knowing that he was strong enough to protect the ones he loved, he drifted back to sleep.

36

Mack woke first; the amount of blood his body had pumped into his now throbbing hard member had a contributing factor to his waking. He was already spooning his lover every possible inch of flesh that could touch at any one time. His cock ached with longing as it twitched between the strong muscular thighs of his man, the shaft pinned in the groove at the base of this most splendid firm ass, the tip pushing underneath his ball sac. He silently thanked whoever may be above for the creation of this wonderful man. Pip stirred; he felt such comfort in this embrace, warmth, and security; he felt loved. He smiled to himself as he realised the sensation, he was feeling between his legs; his own cock became equally as hard. Pip was holding the hands of the arms that held him; he did not let go apart from a short couple of seconds when he had moved his hips forwards and grabbed the pulsing piece of Mack that would make him feel complete as he guided it into his waiting hole. Lay on their sides; pip began to move his hips back and forth, then further back, thrusting his lover deeper inside him; the feeling was one of joy, of ultimate connection. It did not take long before he heard the breath behind him become deeper; he could feel the force of the exhaled air on his neck as Mack rolled him onto his front, released the bear hug grip, lifted Pip to meet his own groin and sank every last millimetre deep inside him, with just a few pounding thrusts Mack gave a guttural roar as he shot his load. Mack fell to his back on the bed and tried to gain his composure and calm his rapidly beating heart; he turned to face his man and mouthed the words, "I love you."

"Up to much today?" Pip enquired, secretly wondering how much of last night's overheard talks would be shared with him.

"Oh, *erm,* just the usual, apart from maybe a trip to the airport."

"What? Why? Where are you going, when? For how long?"

Mack smiled and stood before him, holding his shoulders. "Babe, I'm not going anywhere; you are."

"No, I'm not; I don't have any plans. Besides, besides, there's too much going on."

"Baby, *hush.* It is all set; I bumped into Jacks yesterday a couple of times as it goes. Anyway, she will watch the gym, which you know she does in her sleep, the architects will oversee the final parts of the build, and you, my darling man, are taking a two-week trip, and before you utter one single word from those gorgeous lips of yours, there will be no fighting the decision, it has been made. Jacks are looking for flights this morning, and you ARE taking a break. I'm sending you to the vineyard; my Mum will love having someone to look after, especially you. I'm sure she always secretly wanted you for a son instead of me, blimey; thinking about it, she gets her wish."

"Bu…'

"No buts. No." Mack's eyes began to fill with tears. "Baby, it has taken our whole fucking lives to get where we are now, then to see you yesterday, hunched over alone, injured, baby I was so scared you were dead; my heart broke as I approached you, I cannot live without you, I just can't. So, as your partner I am taking the bull by the horns and taking charge. You are taking a break. You are going to relax. You are going to switch off because seeing you like that, broken, oh, Squeak, no. I'm taking you to the airport and putting you on the plane. Mum will be there at the other end, and for the next three weeks, it will be just you, Mum, my uncle and a fuck load of grapes, no me, no Jacks, no business and no weird fucking husband, oh and if I have to tie you to a chair so you don't run away, then trust me, I will, I still have my cuffs from the force you know."

Pip had to smile. "You teasing bastard, mentioning cuffs and then sending me away, how cruel can a man be?" In his mind, Pip knew this was the best plan; if he were to survive, avoid suicide, and feel any sense of normality, then this escape would be an ideal distraction for a while, but it also posed a little hiccup in his plans for today.

"What time is the flight? I should pack."

"Oh, I asked Jacks to find something evening; I have a couple of things I have to do beforehand and don't worry about packing either; I have pretty much a full wardrobe at the villa; what's mine is yours after all."

"It's all planned then, my God, I'm beginning to wish I had never let you two meet! But then I guess… well… Mack, *erm,* thank you. Thank you for loving me."

"Shush. Just do as you're told. Now, it's already 06.15, bugger off and chill for the day, steam room, massage, anything to start this stress detox. I'll meet you later; oh yeah, don't worry, Jacks has got your passport out of the office safe. All you need is you."

Pip sat on the sofa, stunned at how it felt to be looked after, but it also made him realise even more about his duty to protect his love in the same way. Marcus needed sorting; a timer had now been set, and the countdown to once and for all, silence the man he'd married had begun. Taking long, slow, deep breaths, Pip rehearsed the things that today he would say to Marcus; he recapped the key things he was being falsely accused of the hit and run, the fraud, the acts of treason. Each one he would defend himself against, he would tell Marcus the whole thing was going to be made public by himself, ahead of anything Marcus could do, yes, fight with the fight, enough. Pip stood and headed out to find his husband and end the madness before his love or his best friend did something they would regret.

—

Mack took the quickest of showers and grabbed his rucksack and gave it a small shake to feel the reassurance of the heavy steel object that lay, loaded, at the bottom. He blew a kiss to Pip and stepped out of the door. Jacks observed him through the glass of the gym, nodded in his direction, and gave a beckoning gesture with her hand. He joined her and she led him up to the coffee lounge, still deserted at this early hour.

"Hun, you look a little tired, are you OK?

"Oh, thanks, Mister S, I thought I looked rather fresh," She looked at him with a combined smile and scornful expression. "Of course, I look tired after I left you. I got home and was in bed by half nine; I guess I would have had a cracking night's sleep if the phone hadn't rung off the hook at one this morning."

"What? Who?"

"Never mind, who let us just say a friend of a friend; I told you I did some digging via, we'll never mind. A few favours were called in. Anyway, I've found him."

"Found who?"

"Chris, I've found Chris."

"Well, that is lovely, but Jackie, who the hell is Chris?"

"The poor young lad that Marcus was knocking off, you know, the one that Pip caught naked in the penthouse just before you turned up. It turns out that after he ran away from here, he went over to Worcester to stay with his aunt; she got him a night job at the twenty-four-hour supermarket where she works, so I got up, threw on a tracksuit – and do not tell anyone I left the house with one on – and drove two hours to see him. He was adjusting a shelf when I found him, aisle six, baking goods and coffee. I only had to clear my throat and he froze like a rabbit caught in headlights.

"We spoke for quite a while, and I have to be honest here; I bear no malice towards him; I genuinely believe he had been coerced by Marcus. He had been told an assortment of lies, told that the relationship with Pip was totally open and a marriage of convenience so Pip could use Marcus's connections. He had even told him that he loved him and that once the development was finished and some money had rolled in, they would run away together, but until then, Pip knew everything and was happy about it and even got off on the idea. Honestly, the young chap was broken-hearted; he really must have fallen for Marcus. It really felt like he was in love. Anyway, he ran away because he couldn't face Pip. He'd loved that job, but there was no way he could continue to work there. Chris also said how he had called Marcus to see how they could continue with what he thought would be their eventual future to be told it was all a sham; he wasn't loved at all, but thanks for allowing his beautiful body to be used as often as he liked and also for the passive income from the OnlyFans account, turns out Marcus had filmed Chris doing many things, including things 'performed' on video chats that went straight to the internet. The poor boy! He is so upset, so angry at being used. Chris has said he would do anything to try and make it up to Pip. He is so sad that he was part of hurting the man who gave him a chance and encouraged him at work, so I asked him and he said yes."

"Totally lost here!" Mack's brow furrowed with concentration and attempt at all the possible outcomes of this not quite by chance meeting. "How can this help us? I don't get it; you spoke to the lad that Marcus fucked a few

278

times; how does that get the blackmailing little shit out of our lives? Jacks, I'm putting this gun to his head and I swear if he doesn't promise to fuck off, I'll pull the trigger."

"Calm down there, boy. He said yes to owning up to the affair; he said to clear the air, he would gladly stand in a divorce court and tell all, even return the money that Marcus had given him to save towards a house deposit… OH FUCK!"

"Again, a little lost, why oh fuck?"

"The money, the fucking money, oh shit, how could I have been so blind! All the times Marcus demanded money for God know what trip or gambling debt or to pay off something he had recklessly bought. It has always been from Pip's account or on Pip's card; I don't even have to ask to know how that fucker has lined this one up; I'd put my house on a large transaction showing from Pip direct to Chris, it will look like he has paid for a false witness, Oh God no, wait, oh no, no, no… there's also a transaction from the development account to Pip's private one, so he could transfer money for that god-damned skiing trip, the cunning bastard, hundred to one he's got that one set up and ready to fire as…"

"Embezzlement," Mack finished the sentence and closed his eyes as he sighed. He honestly didn't think that even in his time in the police or even in close security, he had ever come across another that was so calculating.

Jackie's phone beeped; she answered and spoke with the caller. Mack fetched fresh coffee. "Everything OK?" he asked her.

"That was Chris, who just got home after finishing his shift. He wanted me to know that apart from still being scared he was still happy to do the right thing. I've let him know that he shouldn't worry, that we will find another way, oh and to keep the money, use it to make a new start somewhere. He was really angry when I explained how the plan wouldn't work and kept saying that Marcus should pay for everything he had done."

"Christ, all this before breakfast. How did you leave it with him?"

"I didn't. He was still ranting about how Marcus was gonna get it and he hung up! I've tried three times already to call back, but there's no answer."

"I wouldn't worry too much about him; he sounds like a nice kid. I'm sure he will sort himself out; right then, time is cracking on. I think I should walk for a bit before I do my loft installation; if I see the bugger feeling like this, I'm sure I'll thump him, besides I want to get in there as early as I can and hide this little camera; I plan to take away some of the boy's threatening toys."

37

It was nearing ten o'clock when Mack glanced at his watch after once again checking the weight of his pocket assurance that its contents were still in place. He had been plodding aimlessly around for well over an hour, but now he knew he had to get to house number one and face his foe, hopeful that the opportunity would soon arise that somehow, he could find an end to this nonsense. He had left the formidable but frustrated Jackie around 07.30 after thanking her once more for her continued effort in what felt like a war; she shrugged and said she still had a trick or two up her sleeve, wished him luck and said she would look in on Pip and make sure he was OK and not sinking into another downer, Mack thanked her and smiled as he told her he felt sure Pip had had an injection of positivity earlier on… Around eight, she popped her head around the door so as not to wake him should he be resting, but found an empty apartment. Pip was nowhere to be seen. Jacks opened her phone and called him only to hear the buzzing sound of the phone vibrating on the kitchen counter; of course, he'd forgotten his phone, typical. With little else to do, she decided it might be an idea to go and find him; she knew that her friend was still in a very delicate state of mind and couldn't help but worry; after a stroll around the mill, she set off up the valley towards the development thinking about all sorts of things including Chris. Jacks was glad she had found him and met him; it just seemed that it was a tiny bit of closure to one of the ever-evolving chapters in the tangled web that was the life of her friend. The four hours of driving she had done that morning had added to her feeling tired, and she planned to take a nap; just as soon as she had seen her buddy, it was bugging her that she couldn't find him. Her mind replayed the chat with Chris; he was such a lovely young man, naive, yes, easily influenced and maybe not quite as sharp as he could be yet she could hold no malice towards him; he'd been duped, conned by the very evil human that was doing the same to her best friend. She had hated seeing Chris's tears and, even more so the anger in his face when she left.

Jackie sat with coffee in hand and an open packet of thick ginger cookies in front of her. After deciding that a fifth one couldn't possibly cause any more harm than the fourth one did, she bit into it; as she chewed and tasted the sharp, rich spice, she pondered about the call she had made a day or two before. Jackie had mentioned to Mack that she might try to find some numbers and possibly call in a favour to perhaps have Marcus threatened and scared off. Rummaging for a number was far from the truth as she was the kind of woman who could reel off every bauble of Christmas decoration, the list of secret private numbers she had put her hands upon within seconds and without hesitation, she had dialled from the pre-paid phone, the fourth number on the list. After it rang out five times, Jackie hung up, waited for one minute and repeated the five-ring dial. She hung up the phone and waited for one minute; on the sixth ring, a voice answered, *"Patterson's grooming."*

"I would like to book in my Patterdale for a wash as soon as possible, maybe also a cut."

The call was disconnected, as was the form of the code. Her phone rang just a couple of minutes later by a former client of her husband. *"Speak."*

"It's the lawyer's wife," she said calmly.

"Jackie?"

"Yes. I think I need a favour."

"I certainly owe you some! Anything you need, I'm retired, so any time you need me, I'm free. It's good to hear your voice, Jackie; it has been a long time. Let us meet; the old tea room is still running; it will be like old times. Tell me then who you need sorting; the message I heard said you need a wash doing? This is fine, but who has upset you so much that you mentioned a possible cut? I will help you no matter what; tell me all, late today, four p.m." The line went dead at the end of the sentence.

Cookie number six was dunked into the dark liquid, which was nowhere near as hot as she liked, but she continued anyway, her mind churning over whether or not she had made the right decision in the clandestine meeting where she had given a brief outline of the circumstances to a character that was known to the law yet with the help of Jackie's late husband and indeed herself, he had always evaded conviction for crimes that were performed more for passion and morality than for profit. Subject discussed and accepted, it was left to this quite remarkable woman to decide upon the level of action she would like to be performed; the wash was code for warning, to have someone threatened into behaving, a cut was a measure a little deeper which did include a blade and perhaps the need for A&E, but of course, there was also on offer, the full grooming service…

38

Marcus was late; he didn't show up at number one until after 11.30. He reeked of booze and smoke that he had been partaking in until just five hours before with some new acquaintances he had met through Grindr and then met in a bar, 'fun' had certainly been had with all three of them but whatever was rolled into the shared joint combined with the contents of a bottle of Kracken and the bottle of tequila, he had taken to the hovel of a flat two of them shared did mean that if questioned and shown in a line up he wouldn't be able to recognise a single one of them by face or for that matter by the body, in fact, he was beginning to ponder exactly what activities they had all taken part in. Thinking himself invincible partly through his narcissistic tendencies and partly by his substance-soaked brain, he really didn't care. Only part he did remember was bragging about his house and having millions in the bank soon, which the men whom he had visited had been really interested in. He stood in before the open front door of his house, number one, and glanced right then left at some of what he thought were all his houses before going inside.

"Yep, it'll do for now he said aloud in the empty hallway; turning full circle, he remembered the door was already open; whilst wondering if perhaps coffee might be a good idea, he slowly recalled the reason he was there, and once more spoke aloud to himself, "Oh yeah, that fit builder bloke is coming to do the thingy in the loft." With that, he trudged up the sun-bathed staircase.

The difficulty in clearing his thoughts did not become any easier as time ticked away. Marcus was pretty sure that the slow drumming in his ears was indeed that of a grandfather clock, but he was quite sure he didn't own one. As he lay there, staring up at the sky through his beautifully designed light well, he found it almost stunning how the sun was turning pink before the greyness of the outside drew closer in. *Must be raining,* he thought, which would explain the wet feeling on his cheek, he started to brush it away with his hand, well, tried to, he was really confused now, he wondered why his arm didn't do what his brain had told it to, then wondered what that voice had said to him a minute ago, or could have been an hour, either way, he was sure that the words were said to him before and weren't yet to be spoken.

Yes, this made sense to him, of course, he smiled, but wasn't sure if the smile was imagined, he was starting to wonder if his face could move, he began to feel grateful that the pounding in his ears was fading, was slower, quieter, softer, his mind yelled to him, *YES, I know what was said, she said, no, he? It! IT. Ha, IT said, yes, who it was. No, didn't see, behind me? Yes, in the loft behind me, dark, it went dark, too far this time. Yes, yes, that's what it was. Too far this time, no more. You will stop, and you will stop right now. I wonder who that was? I wonder what it meant; where has the sunshine gone? It's dark, isn't it?*

Must be night-time; oh good, I am tired, but it is odd that I don't feel like yawning. I'm glad that the thumping has stopped anyway. I...

Marcus's body lay twisted on the mosaic centrepiece of the hallway. It framed the broken cadaver, the circular edge collecting blood from the smashed skull that had resulted from the very high fall directly from out of the loft hatch to the solid floor.

Minutes passed before the front door was gently pushed closed by a figure that observed the body that lay there, still, silent. The person circled the body, staring at the blood, before backing away and exiting the property from the rear and moving hastily across the fenceless gardens and was gone from sight to sight. A figure lost to the shadows.

Coming soon…

Part Two
33 Houses – The Mothers

Pip continues to live his life striving to find reason, to find peace, to be strong and free from the demons that taunted him.

History, however, continued to unfurl and expose secrets that hold power, enough to change everything…